FRIDAY THE WITCHTEENTH
WICKED WITCHES OF THE MIDWEST BOOK TWENTY

AMANDA M. LEE

WINCHESTERSHAW PUBLICATIONS

Copyright © 2022 by Amanda M. Lee

All rights reserved.

No part of this book may be reproduced in any form or by any electronic or mechanical means, including information storage and retrieval systems, without written permission from the author, except for the use of brief quotations in a book review.

❋ Created with Vellum

PROLOGUE
EIGHTEEN YEARS AGO

"Why are we watching this?" My cousin Clove plastered her hands over her eyes and then created a small gap to peek through. "No!"

As the knife-wielding maniac on the television screen went after the camp counselor with advanced vigor, she slouched low on the couch. "I swear she's torturing us," Clove whined to me. "Do something."

As the oldest cousin, I could see how she thought that fell to me. I, Bay Winchester, was often the boss when it came to group activities ... at least for the youngest Winchester generation. But our great-aunt Tillie was forcing us to watch a string of very bad horror movies, so I had a feeling I wouldn't get a say in the matter.

"What do you want me to do?" I demanded, my upper lip curling with dread when the killer in the hockey mask turned his attention to another teenager. "It's not like I can control her."

"Nobody can control her," my cousin Thistle snapped, fury on full display as she glared at the television. She had her arms folded over her chest in defiant fashion. Nothing scared Thistle, at least overtly. Even if she was feeling discomfort or fear, she would never show it in the presence of Aunt Tillie. "She's the devil. She's getting off on freaking you out. Don't give her the power."

For her part, Aunt Tillie looked amused by Thistle's declaration. "Are you saying you're not afraid?" she asked in a tone that had my inner danger alarm dinging. "Is that what you're saying, Mouth?"

Thistle was never one to back down, even if she knew she was about to step into a trap. "I'm not afraid," Thistle growled. "It's a movie. I know the difference between real life and a movie."

Aunt Tillie's response was a one-shoulder shrug. "I guess we'll see."

I didn't like the gleam in her eyes. She had a plan. What that plan entailed was anybody's guess, but there was no doubt she was going to do something to us. Because I liked to plot myself, I decided our only hope was to weasel the information out of her before she was ready to spring her trap. We were teenagers — well, two of us were officially teenagers — and the other would be a teenager in two months. We would eventually have to start out-thinking her if we didn't want the next five years to be a master class on embarrassment.

"I didn't even think you liked horror movies," I interjected, drawing Aunt Tillie's gaze to me. "Why are you making us watch these?" We were on the third *Friday the 13th* movie in a row, and I was starting to grow numb to the violence but increasingly suspicious of her motivations. Aunt Tillie never did anything without ulterior motives.

"It's Halloween," she replied. "You watch horror movies on Halloween."

"Since when is that the rule?" Thistle demanded. "Last time I checked, horror movies were a choice, not a necessity."

"Are you afraid?" Aunt Tillie challenged.

Thistle's eyes narrowed to dangerous slits. "I'm not afraid of you."

"I didn't ask if you were afraid of me, although your denial makes you stupid. I asked if you were afraid of the movie."

Thistle's eyes drifted back to the scene playing out on the screen, making a face as Jason Voorhees lifted a camp counselor through a window and twisted her head until it came completely off. "Why would I be afraid of that?" She gestured with more disdain than I was capable of mustering. "That's not even remotely realistic. A man can't twist a person's head off like that."

"He's not a man," I argued, surprising myself. "He's a zombie at this point. Didn't you see the start of the movie? They shoved a metal rod into his chest, and it was struck by lightning. That brought him back to life, but he was still full of maggots and stuff. That means he's a zombie."

"Very good, Bay." Aunt Tillie beamed at me.

I swallowed hard. Garnering Aunt Tillie's approval was always a mixed bag. I sensed her motivations were dark this evening. I just couldn't figure out what she had in mind for us. "That doesn't explain why you're forcing us to watch these movies."

"I'm not forcing you to do anything," she countered, wrinkling her nose as if I'd said the most ridiculous thing she'd ever heard. "I'm enlightening you with my knowledge."

"What knowledge?" Thistle challenged. "What is it you're trying to teach us here?"

"How to survive."

"How to survive this?" Thistle jabbed her finger at the screen. "Do you really think we're going to come up against a resurrected serial killer who haunts the same lake and campground movie after movie? I mean ... why would anybody send their kids to that campground? Every time someone does there's a massacre."

"It's not about the little details," Aunt Tillie argued. "It's about the overall theme."

Now she was just talking to hear herself talk. "What theme? I mean ... he's Jason Voorhees. He died in the lake, somehow came back, lived in the woods, and then was triggered when he saw his mother beheaded, and went on a killing spree. There doesn't seem much of a lesson in there."

Aunt Tillie's eye roll was pronounced. "I've clearly fallen down on the job when it comes to enlightening you on how the world works. It's not this specific killer. It's an overall preparedness for what this world will throw at you. That's what you need to get ready for."

She was talking in circles, I realized. She was good at it. When she wanted to confuse us, she threw out a lot of philosophical ideas and rationalizations. They sounded good, but things never ended well for us when she got in these moods.

"Just tell us what you want," I prodded. "It might be easier than pretending we're actually going to learn something from these movies."

"Don't think of them as movies. Think of them as tutorials."

"Tutorials on what?"

"On surviving. What did I just say?" Annoyance flashed across her face. "Get it together, Bay. You need to learn how to survive. You're a witch. Evil will be coming for you. It will kill you if you're not prepared."

"I'm telling Mom you said that," Clove whined, finally dropping her hand from her face. She refused to look at the television and instead focused on Aunt Tillie. "You're not supposed to scare us. You've been warned."

"Yeah," Thistle said, smugness evident. "You've been warned. Do you want to get in trouble?"

"Do your worst, tattletales," Aunt Tillie huffed. "We live in a world where we'll be going to war regularly. It's not my fault you're not prepared."

"War?" Doubt flooded me. "What sort of war do you see coming our way? Do you think we'll be dealing with zombie serial killers or something?"

"Anything is possible. Evil witches. Zombies. Dream monsters. Wraiths. You'll cross paths with them all eventually." She shifted on her chair and gave me her full attention. "You're different from the others. You can see and talk to ghosts. You'll have it the worst."

I tried to remain defiant despite her words. "What do you mean?"

Thistle made a face and vigorously shook her head. "Oh, don't fall for that. She's just messing with you. If she knows she's getting to you, she'll keep at it. That's who she is."

I didn't doubt Thistle's admonition. Still, I couldn't stop myself from asking the obvious question. "What do you think is going to happen to us?"

"Great things are going to happen to you."

The answer was far too easy, and I wrinkled my nose. "That's why you're making us watch horror movies, because you think good things are going to happen to us? That doesn't sound right."

"Along with the good comes the bad. You'll experience great joy, but hardship will follow. You have to learn the balance."

"Now she's just repeating things she read in fortune cookies," Thistle groused. "Don't listen to her. She's mental."

"And you're on my list!" Aunt Tillie jabbed a warning finger in Thistle's direction. Thistle could get under our great-aunt's skin faster than anybody. They both knew it, and they both thrived on it. "If you don't want to survive, by all means ignore my teachings. But if you want to prosper in this world, you must understand what you're up against."

"And we're going to do that with horror movies?" I had serious doubts.

"Of course not." Exasperation wove a tapestry across Aunt Tillie's craggy features. "Horror movies give you the inspiration to fight the good fight."

"What did I tell you?" Thistle was incredulous when she turned to me. "She's just spouting fortune cookie nonsense and you're encouraging her. She's trying to unnerve you. Don't give her the satisfaction."

"That did it." Aunt Tillie hopped to her feet. Sometimes I forgot how fast she could move when properly motivated. "I guess we'll be moving on to our second activity of the evening without proper preparation. That's on you, not me."

Ah. I knew she had something planned. Apparently, she was ready to show her hand. "What's the second activity?" I asked.

"We're going for a walk."

I narrowed my eyes and glanced at the window. Outside, the wind howled and rain splattered the glass. It was late October in northern Lower Michigan. The weather had a mind of its own. One day it could be sixty degrees and sunny. The next it could be thirty degrees and snowing. Tonight, the storm gods had decided to deluge us with rain.

"You want us to go out in that?" I demanded.

"It's time for the practical component of this particular lesson," Aunt Tillie replied. "We have to go outside."

Thistle remained slouched on the couch. "Yeah, I'm not going out in that."

"You are. I'm in charge." Aunt Tillie puffed out her chest. "What I say goes."

"You'll have to kill me to get me out in that." Thistle wasn't going to back down. For once, I was glad to have her belligerent attitude to hide behind. "It's not going to happen."

"What did I just say?" The air between Thistle and Aunt Tillie crackled with energy. "I'm in charge. Me!" Aunt Tillie thumped her chest for emphasis. "What I say goes."

"I think our mothers would have something to say about that," Thistle drawled. "I could call them and ask."

"Go ahead." Aunt Tillie was clearly expecting the suggestion because her smile was feral. "I believe they're down at the fairgrounds for the festival. There's a pumpkin pie contest they want to win. But if you think you can magically get them on the phone, knock yourself out."

Now it was Thistle's turn to frown. "We're not going out in a storm. It's dangerous."

"Which is why it's time to go out there." Aunt Tillie was firm.

"You're survivors. I'm going to make sure you keep surviving. It's time for a game."

I was instantly suspicious. "What sort of game?"

"The sort you have to survive in the woods."

"Survive what?" She was leaving something very important out of the conversation. I'd spent enough time with her to know that she wasn't going to show her hand until she had no other choice. Despite that, I pressed hard. "What are we supposed to do?"

She gestured to the window again. "It's time you go outside and find out."

"In that?" Clove squeaked. "Why do you want us to go outside in a storm? It doesn't make any sense."

"It does when you figure we're dealing with Aunt Tillie," Thistle drawled. "She wants us to go outside so she can scare the bejeesus out of us. That's what this entire evening has been about. That's why she made us watch the horror movies ... and waited until she was certain our mothers were gone. She wants to torture us."

"Torture is a strong word," Aunt Tillie countered.

"Is it the wrong word?" I asked.

She merely held out her hands and shrugged. "Let's find out. Other people say fear is something to be avoided. I say it's something to be embraced before it overcomes you. Let's see who's right."

"We'll get sick if you send us out in that," I argued. "You'll get in trouble."

"I'm not afraid of your mother." Even as Aunt Tillie said it, I saw the flicker of fear in the depths of her eyes. "We should get started. The sooner you overcome the obstacles I've put in place for you, the sooner you can come back inside and celebrate your victory."

"What makes you think we'll be victorious?" I asked.

"Because I've worked overtime to make sure you can overcome any obstacle. I have faith you'll come out the other side."

"Why don't we just assume we'll win and call it a day?" Thistle suggested.

"Because that's not how I operate." Aunt Tillie squared her

shoulders. "This is an exercise in fear. I expect you to always overcome your fears. Don't let me down."

I couldn't believe she was actually going to force us out into this storm. "What if we refuse?"

Aunt Tillie snorted. "Do you really think you have that option?"

I was resigned when I pushed myself off the couch. "Fine, but we're totally going to tell our mothers about this. You're going to be in trouble, so you'd better hope it's worth it."

"Everything I do is worth it."

I shook my head and held out my hands. "What do you want us to do?"

"The name of the game is survival, girls. Let's see what you've learned."

ONE
PRESENT DAY

"We have to go up to the inn."

My husband Landon Michaels — I was still getting used to calling him that — rolled to his side on the couch and looked me over as I stood next to him with my hands on my hips. I was trying to come across as authoritative, but his smile told me he thought I was cute.

"Let's not," he countered. "Let's stay here and pretend we don't remember where the inn is."

I shot him a dirty look. "Yes, because they'll totally believe we forgot how to get there."

"It's possible. We haven't been there much since we returned from our honeymoon."

That was true. Since returning, we'd been holed up in the guesthouse on the family property, consumed with each other. As much as I enjoyed our time together, however, it was time we get back to our everyday lives.

"Landon." I kept my voice firm, bordering on exasperated, and cocked my head.

"Bay." He matched my tone, but his smile was sly. "You know you want to cuddle on the couch."

"It's time for dinner," I reminded him. "Clove and Sam are bringing the baby. He's a month old and we've barely seen him."

"He doesn't do anything," Landon pointed out. "He doesn't even smile. He just gets passed around, cries incessantly, and smells like poop."

"He's a baby. What do you expect him to do?"

Landon shrugged. "I don't know. Babies are supposed to be cute and cuddly. That one is defective or something."

"He cuddles with whoever holds him ... something you haven't yet done."

"I've held him." Landon suddenly sounded defensive. "Why are you saying I haven't held him?"

"Because you haven't."

"I have so. Just this week I held him on the library couch."

"No, I held him, and you sat next to me making faces."

"It's the same thing. You were sort of on my lap. Your leg was on top of mine, so it counts."

"It's not the same." We had a problem, and even though I'd been loath to bring it up, I knew it was time. "Do you not like babies now?"

"I like them fine. But this one doesn't do anything."

"He's too little to do anything. He'll grow fast enough. In a few months he'll be crawling ... and then talking ... and then walking."

"Great. Call me when that starts."

He was far too blasé for my liking. "We need to talk about this."

"I don't want a deep conversation." He groaned as he rolled to his back and covered his face with one of the accent pillows. "We're on our honeymoon. We're supposed to be enjoying ourselves."

"We've been back from our honeymoon for two weeks."

"We're always going to be on our honeymoon." He peeked from behind the pillow, his smile as soft as his eyes. "If you come here, I'll demonstrate how that works."

I emphatically shook my head. "No way. We're going up to the inn." I checked the clock on the mantle again. "Come on. Dinner is in seven minutes. You know what happens when we're late."

"Actually, I have no idea what happens when we're late. We've never actually been late for anything other than what could be construed as a catastrophe, and we get a free pass for those. Let's eat canned soup and live on love."

It was an interesting offer, but I'd made a promise to my mother. I decided to hit him where it hurt and offer the one thing I knew would get him moving. "It's pot roast night."

He immediately swung to his feet and ran his hand through his hair. "We should get going. We don't want to be late."

I made a face. "How did I know that would get you moving?"

"You know me well." His eyes twinkled with impish delight, and he caught my hand before I could move to the closet to grab a coat. "Just one thing, Bay."

"Hmm?" I glanced back at him.

"I love you." He gave me a kiss, one that held a lot of promise for later in the evening. "I'm so glad you're my wife."

He knew exactly how to hit me in the feels. "I feel the same way about you."

"That's why we're the perfect match."

THE WALK TO THE INN WAS FAST. The weather was starting to turn. In Michigan when the sun went down — which was happening earlier and earlier — the temperature dropped quickly. Coats were no longer a choice.

"It will be winter soon," Landon noted as we kept a brisk pace and turned toward the patio. "Christmas will be here before we know it."

"Christmas with a baby," I mused as he pulled open the door to the family living quarters. "That will be kind of fun."

"Will the baby be fun by Christmas?" Landon looked dubious.

I shrugged. "I don't know. He'll still be spoiled rotten."

"I plan to spoil my wife rotten. The baby can play second fiddle."

He really did have attitude about the baby, something I was having trouble wrapping my head around. "I like the idea of being spoiled," I admitted.

"Well, prepare yourself, because your new husband is going to wow you." He slipped his arms around my waist once we were inside and bestowed a heady kiss on me. "If you would be willing to forego family dinner we could go back to the guesthouse and I could get an early start on it," he prodded.

"I thought you wanted pot roast."

"We can steal it and run."

"Yes, because they would never figure that out." I shook my head and let my eyes drift to the empty couch. I checked the clock on the wall to reassure myself that it was the right time and then frowned. "Where is Aunt Tillie?"

Landon didn't look nearly as alarmed as I felt. "Probably causing mayhem in the dining room. Why?"

"*Jeopardy* isn't over." I gestured to the television. "She never misses *Jeopardy*."

"Maybe she found something more entertaining."

"And that doesn't worry you?"

He shrugged. "We're about to eat pot roast, sweetie. There's nothing that worries me when pot roast is on the menu."

"Good to know."

We followed the sound of voices into the dining room. The food was already on the table — the pot roast scent immediately had my mouth watering — but all the adults in the family were grouped around Aunt Marnie as she held baby Calvin and cooed.

"Who is the prettiest baby in the world?" she demanded as the sleepy baby made a series of faces. He had dark hair like his mother, the same ski-slope nose as well, and his eyes were a rich brown.

"He's only going to be the prettiest baby in the world until Thistle and Marcus decide it's time they expand the family," Aunt Twila countered, shooting her daughter a "Don't you dare even argue with me" look when it became apparent Thistle might offer up a complaint.

Instead, Thistle rolled her eyes until they landed on me. "You're late."

"We're right on time," I said as I shrugged out of my coat. "What are you talking about?"

"They've been fighting over the baby for the past thirty minutes," Thistle replied. "Apparently we're expected to be early now if we want to hold him."

That had me smiling. Thistle was abrasive to the point of being compared to steel wool. She'd developed a true love for Calvin, however, and it made me laugh. "Are you bucking for favorite aunt honors or something?"

"I'm already the favorite aunt," Thistle said. "I bonded with the kid when you were off getting tanned and toasted on your honeymoon. You'll never make up the ground I've already covered."

"We'll just see about that," I shot back.

"We will ... and you'll lose."

"Girls." Mom made a tsking sound as she pulled away from Marnie and regarded us. "There's no reason to fight. The baby will love all of us."

"Especially me," Marnie offered. "I'm his grandmother ... and I'm going to spoil him rotten."

"He's going to like me more," Mom countered. "I'm the better cook."

"In your dreams."

I raised an eyebrow as they continued to throw verbal jabs at each other and skirted another look toward Thistle. "This is going to get old quick."

"Definitely." She bobbed her head. "But I figure it's better they fixate on the baby than us."

"Good point." I hung my coat on the rack in the corner and then slid into my usual chair. "Where's Aunt Tillie?" Her chair at the head of the table was empty.

"She's out front with Terry," Mom replied as she straightened. I didn't miss the furtive look of worry that appeared — and then disappeared just as fast. "He told her she needs to have that plow truck looked at so it can pass a maintenance check if she wants to use it this winter. They're arguing."

That sounded fairly normal. "Since when is she required to have the truck pass a maintenance check?"

"Apparently she was always supposed to do it," Mom replied. "She claims otherwise. It's a thing."

Something else was going on. I could feel it. "What's really the problem?" When Mom didn't immediately answer, I flicked my eyes to Thistle. "Seriously. Why isn't she watching *Jeopardy*?"

"And where is Peg?" Landon demanded, referring to Aunt Tillie's tutu-wearing pet pig. "I want to see my girl."

I elbowed him lightly. "I thought I was your girl."

"You're my woman. There's a difference."

"Whatever." I kept my focus on Thistle. "What aren't you telling us?"

Mom started before Thistle could respond. "Your aunt is having a ... moment."

That wasn't much of an explanation. "Like a senior moment?"

"You know she's only middle-aged," Thistle chided. "Come on."

I grinned. Aunt Tillie had certain narratives she liked to stick to. "I need to know what 'she's having a moment' means. If Aunt Tillie is going to go on a rampage, I want to be prepared. Things have been quiet since we got back from the honeymoon."

"You just jinxed us," Landon lamented. He had a hunk of warm bread in his hand and was slathering it with butter. "We've had two blissful weeks with the only excitement falling under the heading of other people's problems. Now we're going to get toasted by a zombie horde or something."

He was being dramatic, which was his way, but he was right.

Since returning from our honeymoon, we'd helped out our friends Scout and Stormy as they fought their own monsters, but we'd been monster-free for the most part. It had been nice ... but it wouldn't last forever. "I'm sure it will be okay." I eyed the hunk of bread. "Do you need all that butter?"

"Oh, don't even." Landon made a face. "Now that we're married, that doesn't give you the right to police my eating habits. We've talked about this."

"We have," I readily agreed. "You eat like a glutton. That's not allowed going forward. You can still eat what you want, but in moderation."

"Shh." He made an adorable face. "You're upsetting the baby."

I wanted to chide him, but I let it go. He was too cute for words sometimes. "So, Aunt Tillie is having a moment," I prodded, hoping to get the conversation back on track.

Mom nodded, letting loose her patented sigh. She was obviously worried. "She seems ... agitated."

"What else is new?" I asked. "She's always agitated."

"Yes, but this time she's agitated about the baby."

"That baby?" I cocked an eyebrow in Calvin's direction. "I would think she'd be thrilled. He's named after her favorite person in the world, and he doesn't cry."

"He cries," Landon countered. "Three days ago, he screamed so loudly we could hear him from one county over."

I shot him a quelling look. "Stop being ... weird." He seemed leery about the baby and it gave me pause. "Don't you want kids now?" Up until this point, we'd been on the same page regarding kids. We wanted one or two ... down the line. Nobody was itching for them right now.

Landon balked at the question. "Of course I do. I want to be a father."

"Then what's the problem?"

"He doesn't do anything. I want a baby that does something."

"Is he insulting my baby?" Clove demanded. She'd been much

calmer since giving birth. We'd been worried about her post-partum hormones doing a number on her, but she was back to her charming self. It was a relief given how obnoxious she'd been in the days leading up to Calvin's birth.

"I don't know," I admitted. "He's being weird."

"I'm not being weird. I just want a baby that does more than ... that." Landon gestured toward Calvin, who had fallen asleep in his grandmother's arm.

"I think he means he wants a circus baby or something," Thistle noted.

I laughed, as I'm sure she'd intended. "All babies are kind of docile when they're first born, Landon. This is normal."

"Yes, but this family isn't normal," Landon argued. "I thought there would be something different about this baby given the things that were happening before he was born. I mean ... he was magically showing you things. Are you telling me you're not surprised he hasn't continued doing that?"

And that's when it hit me. I glanced back at the baby. "You're right. He hasn't shown any signs of magic since joining us."

"I happen to like that," Clove argued. "It would be better if he manifested at an age when he can understand that he shouldn't be showing off."

"It's weird, right?" I asked my mother. "Shouldn't he still be able to do that thing where he controlled our emotions?"

Mom shrugged. "We don't know how it's all going to work out. He's a month old. How about we just let him be who he is and worry about the rest of it when it's time?"

"I'm fine with that," I reassured her, flashing a smile I hoped was friendly rather than frightened. "Is Aunt Tillie worried about that too? Is that why she's having a moment?"

"Oh, no." Mom was grim when she shook her head. "She believes we somehow got the wrong baby. She's in a standoff with the Goddess until it's corrected."

"It's because he's a boy," Thistle volunteered. "She said he was supposed to be a girl. She's all worked up about it."

Calvin had been a surprise. There was no getting around that. Still, he was a welcome surprise. "It had to happen eventually, right?" I asked my mother. "I mean, odds were we'd eventually have a boy."

"Not according to Aunt Tillie," Mom replied. "If you want to know what I think, she's complaining about the baby because she doesn't want to focus on the other thing."

"What other thing?"

"The Bay City Coven wants to send representatives here to get answers on the Minerva situation. Aunt Tillie is putting up a fight."

I cringed. Minerva Prince had served as Clove's midwife, right up to the moment she'd revealed herself to be evil and tried to take the baby. I'd ended her life. I wasn't sorry about it, but in hindsight, pretending there wouldn't be questions was stupid on my part. "Well, if they want to interview me, I'll make myself available."

The corners of Mom's eyes wrinkled. "That's a very diplomatic response."

I held out my hands. "I'm not sorry for what I did. She was a threat to the family. I ended the threat."

Something flashed in Mom's eyes. "You did. We don't know how this will play out. Right now, they're just making noise. If they show up, we'll handle it then."

"And you think that has Aunt Tillie acting weird?" I asked. "That doesn't sound like something she would worry about."

"Who knows what's going on with her." Mom went back to smiling at Calvin. "It's been a quiet few weeks. For all we know, she could be bored. I'm sure she'll snap out of it soon."

I didn't know if I was supposed to wish for that, but anything was better than not knowing. Aunt Tillie was predictable most days. It was when she turned unpredictable that our lives spiraled out of control. "I'm sure it will be fine."

Mom absently nodded. "I'm sure it will. Eat your dinner before it gets cold."

I slid my eyes to Landon to suggest he fill our plates and frowned when I realized he was already elbow deep in pot roast. "Seriously?"

"I need to keep up my energy if I want to romance my new wife," he replied between chews. "I can't help it that your mother provides delicious energy."

"Yeah, we're going to talk about you being a glutton."

"Not tonight we're not."

"Fine ... but soon."

"I look forward to the conversation."

Something told me the opposite was true. I had a bitter battle coming on more than one front.

2
TWO

Part of me thought being married would change things. We'd been living together for a year, so in hindsight, that thought seemed strange. Waking up with Landon as my husband versus my boyfriend or fiancé was no different. It was more of the same ... and I liked that consistency.

"Morning," he murmured as he opened his eyes and found me staring at him.

"Morning. How did you sleep?"

"I had this really weird dream."

"Good or bad?"

"Well ... you were dressed in nothing but pot roast."

I made a face. "We're talking about your eating habits." I hadn't planned for the conversation to go down this morning, but we had time before breakfast. "Now that I have you, I want to keep you — forever. We have to monitor your fat intake."

If looks could kill, I would've been struck dead in that moment.

"I'm serious." I adopted my sternest tone. "I love you too much to lose you to a premature heart attack."

His expression softened marginally. "So, I know you're serious about this," he started.

"Deadly serious."

He continued as if I hadn't spoken. "The thing is, I've given this a great deal of thought and I think you're going about it the wrong way."

"Oh, really?" This I had to hear. "How should I be going about it?"

"You should be looking for a spell that protects me from a heart attack ... or any other human malady that might take me down. That's what we should focus on instead of monitoring my food intake."

My lips twitched but I managed to hold it together ... just barely. "That's not really how it works."

"Oh, no." He wagged his finger. "I've heard you guys talking over the years. You can do anything you put your minds to. This is the route we should go."

"In other words, you want to keep being a glutton."

"You say that like it's a bad thing."

I let loose a sigh. "You're a lot of work."

He grinned. "I'm worth it, right?"

"I guess." When he slid his arm around my waist and tugged me against him, I didn't resist. "Are you doing anything at work today?"

"Why? Are you trying to arrange a little afternoon interlude? If so, I have a few ideas. Now that we have that couch in your office, I was thinking we could get one of those fans that double as a heater. We can raise and lower the temperature accordingly and take regular afternoon breaks together. We'll be prepared for any weather."

"I love how your mind works," I drawled. "It's so you to worry about our napping schedule and a spell that would allow you to eat your weight in cake every night."

"It is so me." He pressed a kiss to my temple. I could sense the moment his attitude shifted. "What do you think the deal is with Aunt Tillie and the baby?"

I wasn't expecting the question, but I'd been thinking about it. "We always assumed the baby would be a girl. It's possible that Sam's witch genes were strong enough to counter our witch genes. We might never know exactly why it happened."

"Yeah, but do you really think Aunt Tillie will keep distancing herself from the baby?"

That was a tricky question. "No," I said finally. "She's never been that interested in babies. If the stories are to be believed, she didn't care about us until we were four or five."

"Really?"

I nodded. "She likes her sidekicks to be more durable. Babies bore her." I shifted to look at his strong profile. "I guess you guys have that in common."

"I'm not bored by the baby."

"That's good because I would still like to have one or two in a few years. Not right now, but down the road ... ." I trailed off, suddenly worried.

"Don't do that." He flicked the ridge of my ear. "I hate when you worry about things that aren't really things."

"I think you hating the baby is a thing."

"I don't hate the baby. I just want him to be more entertaining. Believe it or not, watching the kid suck down a bottle and poop his pants is not fun."

"What do you picture our future looking like when we have a baby?"

"Oh, see, that's a trick question. Our baby will be entertaining the second she arrives."

"What if we have a boy?"

"I'm fine with either, although I do picture a little blond you running around and wrapping me around her finger."

"You'll be cute with him or her."

"I'm going to be a great father. I just want entertaining kids, not boring ones."

"I'll keep that in mind." I pressed my eyes shut and listened to his

21

heart. His fingers tracing light patterns down my spine started to lull me.

"Back to Aunt Tillie," he prodded after a few moments of silence. "You don't think she'll shun Calvin because he's a boy? That would make me sad."

"You don't have to worry about that. She's not worked up about the baby. I mean … she might be a little worked up, but she's not going to freak out or anything. What she's really worked up about is the possibility of the Bay City Coven sending representatives here."

"Why? They can't do anything to you, can they?"

"No. We're purposely coven-less. Or I guess it's fair to say we're our own coven. She doesn't like influence from the outside magic world treading on her turf. That's why she hated Minerva from the start."

"I thought she hated her because she knew she was evil."

"That too. She'll be fine. If the coven does send someone, I'll deal with them."

He angled his head to study me. "They won't try to punish you for what happened with Minerva?" He suddenly looked nervous at the prospect. "Can they do anything to you?"

"They can't touch me." I rolled away from him and stretched my arms over my head. "Besides, I'm stronger than any representative they send."

To my utter surprise, Landon barked out a laugh.

"What's so funny?" I demanded.

"I love that your ego is growing with your powers." He tickled my ribs. "I like when you feel good about yourself."

"You don't think it's obnoxious?"

"Baby, there's nothing you could do that I would ever find obnoxious."

"What about limiting your food intake?"

His smile slipped. "I thought we agreed to go the other route."

"I didn't agree to that."

"I heard you. You can't go back on your word now."

"Landon ... ."

"Bay." He mocked my tone to perfection.

It nudged a sigh out of me. "We're going to keep talking about this, but we have to get ready for breakfast. Mom is expecting us, and I want to talk to Aunt Tillie about a possible coven visit."

"We can talk about it as long as you want," Landon promised. "Just know, I'll continuously derail the conversation until you give up because I'm so cute and you don't want to upset me."

"That's not what just happened."

"It totally is."

"No."

"Bay, have I mentioned I love you?"

"Not today."

"Well, I love you."

I took a moment to let the words wash over me. "That was you distracting me again."

"Just give in to the love, Bay. It will be better for all of us."

THERE WERE NO GUESTS AT the inn, so it was all family when we strolled into the dining room. Unfortunately, certain members of the family had decided the lack of guests provided permission to argue.

"You're in trouble," Mom intoned. She had the pancake platter clutched in her hands and I was momentarily worried she would use it as a weapon against Aunt Tillie.

"What's up?" Landon asked as he plucked a slice of bacon off the platter Twila carried.

"That's one of your three slices," I warned. "I'm counting."

"It doesn't count if it doesn't touch my plate," he argued.

"Says who?"

"Says everybody who matters, which in this case is me." He winked.

"Fine." He was winning the war over fatty foods and we both

knew it. "What's going on?" I feigned brightness as I focused on Mom and Aunt Tillie.

"I like how you put exactly twenty seconds of effort into improving his health," Mom drawled. "You barely put up a fight."

I shrugged. "I can't help it. He's cute and he knows it."

"I am," Landon agreed as he pressed a kiss to my mother's cheek. "You don't want her limiting me when it comes to your food. It will make us all sad. Nobody wants to live in a sad world."

Mom appeared to be fighting the urge to smile. "I guess you have a point," she said finally.

I made a disgruntled sound as I shook my head. "You put up less of a fight than I did."

"He's not my husband," Mom reminded me. "In case you haven't heard, I've limited Terry's fat intake. I seem to be winning my battle. This is your battle."

I frowned as I darted my eyes to Chief Terry, who was elbow deep in sausage links. "Yes, it looks like that's working marvelously." I moved to my regular chair and poured a glass of tomato juice as I turned my attention back to Aunt Tillie and Mom. "What are you fighting about this morning?"

"Thank you so much for reminding her that we were fighting," Aunt Tillie snapped. "She'd forgotten and now she's going to rev up the judgment machine again. You're awesome!" She shot me a sarcastic thumbs-up.

"Don't blame Bay for this," Mom growled. She was clearly in a mood, and even though I had no idea why she was annoyed, there was no doubt Aunt Tillie was in for a lecture. "I wasn't going to forget. Margaret Little woke me up at five o'clock to tell me about your latest trick. Having to deal with that woman before coffee is the worst."

"What did you do to Mrs. Little?" I asked as Landon took the platter of pancakes from my mother. He seemed more interested in food than the argument playing out before us.

"I didn't do anything," Aunt Tillie replied. "I've been accused of something ridiculous, but there's no proof I did anything."

"It seems all of Margaret's unicorns are farting," Mom explained for my benefit.

Landon, a heaping forkful of pancake on the way to his mouth, stilled. "Um ... ."

"Her porcelain unicorns," Mom added.

"I'm familiar with her unicorns," Landon replied. "I've walked into that store and thought all those creepy little faces were possessed and about to gore me with their tiny horns."

Aunt Tillie's eyebrows hopped, as if she was formulating an idea.

"No!" Mom jabbed her finger in Aunt Tillie's face. "Don't even think about that. Somebody could get hurt."

Aunt Tillie was suddenly the picture of innocence. "Why do you always assume the worst about me? It's hurtful."

Mom wasn't about to be swayed. "I'm familiar with your work. Stop whatever you're doing. It's three days in a row of farting unicorns."

"I don't understand," Landon said, syrup on his cheek. "How can you make inanimate objects fart?"

"I can make anything fart." Aunt Tillie beamed at him as she took her chair at the head of the table. "It's not a difficult spell." When Mom cleared her throat, Aunt Tillie darted her eyes in her direction. "Not that I'm responsible for what happened in Margaret's shop on this occasion."

Annoyance danced across Mom's features. "Like we're supposed to believe that a hundred porcelain unicorns just decided to blow confetti out of their rear ends at the same time."

"I think you're looking at it the wrong way," Aunt Tillie wheedled. "Would I use confetti? That's nowhere near messy enough. I would have them blow rabbit poop pellets out of their behinds."

Landon froze with his fork in his mouth.

"She does have a point," I noted, immediately shrinking in my seat when Mom turned her dark gaze to me. "I'm not saying it was good to do, I'm just saying she has a point."

"And I'm saying I'll kill you if you don't stay out of this, Bay," Mom warned.

I opened my mouth to push harder but Chief Terry planted his beefy hand on the back of my neck to still me.

"You're still my favorite," he said in a low voice, "but if I have to get between you and your mother things will get ugly. Don't put me in that position."

Landon studied the pancake platter. "Should I get a second helping?"

The question was directed at me, so I gave him a hard glare. "What do you think?"

"Right." He yanked his hand back. "I'm watching what I eat. That means one serving of pancakes and two of bacon a day."

"Yeah, I don't think we agreed to that either."

"Shh." Landon kissed the tip of my nose. "You're so pretty. Don't ruin it with ugly talk about bacon."

I threw my hands in the air. "This is not going as I planned."

"Welcome to my world," Aunt Tillie said. She darted a dark gaze toward my mother. "Are you still here? You should eat your breakfast before it gets cold."

"We're not done talking about this," Mom insisted. "The confetti was a funny prank. If you'd stopped there, I would've told Margaret to shove it where the sun doesn't shine."

"That sounds like a great idea," Aunt Tillie said. "Let's go with that."

"You didn't stop there," Mom continued. She was like a runaway semi on an icy highway. "No, you made the farts smell like Brussels sprouts on top of everything else."

I pressed my lips together to keep from laughing.

"And then there was the green film left behind, which also smelled like Brussels sprouts," Mom continued. "All that white confetti stuck to the walls ... and shelves ... and unicorns thanks to the green mist. She'll never get that smell out of there."

I had to turn away so that my mother didn't see my smile.

"It's not funny, Bay," Mom barked. "Your aunt has been out of control. Between her placing calls with a voice changer to warn the Bay City coven away to shunning the baby, I'm starting to think she's going senile."

"Starting?" I arched an eyebrow, but I was more interested in Aunt Tillie. "You called the Bay City coven and used a voice changer?"

"I didn't want them to recognize my voice," Aunt Tillie replied. "I was watching a *Scream* marathon the other day and that gave me the idea."

I grinned. "I remember watching those movies with you."

"Yes, and how great did that turn out?" Mom demanded. "You almost got hypothermia because she sent you on a survival mission in the middle of a storm."

"Actually, that was the time she showed us the *Friday the 13th* series," I countered. "After watching *Scream,* she taught us how to identify sociopathic teenagers."

"Ah, yes." Mom's anger flashed again. "That would've been the time we were called down to the school because Thistle tied the entire basketball team to the bleachers and set their shorts on fire to teach them a lesson about sexually harassing classmates."

"It was a lesson well learned," I pointed out.

"It doesn't matter," Mom fumed. "Aunt Tillie needs to get it together. Everybody acts like an adult in this family except for her. It's time she steps up and acts like an adult."

One look at Aunt Tillie and I could gauge her opinion on the subject. "So, Mom put you on a diet." I turned to Chief Terry, who was frowning at an incoming text. "Is something going on?"

"I think so." Chief Terry used the cloth napkins Mom insisted on putting out at every meal, even though it was a waste of time to do the laundry that often, and slowly stood. "I need to head out to I-75."

"What's going on?" Landon asked. He was also standing.

"There's a jumper on the freeway overpass at the Au Sable River Bridge."

My heart skipped. "A jumper? Do you want help?"

Chief Terry hesitated and then nodded. "You might be of help if you can stop this guy from jumping. There's just one thing."

"I won't look if he jumps," I automatically promised.

"That would be good, but that's not what I meant. I don't want any mushy business from the two of you." He moved his finger back and forth between Landon and me. "You're married now. Act like proper adults."

"No problem," Landon said. "We'll be proper adults. You have my word." As if to prove it, he gave my bottom a hearty squeeze as I moved next to Chief Terry, causing me to squeal.

"See," Landon said. "We're totally adults."

"Ugh." Chief Terry was obviously disgusted. "If I didn't need the two of you right now, I'd leave you behind."

"If that's not a ringing endorsement, I don't know what is," I said to Landon.

"Let's move." Chief Terry insisted. "If this guy jumps it'll be a mess ... in more ways than one."

3
THREE

Chief Terry took the back roads. He kept up a steady stream of chatter with Landon as they listened to things unfolding on the police scanner. I didn't say anything. A sense of dread filled me the closer we got to our destination, and I started fidgeting in my seat when we were only a few miles out.

Landon noticed and looked at me. "What?"

"I ... nothing." I shook my head. There was nothing to say. Explaining that I had a feeling wouldn't add anything of substance to the conversation.

"You're worked up," Landon insisted. "What's wrong?"

"I just ... feel agitated."

He studied my face a moment longer and then turned forward. "When we get there, follow your instincts. If you think you can fix this, do it."

I was surprised how easily the words rolled off his tongue. "What if there's an audience?"

"There will be an audience," Chief Terry said. "Just ... be careful. If you can stop whatever is about to happen, we'll figure out a way to explain it after the fact. We always do."

It was nice they had faith in me. I still didn't know what I was feeling. "I just need to see."

Once we arrived and exited the vehicle, Landon put his hand to my back and steered me between Chief Terry and himself for the walk.

"If anybody asks why you're here, we'll just say we were all at breakfast together and nobody had time to drop you off," he said. "We don't need a fancy explanation."

I nodded and increased my pace as we crested a hill. There was so much activity at the overpass I had to take a moment to absorb it.

Three Michigan State Police cars were parked under the bridge. Traffic had been rerouted at a previous exit because there were no vehicles moving in either direction. I turned my questioning eyes on Chief Terry.

"They want to make sure nobody is around to watch," he explained. "Seeing someone jump, even if they were on the other side of the freeway, could cause an accident. They've shifted traffic so it's forced off at the previous exit and doesn't rejoin until the next exit."

As we grew closer, I could make out the man on the bridge. He appeared to be in his early forties and paced back and forth along the bridge. It looked as though he was talking to himself.

"What do we have?" Chief Terry asked as we approached a group of six men. Three of them wore state police uniforms. Three were dressed in street clothes.

"Who are you?" One of the men turned to look Chief Terry up and down. He had an air of authority, and I didn't like the way he looked at us.

"Terry Davenport." Chief Terry extended his hand. "I'm the chief in Hemlock Cove. The bridge is in my jurisdiction."

The man nodded. "I'm Bill Blake. I'm the negotiator with the Michigan State Police."

Negotiator? I looked to the bridge again. There didn't appear to be a hostage.

"He's considered a crisis counselor as well," Landon offered for my benefit as he extended his hand to Bill. "Landon Michaels. I'm with the FBI."

Bill nodded again. "You're the agent stationed out of Hemlock Cove. I've heard about you. I've never understood why you picked that location. Nothing ever happens there."

"You'd be surprised," Landon replied. "As for why I'm stationed there, that's my home." He inclined his head toward me. "This is my wife. She has a business in Hemlock Cove."

Bill turned his attention to me. "What sort of business?"

I opened my mouth to answer but Chief Terry interjected. "Bay owns The Whistler, the local newspaper," he explained. "We were having breakfast together when the call came through. To save time, we brought her with us."

"You brought a newspaper reporter?" Bill's expression reflected doubt.

"I'm not going to cover a suicide," I blurted. "We don't report suicides. I'm just here because it was quicker."

Bill grimaced. "Well, as you can see, we have a situation." He nodded to the man on the bridge. "His name is Chester Hamilton. He's a local lawyer. His vehicle is about fifty feet in the woods that way." He pointed to a stand of trees on the side of the freeway. "We have troopers on the bridge but for now we've instructed them not to get too close. We don't want to spook him."

"Do we know why he's up there?" Landon asked. The set of his shoulders told me he wasn't a fan of Bill.

"He seems to be ranting, but none of it makes sense," Bill replied. "One second he was complaining about the state of the world today, women dressed as men and an amoral society and the like. The next he was going on about all the hatred in the world and how it rains bad luck down on everybody."

"Sounds like a mental emergency," Landon noted.

"That would be my guess," Bill confirmed. "I'll know more in a few minutes. I'm heading up."

Landon flicked his eyes to me, as if asking a question, and I gave an almost imperceptible nod. I needed to get closer. He would do his best to arrange it, but Bill didn't look as if he would be open to a reporter accompanying him onto the overpass. "I can serve as back-up," he said.

Doubt cast a shadow across Bill's face. "I didn't realize the FBI cared about potential jumpers."

If Landon was offended by the comment, he didn't show it. His face remained neutral, but I could sense his unease. "I care that we save this man. I don't want to step on your toes. I would like to get closer to hear what he's saying."

"Fine." Bill's nod was stiff. The Michigan State Police were used to being the big dogs at a scene this far north. "Whatever you want."

Landon allowed Bill to take the lead, but we took only four steps before the negotiator turned to me.

"I'm sorry, but what purpose are you serving here?" he asked.

Landon bristled. "She's with me."

"She's not law enforcement."

"She's my wife and I prefer not being separated from her," Landon shot back.

"I see." Bill's tone told me he didn't see at all. "Well, you're the boss, right?"

"No, you're the boss," Landon countered. "I feel more comfortable with her being here. If you have a problem with that ... ." He trailed off, waiting.

"No problem," Bill replied quickly. "I was just curious."

"Well, let's be curious about Mr. Hamilton," Landon suggested.

I glanced at Landon as we resumed walking. I had questions about Bill's attitude, but they would have to wait. He shot me a reassuring wink, although there was a veil of tension in his eyes. It took us five minutes to get to the top of the bridge, and then another two to position ourselves so we could watch the pacing lawyer. From a closer vantage point, it was clear the man was distressed. His hair was disheveled, his face red and sweaty, and his eyes were wild.

"Wait here," Bill said to Landon and Chief Terry. "I'm going to talk to him. It's best I approach alone so he doesn't feel threatened or outnumbered."

"Of course." Landon's nod was perfunctory. He waited until Bill was a good thirty feet away to speak to me. "Stick close." It wasn't a request. "He's trying to flex, which means he might get off on trying to separate you from me at some point. I prefer that not happen."

I nodded. "I'm not worried about Bill. I'm worried about him." I inclined my head toward the pacing man. "He's ... having issues."

"Meaning what?" Chief Terry asked.

I shrugged. "I ... don't know. There's a shimmer around him."

"A shimmer?" Chief Terry arched an eyebrow. "Are you saying something magical is happening?"

I hesitated and then shook my head. "It's more like an air of despair or something. I don't know how to explain it."

"So it's not magical?" Landon prodded.

I held out my hands. "I don't know that either. Right now, it's just a really bad situation."

Landon leaned in and lightly knocked his head against mine before pulling away. He had to be professional. "Sweetie, if he jumps look away."

For some reason the suggestion grated. "I've seen death before."

"Not like this." Landon was firm. "It's going to be ugly. I don't want you having nightmares."

"I'm a Winchester," I argued.

He slid his eyes to me and managed a smile. "Sometimes you don't have a clear picture of yourself. I don't want you to torture yourself. Protect yourself, okay?"

The earnestness in his eyes softened my stance and I nodded. "I'll be okay."

"Of course, you will. You're the strongest person I know."

We focused on Bill, who pleaded with Chester. The negotiator held both of his hands up, as to appear non-threatening, and his voice was even as he addressed the man.

"If you tell me what's bothering you, perhaps I can help," he suggested. I had to give him credit. He sounded genuinely interested in helping Chester. "I want to help you, but you have to help me do that."

Chester's forehead wrinkled as he turned his full attention to Bill. "Who are you?"

"My name is Bill Blake. I'm with the Michigan State Police. I'm called when there's a crisis."

Chester let loose a hollow laugh. "I'm your crisis today?"

"You are indeed." Bill made an attempt at a smile. "Tell me what's going on, Chester."

Chester's eyes widened. "How do you know my name? Did they send you? I told them I didn't want them near me. I still don't!" He was shrill.

Bill stopped moving. He was about twenty feet from Chester. "Nobody sent me." His tone was grave. "I know who you are because your vehicle is parked over there. The registration was in the glove compartment."

"Oh." Chester looked momentarily taken aback. "I ... um ... no." He vigorously started shaking his head. "You're one of them. They sent you. I'm not falling for that again. I won't let you turn me into someone I'm not." He moved closer to the edge of the overpass, stealing my breath with every step.

"I'm not here to turn you into anyone you're not," Bill insisted as he took five steps toward Chester. "I'm here to give you whatever you need. Just ... tell me what that is."

Chester raised his head and my heart stuttered when I saw the blackness of his eyes. For a split-second he focused on me. Then a muscle worked in his jaw before he turned to face the empty freeway. "I won't be anything other than who I am. I don't care what Lady Luck says. I know who I am. I won't let the darkness take me."

Chester extended a leg to step off the bridge. Bill raced forward to stop Chester's plummet to the freeway below.

I held my breath and watched in disbelief as the shimmer I'd noticed from the ground returned with a vengeance. For a moment — it was almost too fast to be sure I really saw what I thought I was seeing — something, almost an aura, flashed dark around Chester.

Bill grabbed Chester's hand. I believed with my whole heart he would stop Chester from jumping.

It was already too late.

Chester threw himself off the bridge with enough force that Bill's only option was to release the man or risk going over with him. Bill pulled back at the last second, anguish in his face, and then Landon pressed my face into his shoulder and turned his back to the scene.

The sound Chester's body made when it hit the concrete would indeed haunt me. Thankfully I didn't see the impact. I pressed my eyes shut and leaned into Landon as he swayed back and forth.

"There was nothing we could've done," he reassured me. "We were too late."

Even as he said it, I had to wonder. Were we too late or had something else happened?

AN HOUR LATER THE MEDICAL EXAMINER was at the scene. Landon had instructed me to stick close to the woods so as not to draw attention. He'd also begged me not to look at the freeway below, convinced the scene would wreck me. I didn't want to see the aftermath. I kept close to the tree line, my mind busy with possibilities, and when Landon and Chief Terry started moving in my direction, Bill came with them.

"I'm so sorry," I offered awkwardly when the negotiator was standing in front of me.

Bill shrugged. "You didn't cause it."

"No, but ... you really did try," I insisted. "I wish there could've been a better outcome."

"I think that goes without saying." Bill lifted his hand to drag it through his hair and my eyes went to his palm, where an angry red mark was apparent. Without thinking, I reached forward and snagged his wrist.

"What's this?"

Surprise registered in Bill's eyes, likely because he couldn't believe I had the gall to touch him. And then he saw the mark. "Oh, I don't know." He looked genuinely puzzled. "I have no idea."

Neither did I, and yet, it didn't look right.

"It almost looks like some sort of symbol," Chief Terry noted as he took in the squiggly lines on Bill's palm. "Do you know what that is?"

The question was directed at me, so I shook my head. "No. I just saw the red."

"I grabbed Chester's hand to try to stop him," Bill explained. He inclined his head to the hill, suggesting it was time we start down. We were obviously done here. There wasn't much mystery as to what had happened. "I must've grabbed him tighter than I realized. I didn't even feel him digging his fingernails into my palm."

My eyebrows drew together, and I risked a glance at Landon. There was warning in his gaze, causing me to change course almost immediately. "That must be it." I attempted a smile, although I was certain it was flat. "You put yourself on the line. You were very brave."

"I don't feel brave." Bill fell into silence until we reached the bottom of the hill. Then he headed directly to the medical examiner, who had placed Chester's body into a bag but hadn't yet zipped it closed. "I want preliminary toxicology results as soon as possible."

The medical examiner nodded as he fussed with the body. "I'll do my best." As he lifted Chester's arm his palm became evident ... and I sucked in a breath. "It will probably take a few days."

Bill nodded. "This was obviously a suicide, but I need everything I can possibly get for my report."

"You'll get everything I have." The medical examiner closed the body bag.

Bill looked tired, as if he was starting to deflate. Then he turned to Landon and Chief Terry. "Sorry you had to come out here for a lost cause."

"It's part of the job," Landon replied as he exchanged handshakes with Bill. "I'm sorry we didn't have a better outcome."

I was quiet for the walk back to Chief Terry's vehicle, waiting until I was safely ensconced in the backseat to speak again. "We have a problem."

Landon's eyebrows hiked. "What sort of problem?"

"That symbol on Bill's hand."

"The fingernail marks?"

I made a face. "It's a symbol and we all know it. It was on Chester's hand too. I saw it when the medical examiner was closing the bag. Chester's symbol was black, but it was the same symbol Bill had on his hand."

Chief Terry's face was blank. "What does that mean?"

I was grim as I stared out the window. "I don't know, but I'm going to find out."

4
FOUR

Chief Terry parked at the Hemlock Cove Police Department, easy walking distance from The Whistler. Landon caught me before I'd made it to the sidewalk to head to work.

"What's your plan?" he asked. "If this is something more than a suicide we need to know."

"I don't know what it is." That was the truth. "I don't know what any of it is, but I don't think it's normal."

"Suicide is never normal, Bay."

"No, but this felt off from the beginning. I had a feeling when we were driving there."

His fingers were gentle as they brushed my hair from my face. "I've learned never to ignore your feelings," he said. "How can I help?"

"I don't know that you can. I need to do some research."

"On the symbol?"

I nodded. "And other things."

"What other things?"

"You'll be the first to know when I figure it out."

Landon looked torn, as if he wanted to stick with me instead of Chief Terry, but he nodded. He tapped my chin so I would look up. His blue eyes were seeking as he searched mine for some hint of what I was feeling.

"I'm fine," I reassured him. "I'm not traumatized or anything. Well, I guess I am a little. I wish the outcome was different, but don't worry about me. I won't fall apart."

"You never do," he agreed as he kissed me, stroking my hair as he rested his forehead against mine. "It's possible this was just a suicide."

I nodded perfunctorily. "Of course."

"But you don't believe that."

"Nope."

He chuckled. "Well, at least you're honest." He flicked his eyes to Chief Terry, who was making a series of exaggerated faces a few feet away. "I guess we could dig a little too. What's with the faces?"

"You two are supposed to be less mushy now that you're married," Chief Terry replied. "I hate when you're gross. It makes me want to punch you."

"She's my wife," Landon argued. "If I can't be mushy with my wife, who can I be mushy with?"

"How about nobody?"

Landon grinned as he glanced back at me. "He has to adjust, because I'm going to be mushy forever."

He was still riding high on wedding emotions. I was too, truth be told. We would both settle some eventually. "I like mush." I ran my fingers over his cheek. "I need to get to the office. I'll let you know if I find anything."

"I'll do the same." He gave me another quick kiss. "Let's meet up for lunch if we can swing it."

"I'm sure that can be arranged. It will give me another chance to harp about your eating habits."

"Don't push me." He wagged a finger as he started toward Chief

Terry. "I want a magical heart attack cure. You'll pry my pot roast and bacon out of my cold dead hands."

VIOLA, THE RESIDENT WHISTLER GHOST, WAS BUZZING around the office when I bypassed security to enter. She seemed frazzled — actually her normal state — but she was even more worked up than usual.

"What's the word on the street?" I asked as I made my way into the kitchenette. I needed caffeine if I was going to spend the next few hours digging for information on a dead man.

"Well, Margaret is in a tizzy," Viola announced. The television was on in the cafeteria. Viola had been watching her soaps. "She claims Tillie is torturing her with unicorn farts, whatever that means."

I smirked. "I believe that's true."

"Tillie always was a pip. I think she's getting worse in her old age."

"I don't disagree. I don't really care about the unicorn farts. They're harmless."

Viola didn't look convinced. "Have you smelled that corner of Main Street today?"

I hadn't, but it brought up an interesting question. "I didn't know ghosts could smell."

"I've always had a super-sensitive sniffer." Viola tapped the side of her nose for emphasis. "It smells like bad Brussels sprouts down there."

"So I've heard. I'll check it out when I head that way for lunch."

"You might not want to eat afterward."

"I think I'll survive. Anything else going on?"

"You know that Timmy Gibbler kid?"

I took a moment to think. "Janet Gibbler's boy?"

Viola nodded. "He's a senior now, I guess. There's talk that he's going to be expelled from the high school."

"For what?" I was envisioning an answer that revolved around drugs or alcohol. Viola gave me something else entirely.

"Apparently he's been sexually harassing female students and staff. Supposedly he's been grabbing boobs left and right, like it's a contest or something."

I didn't know what to make of that. "Well, if it's true, I hope he's punished. He should keep his hands to himself."

"I believe that's the problem. Janet is uber-religious and says it's a sin for him to keep his hands to himself."

It took me a moment to grasp what she was saying. "Oh, geez. I didn't need that picture in my head."

"Hey, I just share the news. I don't control it."

"Fair enough." I popped the Keurig pod into the machine and slid a mug under the spout. "Anything else?"

"Um ... just one thing."

I waited.

"Bigfoot is living in the woods behind the newspaper."

I blinked several times. She'd delivered the news as if reporting it was going to rain all day. "Bigfoot?" I asked.

She nodded, solemn. "He's in a mood."

"Bigfoot is in a mood?" This was the biggest problem when dealing with Viola. She leaned toward the whimsical. She never outright lied, at least in her mind, but she was prone to exaggeration. "You've seen Bigfoot, have you?"

"Oh, loads of times," Viola said. "We go way back."

"Of course." That was such a Viola thing to say. "And he's in a mood, you say?"

"Yeah. He hates people."

"Who doesn't?"

"Right?" Viola emphatically bobbed her head. "Anyway, that's all that's going on today. What's up with you?"

"A man jumped to his death at the Au Sable River freeway overpass."

Viola perked up considerably. "Was it gross?"

"I didn't look."

"How could you not look?"

"I didn't want to see it." I started toward my office. "I'm going to do some research on him. He had a weird symbol on his hand. Something seems off about the whole thing. I'm determined to find out what's going on."

"Well, if you find anything good, let me know."

"If Bigfoot wants to sit down for an interview about his issues, you let me know."

"Of course, but he's pretty private. I don't think he wants the attention."

"Well, just in case."

ONCE IN MY OFFICE, I STARTED researching Chester Hamilton. The address I found for him was in Grayling, a nearby town. He was hardly quiet online, and his social media profiles were all set to public versus private.

"Anything good?" Landon asked when he appeared in my office about an hour later. He was stealthy when he wanted to be, and I almost jumped out of my skin when I realized he'd entered without me noticing.

"You need to learn to make a noise," I chided as I pressed my hand to my breast. "That was ... freaky."

"Oh, the love is truly gone," he teased as he planted a kiss on my forehead. "You were so focused on your computer you didn't even look up when I was in the doorway. I'm guessing that means you found something."

Had I? "Chester Hamilton recently divorced his wife, Trina. She kept the Grayling house in the divorce. I'm not sure where he was living."

"He was living here in Hemlock Cove. He was renting a place on Plum Street."

I tilted my head, considering, and then nodded. "It's cheaper to rent here than in Grayling. Also, it doesn't look like they had a very amicable divorce."

"Why do you say that?" Landon sat on the corner of my desk and watched me type.

"They aired their dirty laundry on Facebook." I pointed at the screen. "About nine months ago Trina posted that Chester was accusing her of cheating. She said it was ridiculous, but he kept telling anybody who would listen that she was nailing the UPS guy."

"Those UPS guys do look adorable in their shorts," Landon teased.

"They have a teenage daughter." I pulled up Daisy Hamilton's Instagram page. It was full of the sort of filtered model shots that were all the rage in teenage circles. "She's sixteen ... and she posts really sad selfies and laments about her parents fighting."

Landon pursed his lips as he read one post out loud. "Does anybody ever actively wish they were an orphan? I'm at that point in my life. I want some rich guy to swoop in and adopt me — like Daddy Warbucks — and take me away from my parents. They don't deserve me."

"It's a little whiny," I said when he didn't comment. "That's probably a normal mindset for a teenager, though."

His hand landed on my back, and he began to rub. "It was probably difficult for her to watch her parents rip each other apart publicly. Grayling is a small town. Everyone knows everybody's business."

"It's just like Hemlock Cove," I said. "Most of what I found was general complaining by all three of them ... but then things took a turn a week ago."

Landon's eyebrows hiked. "What sort of turn?"

"Look here." I shifted back to Chester's Facebook page. "He goes on a long diatribe about bad luck."

Landon followed my finger, frowning. The block of text stretched for hundreds of words. "Wow. He seems to claim that his luck turned out of nowhere and there's some evil force out to get him."

"He doesn't say what sort of bad luck he was dealing with," I noted. "Thankfully Trina and Daisy weren't shy on social media either." I hit Trina's page first. "She has a long post here about her 'crazy ex' losing his mind. She wonders how she ever fell in love with a man who keeps talking about seven days of torment and then death."

"Seven days of torment and then death?" Landon peered closer. "What do you think that means?"

"I don't know. The first thing that came to mind was that movie."

"What movie?"

"*The Ring*."

"*The Ring*?" He took a moment to think and then his frown grew more pronounced. "The movie about the evil girl trapped in a well who calls you and says 'seven days' when you watch the weird video?"

I nodded. "Are you going to give me grief about it?"

"I haven't decided yet."

"I'm not saying we're trapped in *The Ring* or anything. I'm not an idiot."

"Not my Bay," he readily agreed.

"Maybe Chester crossed paths with some sort of magical entity, maybe a witch or a demon, and that symbol was somehow transferred to his hand in the process. It's possible there's some sort of countdown attached to it."

Landon straightened. "Like in the movie."

"I don't think a malevolent spirit is going to crawl out of the television and convince a man to throw himself off a bridge in seven days, but the countdown aspect is worth looking into."

"You're the expert. If you say it's possible, I believe you. What does that mean for us?"

I lifted one shoulder and went back to staring at the screen. "I am ... flummoxed."

"Only you would use that word." Landon's grin was back. "I like that even in a time of crisis you like to sound knowledgeable."

"That's me. Knowledgeable Bay."

"Sometimes I think you're a genius." He went back to rubbing my shoulders. "What else did you find?"

"Daisy mentioned her father's fraying mental state in a post two days ago." I pulled up the teenager's Instagram account again. "She said that he thought he saw shadowy figures following him, and he was obsessed with bad luck. She's something of an armchair psychiatrist, because she thinks it was some sort of delayed reaction from the divorce, like he was blaming outside elements for what happened."

"But you said he thought his wife was cheating on him."

"She denied it. She claimed he made it all up."

"Is it possible that whatever happened started as far back as then?"

"That was nine months ago. Why would Chester become obsessed with the seven days thing if he was somehow ... infected all the way back then?"

Landon cracked his neck. His mind appeared to be working a mile a minute. "I don't know what to say about any of it."

"That makes two of us."

"Is there a way to track down more information?"

I shrugged. "I'm going to conduct research on the symbol. It looked like a rune of some sort. Just because we find the meaning doesn't mean we'll find the answers we need."

"And you're still convinced we're not dealing with a suicide?"

I pinned him with a dark look.

"It's just a question, Bay." He raised his hands in quick surrender. "I'm not trying to be a pain. I simply want to know what we're dealing with. I don't want you running off half-cocked if there's no malevolent entity to chase."

"And here I thought that's exactly what you would want," I teased. "I mean ... if I'm making it all up in my head, I'll be safe, and you won't have anything to worry about."

Landon looked momentarily torn. "I didn't say you were making it up," he said.

"Yes, because nobody wants to be married to the crazy woman."

He glared. "Bay, I don't think you're crazy. I just don't believe that everything that happens is rooted in magical evil. I want to be open to all options, but sometimes a suicide is just a suicide."

"I don't disagree. I would've written this off as a suicide if it weren't for the symbol."

"Right. The symbol. What if it was just a mark on his hand?"

"How did it transfer to Bill Blake's hand?"

Landon straightened. "Do you think that Chester somehow passed an evil curse to Bill?"

I couldn't deny it. I chose my words carefully. "It's something I want to think about. If there is a time element involved, we don't have to move immediately to save Bill. We can watch him, see if he starts unraveling like Chester."

"And if he does start unraveling?"

I shook my head. "We need to come up with a plan so he doesn't join Chester." I reached over and rested my hand on Landon's knee. "We don't know anything yet."

The sigh Landon let loose was long-suffering. "Well, let's keep digging. If I've learned anything since falling in love with you it's that your instincts are never wrong. I don't even know why I'm arguing this point with you."

I knew. "It's because you want to keep the honeymoon train rolling. It's been quiet for a few weeks. You've been happy."

"Aw, Bay." He shook his head. "You're my happiness. Our family is my happiness. I don't expect it to be smooth sailing when it comes to external forces forever."

"You wouldn't complain about another week of quiet though."

"I wouldn't complain about anything where you're concerned."

I was relieved that his first instinct wasn't to melt down. "So, we keep researching?"

He bobbed his head. "Absolutely. If you're right, which you usually are, we need to get ahead of this."

"I'll keep digging," I promised.

"And I'll ask around the local courthouses. Maybe some of the other lawyers will be able to give me an idea of where Chester's head was at in his last days."

5

FIVE

Landon stayed with me for an hour before heading out to do some digging of his own. I could tell he was concerned, but we were in that weird limbo where we had nothing but a hypothesis without anything to back it up.

I spent hours poring over social media posts. Chester's postings read as though he were growing increasingly unhinged as the days progressed, but there were no direct statements about evil entities. He railed about bad luck and people judging him.

Landon and Chief Terry were called out to a domestic dispute on the outskirts of town, so I wandered over to Hypnotic to catch a ride to the inn with Thistle. I'd completely forgotten about the farting unicorns until we were directly in front of Mrs. Little's store. The chaotic scene inside drew my attention, and it took everything I had not to bend at the waist and start guffawing when I saw the woman melting down inside.

"Stop it!" she screamed as the clock struck six and the unicorns started farting as if on cue, glitter and confetti shooting everywhere. The scent that followed was enough to turn my stomach.

"Oh, gross." I covered my nose. Thistle had changed her hair color sometime in the last twenty-four hours. Now it was a rich green. "That is ... horrifying."

Thistle grinned. "Yeah. It's pretty great."

I made a face. "You can smell it from blocks away."

"Yeah, but the scent lasts only five minutes and then it's quiet for another hour. Mrs. Little spends that hour complaining and threatening Aunt Tillie with death, and then it starts all over again."

"It's kind of mean," I lamented.

Thistle's only response was a shrug.

"You don't think it's mean?" I challenged.

"Mrs. Little gets off on being mean, so it sort of feels like karma."

"Would you feel the same way if Aunt Tillie was doing it to someone else?"

"I guess it would depend on the person. But it's Mrs. Little so I'm fine with it."

I shook my head. "You would be. Are you ready? You're my ride."

"Landon texted," she said. "He wanted to make sure I didn't leave without you."

"Like I can't secure my own ride," I groused.

"It's kind of cute."

"Since when?"

"Since now I guess. You two are pretty adorable together. I don't know if it's adding a baby to the mix or not, but I feel softer inside when I think about the world."

That was the most ludicrous thing I'd ever heard. "Do your ovaries ache or something?"

She laughed and then rolled her eyes, assuring me the real Thistle was still in there somewhere. "I'm fine waiting. Given everything that happened with Minerva, I can't help feeling grateful for how things turned out. I don't know how to explain it."

I didn't either. "You're kind of freaking me out," I admitted.

"I'm kind of freaking myself out," she said. "I've decided to just go with it for now. I'm sure I'll be over it in another week or two."

We fell into step with each other as we crossed to her car. "So, something happened today." I launched into the tale of Chester Hamilton and his suicide. When I got to the part about the symbol, Thistle's demeanor changed.

"What do you think that was about?"

"I don't know, but I don't think it was a coincidence."

"We can check the books in the library at the inn. There might be something there."

"That's the plan."

"I'm sure our mothers — especially your mother — will be on a rampage with Aunt Tillie. It will give us an excuse to hide."

"I'm always looking for one of those."

"You and me both."

RAISED VOICES WERE OBVIOUS WHEN WE entered the inn through the front door. We skirted down the far hallway and locked ourselves in the library. Thistle mixed drinks for us and then we got to work.

"I don't know what I'm even looking for," she said as she flipped through a heavy leather tome. "Can you give me a description?"

I pursed my lips and thought back to the symbol. "There was like a half-circle on the top ... and some wavy lines. There were a few other lines too."

Thistle shook her head. "Well, that certainly narrows it down."

"I don't know how to describe it. I just know I'll recognize it if I see it again."

"Okay. If I see anything with half circles and lines, you'll be the first to know."

We focused on our work, tuning out the yelling that kept cropping up. It wasn't just Mom demanding that Aunt Tillie get it together. Marnie chimed in too.

"Notice my mother isn't giving Aunt Tillie grief," Thistle said. "She's either incredibly smart or too lazy to bother."

We stared at each.

"Too lazy," we said at the same time, and then laughed as if it was the funniest joke in the world. We were still laughing when the library door opened to allow Clove and a swaddled Calvin entrance.

"Don't stop laughing on my account," she drawled as she flopped on the couch next to me. "It's not like I don't already know that you guys prefer spending time together these days. I'm the odd cousin out."

"Oh, here we go," Thistle muttered as she inched closer to Clove and extended her hands. "Give me that baby."

Clove gladly acquiesced and handed over her sleeping son. "I'm on to you," she warned in a low voice. "You think holding my son will prevent me from yelling at you. Well, it won't. If I want to yell, I'm going to yell."

"Do you want to yell?" I asked.

She shook her head. "No. Oddly enough, I feel so much more mellow now that I've had the baby. I thought for sure I would melt down constantly because I felt overwhelmed — you know, hormones and the like — but I've been perfectly fine. Can you believe it?"

Actually, I couldn't. I looked to Calvin, who was happily sucking a pacifier as he stared into Thistle's eyes. There were times he cried — there was no escaping that — but for the most part he was a mellow baby. "Let me see him." I held out my arms so Thistle could transfer the baby to me.

She balked. "I just got him."

"I'll give him back," I reassured her. "I just want to see him for a second."

"Fine." Thistle made a disgruntled sound deep in her throat as she relinquished Calvin. "I'm timing you."

"Yeah, yeah, yeah." My eyebrows drew together as I took in the baby's placid features. He was ridiculously cute — and not just because he was related to me — but there was something otherworldly about him. "You're really ... something ... aren't you?" My fingers were gentle as I pressed them to his forehead in the hope I could see inside his head. To my surprise, I initially found a wall. He stared at me hard as I tried to find a way around the wall, and then ultimately let me inside.

"Well, well, well." I grinned at him as he contentedly sucked his pacifier. "You're magical after all."

"He is?" Clove's eyes went wide.

"Definitely." The baby's skin was ridiculously soft as I ran my finger over his cheek. "He was something of a mood-altering presence when he was in the womb. I think he's still doing it."

"But ... no." Clove shook her head. "He upset us when he was in the womb."

"I think he's doing the opposite now. He's mellowing you out. I mean ... why else wouldn't you be freaking out? We were all prepared for you to be a Momzilla of the highest order. Instead, you're calm and completely put together."

"I think there's an insult buried in there," Clove said darkly.

"And I think it's interesting. He's mellowing Thistle out too."

Thistle narrowed her eyes. "I've always been mellow."

Clove and I snorted in unison.

"I have," Thistle insisted. "I'm the only one who doesn't freak out when something big is happening."

"Actually, I think that's Bay," Clove countered.

"No way." Thistle was adamant. "Bay's a whiner."

"I think that's Clove," I countered.

"Hey," Clove shouted. "I'm a mother now. You can't call me a whiner."

I turned back to the baby, who looked to be concentrating. Or maybe he was crapping his diaper. It was always hard to tell. "I think the baby likes when we're calm and exerts himself to make sure it stays that way."

"But ... why?" Thistle's expression was hard to read. "He made us cry and get upset when he was in the womb."

"Did he?" I glanced up at the sound of the door opening. Landon,

Marcus and Sam were making their way inside. "Or did he just make us feel what his mother was feeling?"

"What are we talking about?" Sam asked as he moved over to Clove and kissed the top of her head.

"Your baby," I replied as I scooted so Landon could sit. He seemed to want to be close to me but wasn't all that keen to hang out with the baby. "I think he can control the emotions of others."

Sam looked as if I'd said something in another language. "Come again."

"I think he's making Clove and Thistle calm."

"Seriously?" Landon leaned forward to stare at Calvin. "That's a little less boring, buddy." He shot the infant an enthusiastic thumbs-up. "Keep it up."

"Stop saying my baby is boring," Clove hissed.

Landon waved the comment away and then glanced at the book I'd dropped on the floor when Calvin had garnered my interest. "Did you find anything on your magic symbol?"

I shook my head. I was much more interested in the baby at present, although I knew it wouldn't last. "Not yet. We didn't get a chance to look all that long."

"But you're still convinced there's a magical angle to what happened."

"I am." Slowly, I shifted my eyes to him. There was something akin to worry in his eyes. "But you're not. You think I'm crazy."

"I would never say that." He emphatically shook his head. "It's just ... Terry and I were talking, and the cause of death is going to go down as a suicide no matter what."

"I don't really care about the cause of death," I pointed out. "I care about this ... contagion, if that's what it is ... spreading."

"We have no proof there is a contagion," Landon argued.

"I saw Bill Blake's hand," I insisted. "He had the same symbol as Chester Hamilton, and in the same spot."

"Okay. Fair enough." Landon held up his hands, telling me he wanted to stave off a fight, not that he was surrendering. "Here's the thing...." He broke off and licked his lips. "We went to the medical examiner's office to look at the body. We didn't see a symbol on the hand."

"I saw it."

"Maybe you just think you did." Landon looked pained. "I don't want to tick you off, Bay, but it was a stressful morning. The body wasn't in the best shape when you saw it. Isn't it possible that what you saw was blood?"

"No."

Landon blinked twice and then held out his arms. "Hand me that baby."

"No." I clutched Calvin closer to my chest. "You don't even like him."

"Don't say that." Landon made an exaggerated face. "He'll develop a complex. I like him fine. I just want him to start doing things. And what do you know? He has been doing things all along."

My eyes were slits of annoyance as I regarded him. "I need to take a walk." I stood with the baby and frowned when Landon stood with me.

"Let's take a walk," he agreed.

"I don't want to take a walk with you." I begrudgingly handed Calvin to Thistle. He didn't need to witness a fight.

"Oh, don't be like that," Landon whined. "I didn't say it to hurt you. I just don't want you wasting your time. Sometimes a suicide is just a suicide, Bay."

I hissed something dark under my breath.

"There was nothing there," Landon insisted. "I'm sorry. It was just a horrible tragedy."

I could've argued further. I could've dragged out the fight. Instead, I plastered a fake smile on my face. "Okay. It was just a suicide. Excuse me." I pushed him out of the way to exit the library.

"You're in trouble now," Thistle sang out, grinning at the baby as she swooped her arms left and right. "Uncle Landon is going to get punished."

Calvin was too young to smile but I swear he wanted to. Apparently, Thistle's glee was enough to provide oodles of entertainment for an infant.

"I'm not going to get punished." Landon was adamant as he followed me into the hallway, where we ran into Aunt Tillie, who was racing across the hardwood floors on her scooter, Peg trailing in her wake.

Snort. Snort.

"Oh, there she is!" Landon brightened as he collected the pig in his arms.

"There she is," I agreed as I shook my head. I was anxious to get away from him, something I could rarely say.

"Bay." Landon abandoned Peg when he realized I was still walking and chased after me, not catching up until I was in the dining room, which, thankfully, was empty.

"What do you want?" I demanded.

"I want you to not be angry with me."

"Well, I am."

"I didn't want to hurt you. I promised Terry I would talk to you. There's no case to waste your time on here."

"Weren't you the one who always told me you had faith in my instincts? I believe that was you, and only a few hours ago."

He licked his lips, doing his best to ignore Peg as she wrapped herself around his ankles. "I trust your instincts," he said.

"Obviously not. It's fine. I'll handle this one myself."

"Don't say that." His frustration was evident. "If you want to stick with this, we will."

"Even though you believe we'll be wasting our time," I challenged.

"I ... ." He didn't finish. He didn't need to.

"Play with your favorite girl." I inclined my head toward Peg. "I'll be back in a few minutes."

"Bay."

"It's fine." I didn't mean it. I was annoyed but had no idea if I had the right to be. He had an opinion on the subject, and he was entitled to it. It was rare these days that we weren't on the same page. "I'm fine. We're fine. Everything is fine."

"Why don't I believe you?"

"Because she's a terrible liar," Aunt Tillie replied as she appeared in the doorway. "What's going on?"

"Nothing important," I replied. "It's just a difference of opinion."

"This isn't you two faking a fight just so you can make up later?" she asked, her nose wrinkling. "I hate when you guys are gross. There's no reason to fake fights if you want to have sex. You're adults. Just freaking do it already."

"Oh, geez." Chief Terry slapped his hand over his eyes as he appeared behind Aunt Tillie. "Why can't I ever walk in this house and hear a nice conversation about bunnies? Is that too much to ask?"

"Well, bunnies like to do it all the time too, so we could've been talking about bunnies for all you know," Aunt Tillie said.

"Ugh." Chief Terry looked as if he wanted to start drinking. Funnily enough, that's how I felt.

"Bay's upset," Landon volunteered. "I told her that we believe it was a straight suicide."

Now Chief Terry looked upset for a different reason. "We checked the body, sweetheart. There was no symbol. I think you imagined it."

"I didn't imagine it."

"What symbol?" Aunt Tillie asked. "You know what? Never mind. I agree with Bay. Something evil is afoot."

That was so typical. "You're just saying that because you want something to focus on that will get Mom off your back," I groused.

Aunt Tillie didn't look bothered by the charge. "You say that like it's a bad thing. What's important is that I'm on your team." She leaned in conspiratorially to impart some wisdom. "Unlike these two, who think you're full of crap. They're not on your side. I'm on your side. Put your faith in Tillie."

"She won't fall for that," Landon said. "We have faith in her. There's just nothing to chase."

"Don't listen to him," Aunt Tillie insisted. "He's your enemy. You don't need him. You have me."

"Bay." Landon's hands landed on his hips. "Don't let her get you worked up."

It was too late. "I know what I feel. Something forced him to do it. I don't expect you to stand with me. I'll handle this one on my own."

"Oh, here we go." Landon threw his hands in the air and glared at Chief Terry. "I told you she wouldn't like this."

"I knew she wouldn't like it," Chief Terry barked back. "Why do you think I made you tell her?"

"Well, now we're both in the doghouse. I hope you're happy."

"Yes, I hope you're both happy," I agreed as I sulkily sank into my chair. "We're just one big happy family. Nothing to see here. Move along."

Landon didn't respond but I saw the determination in his eyes. This was nowhere near over.

6
SIX

"What's the plan for today?"

One week later, Landon caught me in the parking lot outside the inn before we split for our jobs. Things had been quiet the entire week, as he predicted, and nothing out of the ordinary had happened. I remained on edge, although I was careful not to show it. I didn't want him getting upset, especially since he had apparently been right.

As far as I knew, Bill Blake was the same man he'd always been. Landon had reluctantly checked several times during the week, and the man wasn't acting out of sorts, according to Landon's sources with the Michigan State Police. My suspicions had been wrong. Thankfully, my new husband was gracious enough not to bring that up.

"I have a store opening to cover," I replied as I checked my bag for a reporter's notebook. I stashed them everywhere most days, which was a benefit because I often lost them. "Kristen Donaldson's store is already opening as something else."

"Really?" Landon's eyes gleamed with interest as he brushed my hair from my face. Kristen Donaldson had been working with an evil midwife to steal Clove's baby and wreak havoc on our lives. She'd been in town only a few weeks when she died. Now her store was being converted to something new, providing a new source of gossip in town. "What sort of store are we getting now? Hemlock Cove needs witchy lingerie. Please tell me we're finally getting that."

I didn't allow my expression to change even though it took everything I had not to grin. "Witchy lingerie would cut you funny, but you do you."

"Ha, ha." He tapped the end of my nose and leaned in for a kiss. We'd made up almost immediately after our fight — I could never stay angry with him long — but he'd been watching me closely the past week. It was as if he was waiting for a bomb to go off.

"I'm fine," I blurted, immediately wishing I could drag the words back into my mouth. "There's absolutely nothing to worry about. I'm ... perfectly cool."

"You're way better than perfectly cool," he countered as he stroked the back of my head. "It's just ... we don't really fight."

"We fight all the time. I thought you were fine with it because you like to make up."

"Oh, I love making up." His grin turned devilish. "But our fights are always minor."

"Not always." I thought back to a few we'd engaged in because his job and mine collided. We'd mostly gotten past that — we'd both done some compromising — but I didn't particularly remember those fights being nothing.

"Lately they've been nothing," he countered. "We worked through all that stuff. I like our minor skirmishes, the ones that aren't real. Those are the ones I like to engage in simply so we can make up. The other stuff ... ." He trailed off.

"It's fine, Landon." I meant it. It was best to get this conversation out of the way now. "You were obviously right. Bill Blake is still alive. You said you checked on him at the state police outpost yesterday. There was no symbol on the palm of his hand, and he wasn't acting erratic."

"He wasn't." Landon's gaze was sincere. "He was his normal self."

"Well, that's awesome ... especially for him. I'm glad."

Landon didn't look convinced, but he nodded. "I love you." He pressed a kiss to my forehead. "I'll let you know if I hear anything. We should be in the clear today if that seven days thing is correct."

I nodded. "Yeah. My theory turned out to be crap. You can do your victory lap."

He shook his head, solemn. "I don't want to be right. I want you to be happy."

I had news for him. The niggling worry that had started creeping through me the day we went to the overpass hadn't gone anywhere. I'd simply been doing my best to pretend I wasn't wound up and ready for Armageddon. I had no idea if Landon was truly buying it.

"I'm happy," I reassured him despite the way my stomach clenched. "Don't spend your day obsessing about me."

"I always do that." He cupped the back of my head and made a grand gesture of bending me back for a Hollywood kiss. It made me laugh. "You're my favorite thing to think about," he whispered.

"Oh, don't be gross," Chief Terry barked as he exited the inn. He and Landon were driving in together. I'd left my car in the parking lot the night before so it would be handy when it came time to head to town. "You guys are always so ridiculous it drives me nuts."

Landon gave me another smacking kiss before righting me. "Yes, because we live our lives for you."

Chief Terry rolled his eyes until they landed on me. "New witch store today, right?" He looked concerned for an entirely different reason, and I knew what was worrying him.

"Voodoo store," I corrected.

"What?" Landon's shoulders suddenly went stiff. "You didn't mention that." His tone was accusatory.

"I didn't think it was a big deal."

"Voodoo is evil magic."

I made a face. "Like anything else, voodoo is what you make it. If you're a good person, your magic will be good. Don't be all ... you." I waggled my fingers, earning a stern look. "It's a voodoo store, not the end of the world. I'm actually kind of excited. Hemlock Cove needs something new."

"If you say so." Landon pulled me close for another hug. "I just want you to be happy."

"I'm totally happy," I reassured him.

"It's because you have the best husband in the world." He rubbed his cheek against mine, eliciting a smile.

"I do have the best husband in the world," I agreed. "I love him more than anything."

"Right back at you." Sincere adoration shone through his eyes as he pulled back. "I want to hear about the voodoo store later. I feel as if that's a bigger story."

"It's just a store. There's nothing to worry about."

EMORI CLARK WELCOMED ME INTO her store an hour before it was set to open and stepped to the side as I took several photos of her shelves. I could feel her eyes on me as I perused the offerings, but there was nothing malevolent about her aura or attitude ... at least not yet.

"So, you lived in New Orleans for a spell?" I asked. We'd gone over her background during a phone conversation. I still had questions.

"I was born in Detroit, but my mother grew up in New Orleans," Emori replied. She was in her late-thirties, maybe early-forties, and had one of those winning smiles that light up entire rooms. "My father was a salesman and met my mother in New Orleans when she was twenty. She didn't leave with him right away, of course — she said love at first sight was a myth — but she went to dinner with him when he came to town on business.

"At first he only visited every other month," she continued. "Then it was every month. Soon, he was somehow managing to get to town once a week. My mother realized she looked forward to each visit, so eventually she agreed to move to Detroit with him because being together was more important to her than holding onto a city."

"That must've been quite the change from New Orleans," I mused. I'd never been but I'd always wanted to visit. Landon had promised we would go soon.

"I don't think she minded." Emori took on a soft smile. "They're still in love to this day, almost forty years after they met. As for me, I visit family in the Quarter at least once a year. I try to make it more often, but it doesn't always work out that way."

"At least you get to see them." I managed a tight smile. "I've always loved the photos I've seen of New Orleans. Not the Mardi Gras photos, but the cemeteries and other places. I want to visit one day."

"What's stopping you?" Emori looked genuinely curious.

"Nothing really. I just got married. My husband wants to go with me. We need time to plan, arrange his time off work. I do most of the heavy lifting at The Whistler, so I'd have to work ahead to cover that."

"Yes, being the only person doing the work is difficult," Emori agreed, her eyes roaming my face. "You would love the city. They're fond of witches there."

I went still and swallowed hard as I fought to collect myself. "Witches?" I pasted what I hoped was a curious smile on my face. I didn't want her to know she'd touched a nerve. She had a certain shimmer about her, one I'd grown familiar with since I'd begun crossing paths with magical beings more frequently. Whatever she was — good or evil — she had genuine magic. How much was the question.

"Oh, you're cute." Emori made a tsking sound and shook her head. She'd dressed in a brightly-colored wrap dress for her opening, her long braids arranged in an intricate pattern around her head. I found everything about her interesting.

I was also leery. I'd been burned a few too many times by new witches moving into my town. They almost always had ulterior motives.

"People in this town talk," she continued. "The woman across the road talks more than most." She inclined her head toward Mrs. Little's store.

I shifted toward the window to look across the street. The unicorns were still farting — Aunt Tillie refused to remove the spell, though she did adjust it so they only farted four times a day instead of twenty-four — and the smell of Brussels sprouts clouded the street.

"What has she said about us?" I asked, struggling to keep my tone even. "I mean ... has she been trying to turn you against us?"

Emori's laugh was hollow. "I can read people, Bay. That includes Margaret Little — and you. I know you're a good person. I also know you're powerful. As for Margaret, she has a very specific opinion of your family."

I had no doubt that was true. "She and Aunt Tillie have been at each other's throats for a very long time," I confirmed.

"Oh, I have no doubt." Emori's features brightened. "Your aunt is ... interesting. She likes attention. That's why she has the scooter ... and the cape ... and the combat helmet ... and those ridiculous leggings ... and the whistle ... and the pig."

"Don't forget the stick," I added.

Emori barked out a laugh. "I could never forget the stick. She's the real deal, though, and she covers for being the real deal by being flamboyant. She wants people to think she's a kook."

"Actually, her motivations are ... shakier." A small smile played at the corners of my mouth as I turned my attention back to Mrs. Little's store. There was no movement inside, which meant the unicorns were dormant ... for now. "Aunt Tillie is impossible to read. In fact ... ." I trailed off when a figure appeared in the middle of Main Street.

At first, I didn't know who it was. Then the man, who appeared disheveled, turned to look directly at the voodoo store. Directly at me.

I let out a breath when Bill Blake's agonized features swam into view. "Oh, no."

"Do you know him?" Emori was instantly on alert.

I nodded as I moved toward the door, my heart pounding loud enough to drown out the noise on the street as I emerged onto the sidewalk. Emori followed.

"He doesn't look good," she noted. She didn't sound alarmed as much as curious. "Where do you know him from?"

"He's with the state police. He's a crisis negotiator." I looked up and down Main Street, debating, and then pulled my phone from my pocket. My hands were surprisingly steady as I pulled up Landon's name on my contact list. Before I could hit it, Bill began to speak.

"You're all idiots if you think you're safe here," he seethed. Flecks of foam gathered at the corners of his mouth. "You don't know the danger of living in this world, in this town. It's not safe here. The bad luck will find you, just like it found me. They're coming."

"Who is he talking about?" Emori asked.

"I don't know." I hit Landon's name. He answered on the second ring.

"Miss me already?" Landon's tone was jovial.

"Where are you?" I demanded.

"I'm with Chief Terry on Dunham Street," Landon replied. He quickly picked up on the tension in my voice and was no longer messing around. "Where are you?"

"Main Street. Bill Blake is here."

He was silent.

"Are you still there?" I snapped, my anxiety getting the better of me.

"Yes." Landon sounded calm and yet I knew better. He was likely already signaling Chief Terry that it was time to leave. "Tell me what's happening." He leaned into his training.

"He's ranting. He's pacing. He says nobody is safe. I don't think he's slept in days."

"Can you see the mark on his hand?"

"I'm not close enough."

"Well ... don't get close enough. We're ten minutes out."

Bill withdrew a knife from the pocket of his coat. "Oh, no." I took an inadvertent step forward.

"What is that?" Emori demanded. "What is he doing with that knife?"

Landon obviously heard the question because he was suddenly snapping out orders. "Don't touch him, Bay." His fear was palpable enough, even from a distance, to fill me with dread. "Don't go near him."

The street was filling with people, shop owners and locals. All eyes were on Bill. "Landon, I can't let him hurt an innocent."

"Stay away from him, Bay." The order was issued on a growl. "If he's sick, Chester somehow transferred the sickness to him. We both know how."

We did, but I couldn't stand by and watch a man kill himself ... or others. "Get here as soon as you can." I disconnected the call before Landon could argue further and exhaled heavily, my eyes darting left and right.

"What are you going to do?" Emori asked as I stepped off the sidewalk onto the street.

"I'm going to try to talk him down," I replied. "Keep everybody away. The police are on their way."

"But ... ."

"I need to get that knife from him." I was firm. "It's my only option."

"I think Mrs. Little has the same idea," Emori noted. "Maybe you can work together."

Mrs. Little? Even hearing her name made no sense. When I snapped my eyes back to Bill, I saw her approaching him from behind ... and she didn't look happy.

"You can't just stand in the middle of the road," she snapped. She couldn't see Bill's face. I was almost positive she couldn't see the knife either. "You're obstructing traffic ... and cutting off people from my business. You need to move along."

Bill swiveled at the sound of her voice. I opened my mouth to call out, but it was already too late. Bill swiped at her with his right hand, the one without the knife, and I caught a glimpse of his palm. The symbol was back ... and it was glowing a dark red that bordered on black.

"Stop that!" Mrs. Little swatted at his hand.

"No!" I yelled, my voice finally breaking free as I took two steps toward Mrs. Little. "Don't touch him!"

"Don't tell me what to do, Bay," Mrs. Little fired back as Bill reached out for her a second time. "You're not my boss. While you're here, let's talk about your aunt." She slapped Bill's hand away again. This time I was positive they made contact.

Bill seemed satisfied with the slap, because he stopped trying to make contact with Mrs. Little and instead focused his full attention on the knife, which he transferred from his left hand to his right hand.

I reacted on instinct, drawing enough magic that I stopped Bill from using the knife against his own throat. His eyes went wide when he realized an outside force stopped him from slashing his throat.

"You don't even realize what's to come." Slowly, he raised his eyes until they were trained on me. "You don't understand that you're already lost, you're already in the midst of a dark plague. The bad luck is coming for you, all of you."

"Just ... don't do anything," I pleaded.

He didn't respond with words. Instead, he moved two steps in my direction and grinned. It was the smile of the damned and it made my blood run cold. I opened my mouth to call out to him, stop him, but it was already too late. The car pulling out of the bank barreled into him.

The sound of the vehicle hitting Bill had my stomach constricting, and I shut my eyes so I wouldn't have to see the result. That didn't stop the horrified screams echoing up and down Main Street as the locals realized what had happened.

Those screams would live with me a long time. Maybe forever.

7

SEVEN

I was still sitting on the curb in front of the new voodoo store when Chief Terry and Landon arrived. They parked in the street to cut off traffic from one direction, and Chief Terry hit the pavement running. He started barking orders to his officers. Landon headed directly for me.

"Hey." He hunkered down in front of me and stared into my eyes. "Are you okay?"

"I tried to stop it," I offered. "He was going to stab himself. I used my magic to stop him but ... I didn't see the car."

"Oh, baby." He slid his arm around my neck and pulled me in for a hug. "This isn't your fault. You can't blame yourself." He rubbed his cheek against mine. "This is my fault."

I was caught off guard. "What?" When I pulled back, I found sincere regret reflecting from his sad eyes.

"You knew," he said. "You knew something bad was going to happen. I should've listened."

I'd been angry with him when he said it was just a suicide. Like ... legitimately angry. All of that emotion drained from me when I saw the guilt in his eyes. "You couldn't have known. I didn't really know either," I said. "It was a hunch."

"It turned out to be the right hunch."

"Yes, well, we have another problem." There was no sugarcoating this for him. "He touched Mrs. Little. I saw the symbol on his palm when he was flailing about. She came out to shut him up. Before I could stop her, she swatted him away. I know they made contact."

Landon jerked his eyes over his shoulder, to the Unicorn Emporium. "Where is she now?"

"She retreated inside. She was understandably upset."

Landon rubbed his jaw. "We need to talk to her."

I cringed. "Do we have to?"

His lips quirked at my whine. "It's for the best."

"She's going to be obnoxious."

"What else is new?" He pressed a kiss to my forehead and stood, extending his hand to help me up from the curb. "Who is that?" he asked.

I looked and then inclined my head in acknowledgement when I realized Emori was watching us from in front of her shop. "That's Emori Clark. She's the owner of the new store."

"The new voodoo store."

"She seems okay. I didn't get a chance to talk to her long before everything went down."

"Let me ask you something." He licked his lips and kept his voice low. "Do you think she's involved in this?"

"Why would she be?"

"It's voodoo."

"Like I told you before, voodoo itself is not evil. It all comes down to the practitioner."

"So you don't think she's evil."

"I don't know her," I countered. "I haven't seen any outward signs that she's evil, but I rarely do at the start. That's when everybody is on their best behavior. She seems fine ... for now."

Landon nodded and gripped my hand tighter. "Okay, well, let's talk to someone we know is evil."

I wrinkled my nose. "She's awful."

"I don't think that matters if you're right, Bay. She might be evil — heck, we know she is — but we can't sit back and do nothing if this curse, or whatever it is, has marked Margaret Little next. We have to be proactive."

I'd already come to that conclusion. "Yeah." I blew out a sigh. "Let's talk to her."

Landon led me across the street. I was careful not to look at Bill's face. I didn't want to see the death mask that I knew was waiting for me there. Instead, I focused on his hand. The symbol was still evident, but quickly fading. I took out my phone and snapped a photo, jolting Chief Terry in the process.

"What are you doing?" he hissed, pinning me with an admonishing look. "You can't photograph a body, Bay. That can't go in the newspaper."

Now it was my turn to glare. "I'm not putting it in the newspaper. I need a photo of that symbol for research before it disappears again."

"Oh." Chief Terry looked properly abashed. "I'm sorry. I didn't mean to bark at you."

I knew that was true. He never yelled at me. Even when I was a child, he rarely raised his voice. He was often stuck being the disciplinarian because my mother and aunts were busy starting a bed and breakfast. Aunt Tillie regularly got us into trouble, and he had to be the one to explain why we were doing something wrong.

"It's fine," I said automatically.

"No, it's not." He shook his head. "I'm just ... shaken ... by this. I shouldn't have said that. I know you better than that."

He did, but I wasn't going to make a thing out of it. "We're going inside to talk to Mrs. Little," I volunteered. "Bill touched her before ... well, before the end came. I'm worried she has the same symbol on her hand."

"Which means what?" Chief Terry's demeanor shifted in an instant. "What are you suggesting, Bay?"

"Chester Hamilton clearly passed ... something ... along to Bill Blake," I replied. "It happened fast. I saw the symbols. They might disappear after the fact, but they're there initially ... and at the end. I need to see Mrs. Little's hand."

"And if she has the symbol?"

This was the part I dreaded most. "Then I think we have one week to save her."

Chief Terry worked his jaw. "Well, isn't that just a kick in the pants?" He flicked his eyes to Landon. "Do you think that's what we're dealing with?"

Landon nodded. "I'm not doubting Bay again. Her instincts were right. If we'd listened ... ." He trailed off.

"Oh, you're going to blame me for this," Chief Terry complained.

"No." Landon was firm when he shook his head. "I don't blame you. We talked about it and thought she was shaken by what happened, thought that was the reason she was jumping to conclusions. It's on me that I didn't believe her. I know better than to question her instincts."

Chief Terry looked drained. "Talk to Margaret. Tell her you need to get a witness statement. Ascertain what you can. We'll go from there."

"That's the plan," Landon agreed, his hand on the small of my back. "I'm sure she's going to be an absolute delight, but if we know she's going to die, we have to stop it. I don't know that I'll ever get over the fact that we could've stopped this and didn't." He gestured toward Bill's body. "We can't fail again."

THE BELL OVER THE UNICORN EMPORIUM door jangled as we let ourselves in. Otherwise, the store was completely silent. The lingering smell from the spell Aunt Tillie had cast lingered, however, and I gagged when it hit me head-on.

"Oh, don't do that," Landon chided, making a face. "You know I'm a sympathetic puker. If you get sick, I will too."

"I'm sorry. I like Brussels sprouts. They just leave a very pungent after ... smell."

Landon smirked. "That's why it's one of her go-to scents."

Footsteps behind the counter had both of us jerking our heads in that direction. Mrs. Little's nose wrinkled in disgust when she saw who was darkening her doorstep. "Oh, it's you."

"Good afternoon, Mrs. Little," Landon drawled. He gave my shoulder another squeeze and stepped to the counter. "We were just discussing the lovely scent. Is that some new type of fragrance you're testing?"

If looks could kill, Landon would be dead. The glare Mrs. Little graced him with was straight out of a mafia movie. "You're so funny."

"I'm serious. It's a very unique scent."

"It's Tillie," Mrs. Little barked. "She's been wreaking havoc all week. I'm sure you know nothing about that, though."

Since the statement was directed at me, I merely shrugged. "I don't. I'm sorry."

Mrs. Little dusted off her hands. I could make out a flash of red in the palm of one of them, the one that she'd used to bat Bill away. I would need to get closer. "What do you want?"

"We want to talk to you about that." Landon gestured to the front window, where Chief Terry was working with the medical examiner. "I understand you were outside when it happened."

"As was your girlfriend," Mrs. Little drawled in challenging fashion.

"Wife," Landon corrected.

"What?" Confusion lined Mrs. Little's forehead.

"She's my wife," Landon said. "You're well aware of that fact."

"Does it matter?" Mrs. Little was in fine form. "What do you want from me? There's nothing I could've done to stop what happened. If that's why you're here, you can just take your questions and shove them."

"I don't blame you for this," Landon replied calmly. "I simply need to get your statement. Even though it was obviously an accident, we have reports to file. The driver of the car will have to give a statement ... and deal with the horror of being behind the wheel."

"It wasn't his fault," Mrs. Little insisted. "It was Ned Brower. He was coming from the bank. There was no way he could see what was happening given his location. He's not at fault."

"We really should remove that weeping willow," I murmured, more to myself than anybody else. "It's been causing problems for years."

"That tree is older than you," Mrs. Little fired back. "It's not going anywhere."

"We'll let the road commission make that determination," Landon countered. "I need to know what you saw before the accident, Mrs. Little."

"I didn't see anything," she insisted. "I didn't even know he was out there until two customers came inside and said there was a crazy person in the street. He was ranting about bad luck or something."

"Bad luck?" Landon cocked an eyebrow. "What sort of bad luck?"

"I have no idea. They just said he was talking about bad luck, that we would all realize we didn't belong here and couldn't keep ourselves safe, and then I went out to see if I could help with the situation."

It took everything I had not to scoff. Mrs. Little was rarely helpful.

"What did you see when you walked out onto the street?" Landon asked. He had his FBI face on.

"I just saw him." Mrs. Little held out her palms and I saw the symbol. It was faint, but it was there. Whatever had plagued Bill Blake was now Mrs. Little's problem.

"Did you talk to him?" Landon asked.

"Not really. I told him to stop what he was doing. I swatted at him when he tried to touch me." Her accusatory eyes slid to me. "You were there. Why didn't you tell him all of this?"

"She did," Landon replied. "I need confirmation from you."

"But she's your wife." Mrs. Little's tone was smug. "Don't you always believe your wife? History would suggest you believe her to the detriment of all others."

Landon touched his tongue to his top lip, clearly debating, and then slid his gaze to me. He clearly needed direction.

Even though it wasn't my place, I took a step forward and fixed Mrs. Little with a serious look. "How are you feeling?"

She clearly wasn't expecting the question. "Are you serious?"

"Yes." I couldn't explain to her what worried me. Her initial reaction would be to dismiss it — just more Winchester nonsense — but as the week progressed, she would start to panic when the bad luck began piling up. I didn't want to put her through that.

"Well, Bay, I'm doing pretty poorly," she shot back, sarcasm on display. "Every few hours my unicorns — which are inanimate objects, mind you — shoot confetti and glitter out of orifices that don't even exist and fill my store with the scent of Brussels sprouts. It's a very distinctive scent that seems to scare people off."

"I understand that you're frustrated with that." I chose my words carefully. "I wasn't really talking about the farting unicorns, though." A quick glance at Landon told me he was trying to hide his smile. "It was more of a general question. Like ... how are you feeling in the wake of what happened to Bill Blake?"

"I don't know who that is," Mrs. Little shot back, her eyes flashing with annoyance. "What's going on here?"

"Bill Blake was the man who died in the street." Landon took control of the conversation. "He was a negotiator with the state police crisis intervention team. He was a good man."

"Oh." Mrs. Little looked taken aback. "It's awful what happened to him, but there's nothing I could've done. I swear it looked like he was going to stab himself, and then he shot his arm out in a different direction. I think he may have been drunk."

"Well, thank you for your time." Landon grabbed my shoulder and squeezed as he directed me toward the door. "I'm sorry you had to see what went down, but I'm glad you're okay."

"I won't be okay until somebody reins in Tillie," Mrs. Little shouted. "That's the only way I'll be okay."

"We'll get right on that," Landon promised as he led me outside. He waited until the door was fully shut to speak again. "She has the mark on her palm."

"I saw it." I glanced over my shoulder, frowning when glitter and confetti started spewing in every direction. The scent permeating the street grew in scope until I thought I might throw up. "Oh, no way."

"Here." Landon wrapped his arm around my waist and dragged me across the street, not stopping until we were in front of the diner. "Bend over. Breathe deep."

I gagged again. "Aunt Tillie really is going above and beyond with this curse. That is ... rancid."

"It is," Landon agreed as he rubbed my back. "If she was torturing anybody else like this, I'd order her to stop."

"I think we should tell her to stop anyway."

"Why? It's just Margaret Little."

"Because we need to start watching her for signs of bad luck. This is a huge sign of bad luck, but it's been going on for days. We need to clear whatever curses Aunt Tillie has working and keep an eye on Mrs. Little. It's our only option."

"How easy do you think that's going to be?" Landon asked. "I mean ... getting Aunt Tillie to work with us?"

It was a fair question. "I don't know, but we have to make it work. We're officially on a timetable."

I thought Landon might argue but he nodded. "I really am sorry," he offered. "I should've believed you."

"It's not that you didn't believe me. It's just ... there was nothing to back it up. We know more now."

"We need to make sure we're on top of it this time. I don't want to have to watch Mrs. Little die. As horrible as she is, nobody deserves what's happening here."

I straightened and rubbed my neck. The nausea was diminishing. When I glanced across the street, I found Emori watching us. She wasn't even trying to hide her stare. "I think she has real magic."

Landon followed my gaze. "Is she doing this?"

"I have no idea, but the odds seem long. The last woman who leased that space tried to kill us. I can't imagine that it's going to happen again."

"If you remember correctly, there was a witch in there before Kristen who wanted to hurt us too. Maybe it's the space. I don't think we can rule her out."

"Fine. We can't rule her out." I had no problem keeping an eye on the woman. "We have to be smart about this."

"How do we start being smart?"

It was a fair question. "Research," I said. "It's all we have."

8
EIGHT

"Let's not panic."

Chief Terry was less than thrilled when I laid out my full hunch for him in his office after Bill's body had been transported to the medical examiner's office.

"Nobody is panicking," Landon replied evenly. "We are trying to get ahead of this."

"No, you're trying to make me believe that Margaret Little is about to have a run of bad luck that will lead to her death," Chief Terry shot back. "I hate to break it to you, but Margaret's life is riddled with bad luck already thanks to Tillie."

"We're aware," I agreed. "I plan to talk to Aunt Tillie, have her back off a bit."

"Oh, right." Chief Terry rolled his eyes. "Tillie will suddenly stop torturing Margaret just because you ask."

"She's not as bad as you think," I insisted. "If she knows something bad is going to happen, she'll stop."

Landon shot me a dubious look. "Are you sure?"

"Yes. And if she doesn't do as I ask, I'll have Mom deal with her."

"There it is." Chief Terry let out a heavy sigh. "Bay, I'm not saying you're wrong."

"But you think it," I muttered.

"No." He shook his head. "I just want to be sure before we cause a panic."

"How can you be sure?" I demanded. "We don't have time to mess around. If I'm right, Mrs. Little will kill herself in a week."

"And in dramatic fashion," Landon added. "That's one thing both of our deaths have in common."

"It could still be a coincidence," Chief Terry looked pained. "We don't know that something magical is happening."

I refused to let him believe that. "I saw the symbols. I'm certain. Whether you're willing to help me or not, I'm going to stop this." I was defiant as I planted my hands on my hips. "I'm going to do what I have to do."

Chief Terry dragged a hand through his hair and shook his head. When he looked at me again, a small smile curved his lips. "You look like your mother when you do that."

"That's the meanest thing you've ever said to me," I complained.

He barked out a laugh. "I didn't mean it as an insult. You're just ... really bossy when you want to be."

I adjusted my tone to match his. "I don't mean to be bossy. I just need you to understand. I can't do nothing."

"I don't expect you to do nothing." He stroked my hair in fatherly fashion. When Landon did the same thing, it was to signify intimacy. Chief Terry's ministrations were always paternal. "Okay, I have a suggestion. Why don't we go to Bill's house to make notification together? We can ask some questions, see if you're on the right track."

"I have no objection to that," I assured him. "I just want to make sure that we do this the right way. If Mrs. Little dies ... ."

"Then it won't be your fault," Landon insisted. "You didn't cause this, Bay."

"I had my suspicions and did nothing. That's on me. You can't convince me otherwise."

"Let's just take it one step at a time," Chief Terry argued. "We can't come up with a plan until we know exactly what we're dealing with."

SHANNON BLAKE MET US AT the door. I positioned myself behind Chief Terry and Landon because they were the official presence. The second she saw who was interrupting her day she knew.

"What happened?" she demanded.

"I have some bad news." Chief Terry was calm, his tone measured. He'd done this before. I never thought about how it was for him to tell people they'd lost a loved one when I was a kid. It wasn't until I was an adult and had to watch him do it at an accident scene when a father showed up to ask questions about his teenage daughter that I truly understood. This was the part of his job he hated. He once told me that the good he got to do made up for it. I wasn't so sure.

"It's Bill, isn't it?" Shannon's lower lip trembled.

"It is," Chief Terry confirmed. "Can we come in?"

"Just tell me one thing." Shannon was surprisingly stoic. "Did he do it to himself?"

"It's ... complicated."

Shannon absorbed the news for several seconds before nodding. "Come in. The kids are still at school."

We followed her into a small kitchen but declined her offer of coffee. We sat. She nervously walked a small space between the cupboards and table.

"Tell me," she instructed.

"I wasn't there for the end," Chief Terry explained. "Bay was. She was interviewing the owner of a new store downtown and saw Bill on the street. He was going on about how we weren't safe, that something bad was going to happen. There was also something about bad luck."

Shannon released a heavy breath. It almost sounded as if she was laughing but I knew better. She was trying to hold back a sob. "Bad luck. He wouldn't stop talking about it the last few days. He said he was cursed."

"Cursed?" I didn't mean to speak out loud.

Shannon's eyes were dull when she bobbed her head. "It started after that guy jumped from the bridge out by the Au Sable. He was wrecked about that. I've seen him lose people before, and he always took it hard, but there was something different about this one. He just ... couldn't seem to understand what happened."

"We were there," Chief Terry offered. "He did his best to stop it."

"He didn't believe that." Shannon was matter-of-fact. "He said that he didn't get enough time. He was convinced that if he'd known more about what was bothering that man, he could've stopped it. He talked about it that entire first night ... and then he started talking about other things."

I leaned forward with anticipation. "What other things?"

"He stubbed his toe. When he did it, he ripped off a piece of trim from the dining room. I'm the one who called it bad luck first. Then he hurt his shoulder pushing open the screen door."

"Those just sound like minor accidents," Landon pointed out.

"To start," Shannon agreed. "Then the engine on his truck died. We got a note from the mortgage company that said we were delinquent, even though we pay on time every month. Our daughter was accepted to Central Michigan University three months ago, but we got a letter two days ago saying it had been a mistake and even if they accepted her — which wasn't a given — all the financial aid she qualified for would be yanked. She's a straight-A student."

I ran my tongue over my teeth, absorbing.

"Is that everything?" Landon asked.

"Not by a long shot. The dog ran away. A rabid raccoon bit the cat. The step on the back porch rotted and he fell through it. Not everything that happened was big. Not everything that happened was small. But it was nonstop."

"How did Bill react to what was happening to him?" Chief Terry asked.

"At first he tried to laugh it off. He was hurting from what happened on the overpass, but it was all so ridiculous. After a few days he started thinking it was more than that. The girls, they didn't want to be around him because he was so angry. He started ranting."

My heart went out to her.

"And this morning?" Chief Terry prodded. "How was he the last time you saw him?"

"Ragged." Shannon blinked back tears. "I'd come to the conclusion that he was having some sort of mental health crisis. I planned to get him some help after he got off work today – he was putting on a show so the people at work wouldn't see him falling apart. I guess I didn't move fast enough."

"You can't take this on yourself," I said. "It's not your fault. It's just ... ." Just what? What was I supposed to say to ease some of the horror she was feeling?

"Bad luck?" Shannon arched an eyebrow. She looked numb, beaten down. The true scope of what had happened to her family wouldn't hit her until later. "You still haven't told me how he died," she reminded Chief Terry, sliding her eyes to him.

"He was downtown," Chief Terry replied. Now he sounded like he was reading recipe instructions. "He was ranting in the middle of Main Street. He had a knife and appeared as though he was going to hurt himself. Before he could, a car hit him. It was an accident."

"Except he would've done it to himself." Shannon's fingers trembled as she brought them to her mouth. "What am I supposed to tell my girls?"

"I don't know," Chief Terry replied. "I'm truly sorry for your loss."

. . .

WE MADE MOST OF THE DRIVE back to town in silence. It was only when we crested the hill to the downtown area that I spoke.

"We have to watch Mrs. Little very closely," I said. "She's going to be a danger to herself, and quickly, if Shannon's story is to be believed."

"There's no reason not to believe her," Chief Terry offered.

"We obviously didn't dig hard enough," Landon noted. "If we'd tried to talk to Bill more, dig a little deeper ... ."

"We can't keep going around in circles," I interjected. "We're all dealing with a certain amount of guilt, but we have to move forward. That means saving Mrs. Little."

"Any idea how?" Landon asked. "I don't want to make things more difficult for you, but ... well ... you're the witch. You know more about this than we do."

"I know nothing." And that, I realized, was what bothered me most. "I need to talk to my mother and aunts." This last part was the hardest to admit. "I need to talk to Aunt Tillie."

"Then we'll do that," Landon said as Chief Terry pulled into his regular parking spot in front of the police department. "We'll figure it out."

"In time?" We were working against a deadline, and while I sometimes thrived under pressure, there were moments it froze me in my tracks.

"In time," Landon promised.

"How can you be so sure?"

"Because you're a super witch. You have me convinced that you can do anything."

"But no pressure," I drawled.

He smirked. "Don't get worked up, Bay. We have time."

That was easy for him to say. It wasn't as easy for me to absorb. I stewed in his words until I was out of Chief Terry's truck, and then joined them on the sidewalk. Noise across the street at the Unicorn Emporium drew my attention.

"Make it stop!"

I recognized Mrs. Little's voice but didn't immediately see her. I could smell what was going on, though, and it wasn't pretty.

"Is that ... ?" Chief Terry made a face and then leaned over, his throat convulsing.

"Don't," I warned, forcing myself to look away from him. "I'll throw up if you throw up."

"It's not something I can control," Chief Terry growled.

I had to move away from him. The sounds he was making in his throat were pushing me to the edge. I crossed the street, keeping my eyes on the Unicorn Emporium. I was halfway there when I realized the door to the store was open. I saw Mrs. Little inside, flapping her arms like a bird trying to take flight.

"I'm going to kill you, Tillie!" The threat was barely out of her mouth when the huge pink unicorn on the shelf next to her blew glitter out of its behind. The huge magical puff smacked her in the face ... and then the smell started in earnest.

"What is that?" I slapped my hand over my mouth and sucked down a heave.

"That would be sour herring," a voice said from my right.

I found Aunt Tillie standing between two parked cars. I hadn't immediately seen her because she was so short. Today she was dressed in a purple camouflage ensemble — including a matching hoodie — and a football helmet instead of her usual combat helmet. She was focused on the store rather than me.

"Sour herring?" I was incredulous.

"I Googled the worst smelling scents in the world. There are entire message boards dedicated to it. The Brussels sprouts were no longer garnering the desired effect. I had to start thinking outside the box."

She sounded so calm, so sure of herself, it irritated me.

"Well, you have to stop," I ordered, sucking back another heave as the lunch I ate so long ago threatened to make an appearance. "Seriously, you're going to earn the town a million bad reviews on Yelp. Do you want that?"

Aunt Tillie didn't look bothered in the least at the possibility. "It won't keep people away. It's just a temporary blip. Besides, I hate tourists."

"Our family — as well as everybody else in this town — makes their living from tourists. Stop being you!" I had to open my mouth to scream, and it was a mistake. This time when the heave came, there was no holding it in. I lost the contents of my stomach on the sidewalk directly in front of the Unicorn Emporium.

"Oh, that is really foul," Aunt Tillie intoned as she stared at my offering. "You have to clean that up. If you think the tourists hate the smell, they're really going to hate that."

"Thanks so much for your support," I drawled. "Now, stop this."

"Yeah, I'm good." Aunt Tillie beamed at me. "I guess the people who said that sour herring was the worst were right. I was going to go with fermented soybeans because a bunch of people mentioned them, but I went the fish route and I'm not sorry."

"You have got to stop this," I shouted. "You don't understand what's happening. Mrs. Little is cursed."

The look Aunt Tillie shot me was incredulous. "Of course, she is. I cursed her. It's fun."

"Not this." I waved vaguely toward the store, to where Mrs. Little was flailing her arms. I cringed when she slapped at the offending unicorn, one that served as an enduring focal point in her store. She hit it hard enough to tip toward the edge of the shelf. That bit of movement was enough to cause all the unicorns on the shelf to tilt to the side.

They hit the floor with a deafening roar, the sound of glass breaking everywhere … and still the remaining unicorns that hadn't fallen by some miracle continued to blow confetti and glitter in every direction.

"What was that?" Landon demanded as he appeared at my side. He looked as pale as I felt.

"Look out." I pulled him away from my puke. "Don't step in it. I'll get sick again."

He shot me a sympathetic look. "Terry and I did the same on the other side of the road. Is this Aunt Tillie?"

I gestured to the woman in question. "What do you think?"

Landon flicked his eyes to her and shook his head. "Can you make her stop?"

"Are you kidding me?" Fury bubbled up. "When have I ever been able to make her do anything? She does what she wants when she wants. That's who she is."

"You know it." Aunt Tillie fashioned the fingers on her right hand into a gun and fired it at us. When she did, another large unicorn let loose what sounded like a belch. The scent was back with a vengeance.

"Stop it!" I was at the end of my rope. "You have to stop it right now. This is too much."

"It's never too much."

Perhaps Mrs. Little heard me yelling. Perhaps she finally realized Aunt Tillie was outside watching the show. She raised herself up to her full height, which was only about two inches taller than Aunt Tillie, and stormed through the door.

She had murder in her eyes. In that moment, I knew she would kill Aunt Tillie if she could get her hands on her.

"Don't!" I held out a hand to stop Mrs. Little, but it was too late.

The second her shoe hit the vomit on the pavement she started to slide. She didn't catch herself. She didn't manage to break her fall. No, she just slid into the vomit, landing solidly on her rear with an emphatic splat.

"I'm going to kill you, Tillie Winchester!"

For once, I was on Mrs. Little's side. I had to get this situation under control, and fast.

9
NINE

I was tired when we got to the inn. I would've preferred going home, crawling into bed, and attacking the problem fresh in the morning. That wasn't an option. I needed help, which meant tapping the other witches in my family.

"Come here." Landon snagged me around the waist before we went inside and pulled me against him. There was concern in his eyes. "Are you still feeling sick?"

I managed a wan smile. "Believe it or not, once we got away from Aunt Tillie's scent experimentations, I felt fine."

He leaned his forehead against mine. "I want to kiss you."

"We're married. I think that's allowed."

"We both puked, Bay. I love you, but come on."

That made me laugh. "Good point." I tapped his chin. "Mom keeps extra toothbrushes in the supply closet. Let's brush first."

"Good idea." He pressed a kiss to my forehead and then followed me into the inn. Things were quiet — this was a rare off week when we didn't have many guests before the Halloween rush started in earnest — and I was grateful for the lack of outsiders.

I found the toothbrushes and took over the guest bathroom with

Landon. I found it funny that we had to brush our teeth thanks to Aunt Tillie's curse and started giggling halfway through. Landon shot me a look but ultimately joined in. By the time we finished, toothbrushes discarded in the trash, I was feeling more relaxed. That lasted until we wandered into the dining room ... and found World War III playing out between Mom and Aunt Tillie.

"Do you know how many people called me today?" Mom demanded, fury etched across her face as she regarded Aunt Tillie with the sort of glare I remembered well from childhood. She meant business this evening.

"Honestly? I can't be bothered to care." Aunt Tillie sat in her usual chair, a glass of wine in front of her, and appeared unbothered by Mom's fury. That wasn't a good sign. "I'm proud that you have friends. I mean ... nobody wants a loser who can't hold down a friendship as her niece. That's about all I can say."

I pressed my lips together and jerked my eyes to Landon. He was smiling. That was also not a good sign. Before I could pinch his flank and get him to cover, Mom turned to us.

"Do you find this funny, Landon?" Mom asked in her deadliest voice.

Landon was an observant man — at least most of the time. He straightened quickly but it was already too late. "Of course not." He sounded appropriately contrite. "This is a travesty of epic proportions."

"Oh, really?" Mom folded her arms across her chest. "What are we talking about?"

"What an absolutely amazing woman you are." To my utter surprise, Landon slid closer to her and kissed her cheek. "Marrying Bay was the greatest moment of my life. Not just because she's the best wife I could ever ask for, but also because you're the best mother-in-law."

I rolled my eyes, expecting my mother to do the same. Instead, she smiled.

"You have so much charm it flies out of your butt like monkeys,"

Mom said. "Most of the time that wouldn't work on me, but it's been a long day." She patted his cheek as my mouth dropped open.

"I cannot believe you just fell for that," I hissed to my mother, horrified. "I'm so ... disappointed."

Mom swished her lips back and forth. "You have a lovely man, Bay. You should be appreciative."

"See, Bay." Landon winked at me from an angle Mom couldn't see. He was smug to the point of obnoxiousness. "You should appreciate me."

"Oh, whatever." I skirted around him and threw myself in my usual chair. "We have a problem."

"Of course, we do." Mom was matter-of-fact as she went back to glaring at Aunt Tillie. "Your great-aunt has been wreaking havoc on the downtown area for a week. Each day she unleashes something worse. It is ... unbelievable."

"She says that like it's a bad thing," Aunt Tillie noted in an aside to me.

"It is bad," Mom growled. "This is an off week for tourism. It's one of those weird lulls when we don't have a festival. We've lucked out so far. You need to put an end to this. If you have a measured effect on the tourism, your punishment will be severe."

Aunt Tillie's eyes narrowed. "Was that a threat?"

"It was a promise."

"What exactly are you promising?"

"You know what I'm capable of," Mom warned. "You need to stop this ... now."

Chief Terry picked that moment to wander into the room. He looked as weary as I felt. He'd remained behind in town to settle a few things at the office — if I had to guess, he'd ordered his officers to pay special attention to Mrs. Little and used her ongoing fight with Aunt Tillie as a reason. In those twenty minutes, he'd aged a good ten years. He clearly needed some rest.

"I take it you informed your mother what's going on," he said as he crossed to her. He gave her a sweet kiss that had me looking away in discomfort. He was my father figure. I wanted him to be happy, but it always grossed me out when he and Mom kissed. It was freaky. "Have you guys come up with a plan?"

Mom completely missed the fact that we had a bigger problem than she realized, because she barreled forward in oblivious fashion. "I'm going to punish Aunt Tillie if she plays one more prank on Margaret Little. I believe the punishment will come in the form of losing her scooter ... and that pig she loves so much."

Landon, who had just settled next to me, straightened. "You can't do anything to Peg. It's not her fault that Aunt Tillie is mean. Peg is innocent."

"Peg has been running roughshod over this inn," Mom countered. "She's very cute. She's also very destructive. It's time she moved outside."

"No way." Aunt Tillie vigorously shook her head. "She's part of the family. You can't move her outside. Winter is coming."

"I hate to agree with Aunt Tillie," Landon interjected.

"Then don't," Mom hissed.

Landon loved my mother, respected her to a fault, but he adored Peg. He would melt down at the mere thought the pig might somehow be cold or feeling abandoned. "She's a pet. You don't just lock a pet outside in the cold. It's uncivilized."

Mom shot him a withering look. "Landon ... ."

"No." He crossed his arms over his chest, defiant. "If you try, Bay and I will have to move her in with us."

I tried to imagine what that would look like. "She's staying here," I argued. "She's Aunt Tillie's pet. Landon is right. You can't lock her outside and hope she doesn't freeze to death when the snow hits."

"Oh, don't be melodramatic, Bay," Mom snapped. "I'm not going to lock her outside. I'm going to have her moved to the greenhouse. It's heated."

"It's also empty," Landon said mournfully. "You can't lock her in an empty greenhouse. She'll be lonely."

"Oh, good grief." Mom shook her head. "You guys are unbelievable."

"People love her," I pointed out. I knew I was risking a potential fight with my mother, but I didn't care. "She's mentioned in all the recent reviews. She's a fixture now. I don't disagree with punishing Aunt Tillie."

"You're on my list," Aunt Tillie growled.

I ignored her. "You can't take out your frustration with Aunt Tillie on Peg," I said. "It's not fair."

"It's not," Landon agreed. "Speaking of Peg, where is she?"

"Twila has her in the kitchen," Mom replied. "She's giving her snacks. She was upset when I mentioned moving Peg to the greenhouse."

"Twila or Peg?" I asked.

"Both."

"Well, I think that's your answer." I smiled. "If you want to punish Aunt Tillie, take her scooter away. You could also ransack the greenhouse and take all her potion ingredients away. That freaking curse she unleashed today was foul."

"Yes, but it's Margaret," Aunt Tillie insisted. "Have you forgotten that she's evil? Also, you're definitely on my list. You can't suggest punishments for me. I mean ... are you suddenly new?"

Landon perked up. "Can I put in a request?"

"If you want me to curse her to smell like bacon, you're fresh out," Aunt Tillie countered. "I was thinking more along the lines of sour herring."

"That won't stop me from loving her," Landon warned. "Besides, I was on your side about Peg. You won't punish me. You want to reward me. Just for the record, I don't want her to smell like bacon. I'm looking for a change."

"Oh, really?" Aunt Tillie eyed him with suspicion.

"I'm thinking pot roast. It's fall. Pot roast is comfort food."

"We'll see how this conversation goes," Aunt Tillie replied. "As for the curse, don't worry about it." She turned her attention back to Mom. "I've got everything under control."

"Heather Martin said that people were puking on the street," Mom sputtered. "That's hardly having the situation under control."

"That was them!" Aunt Tillie jabbed a finger toward Landon and me. "It's not my fault you raised a daughter with a weak stomach. This is on you."

"You're the one who puked?" Mom looked dubious. "That doesn't sound like you."

"You have no idea the smell she unleashed," I countered. "As much as the curse sucked — and it did — we have another problem." I decided to take control of the conversation. "Aunt Tillie has to stop cursing Mrs. Little for the foreseeable future."

The laugh Aunt Tillie let loose was bone-chilling. "Fat chance."

"It is." I was adamant. I didn't care if she cursed me to smell like sour herring. Well, I did, but Mrs. Little's life was hanging in the balance, and I had to take a stand. "There's more going on here than you realize."

I explained everything. When I finished, Mom sat in her normal chair with a heavy sigh and pressed the heel of her hand to her forehead.

"Well, this isn't good," she lamented.

"Definitely not," I agreed.

"I didn't even know a bad luck curse was a thing."

"I never gave it much thought," I said. "We have to figure out how it originated. I think I know how it's being passed, but it had to start somewhere."

"We'll figure it out," Landon promised. "We have time."

"Not that much time." I shifted my attention to Aunt Tillie. She'd been quiet since I started explaining things. "What do you think?" I asked when she hadn't spoken for a good stretch.

"Luck curses aren't easy to cast." She was deadly serious now. "Whoever managed to set this in motion knew what they were doing. That's a very specific curse."

"You cast bad luck spells all the time," Landon argued. "You're constantly messing with Mrs. Little."

"Not the way you think," Aunt Tillie countered. "I cast specific spells to mess with her. I don't cast general bad luck spells. They're too dangerous. They spread like a contagion. I'm her bad luck. The spells I cast to mess with her are specific."

"Bill Blake's wife gave us a laundry list of things that happened to him," I offered. "Dead pets, accidents, cars breaking down, banking records going missing. His kid lost her college scholarship on top of everything else."

"That's bad," Aunt Tillie agreed, all traces of belligerence gone. She liked to be obnoxious — heck, there were times I was convinced that messing with other people kept her young — but she was sober now. "I don't even know where to start on this one."

"I took a photo." I pulled out my phone and scrolled until I found what I was looking for and then handed it to Aunt Tillie. Mom peered at the screen over her shoulder. "That's the symbol. It appears on the palm of the victim's hand when it's first transferred and then disappears. Mrs. Little has it right now. It will be gone shortly."

"And then it reappears in death?" Mom asked.

I held out my hands. "I saw it on Bill Blake's hand right before he died."

"And those suffering under the curse kill themselves," Mom mused. "That is a really specific curse."

"We need to end it." I was firm. "We can't let it spread."

"That's all well and good in theory," Aunt Tillie noted, "but you're assuming your victim only spread it to one person. What if he can spread it to more than one person?"

I was taken aback. "Wouldn't we know if that were the case?"

"I don't know. Have there been an uptick in suicides?"

I slid my eyes to Chief Terry, who looked concerned.

"I don't know," he said. He had his hand on Mom's shoulder and seemed lost in thought. "I'll have to check."

Landon shifted on his chair. "If we do have an increase in suicides, what do we do?"

I didn't have an answer. "All we know right now is that those infected have an increase in bad luck. After seven days, the bad luck is so catastrophic they end up killing themselves. It's a compulsion they can't seem to fight off."

"If Margaret is the only one infected, even if we can't save her, as long as we don't let her transfer it to someone else, shouldn't it end with her?"

I felt mildly sick to my stomach. "We can't just let her die."

"Of course not, Bay." Mom shot me a 'Well, duh' look. "We'll do our absolute best to save her."

"Speak for yourself," Aunt Tillie muttered.

Mom continued as if Aunt Tillie hadn't spoken. "If something happens and we can't stop this, containment has to be our top priority. We have to make sure this ends."

"It's possible the curse is only transferred at the end," Aunt Tillie noted. "If so, that's lucky for us. It means Margaret can't infect anybody until right before she offs herself."

"What a lovely way to put it," Mom drawled, annoyance obvious.

"I'm just being practical," Aunt Tillie snapped. "We don't know anything. Bay had a hunch but didn't chase it with Bill Blake. Now he's dead and we're left to clean up the mess."

"Hey!" I shouted. "I did my best. Landon and Chief Terry checked on him. They said he was acting normal."

"His wife said otherwise," Aunt Tillie noted. "Obviously they missed something."

"I can't help feeling there's an insult buried in there," Landon drawled.

"It wasn't buried," Aunt Tillie shot back. "The guy was obviously floundering. People noticed but assumed it was temporary. We have to be better about watching this time."

"Let me guess," I said. "You want to volunteer for shifts watching Mrs. Little."

"I can't say I'm not curious," she said. "That whole 'slipping in the vomit' thing was amazing. I want to see more of that if it happens."

"Let's not talk about vomit before dinner," Chief Terry suggested. "I instructed my men to keep an eye on her store. I also asked them to drive by her house during rounds. I don't expect anything to happen immediately, but I want to keep an eye on things."

"That's smart." Mom patted his hand. "You're on top of things. That's good."

Chief Terry winked at her. "I like being on top of things."

My stomach curdled at the double entendre. "Let's not be gross," I groused.

Chief Terry snorted. "Oh, please. I've had to listen to you two gush over each other for almost two years now."

"That's not what we should be focused on right now," Landon said. We need to focus on Mrs. Little. We have to watch her, keep her safe if we can, and find a way to end this ... and we only have a week."

"No pressure," I muttered.

Landon squeezed my knee under the table. "We've faced worse than this, Bay. We'll figure it out. We just need to focus and start breaking things down. It will all come together."

"Research is the key," Mom insisted. "Between Hypnotic and here, we have hundreds of books. I'm willing to bet the answer is in the books."

It was the most logical place to start. "Then I'll be down here tomorrow morning to scour the books in the library. I should've kept at it when I started last week. I won't get distracted again."

"It's a start," Landon agreed. "We'll keep an eye on Mrs. Little while you're doing that. I think that's our best course of action."

It didn't sound like enough, but we had nothing else. We needed a direction.

10
TEN

Two days later we were still mired in research and getting nowhere. It made for a tense family dynamic.

"You can't tell me what to do!" Aunt Tillie stomped her foot at the head of the breakfast table and openly glared at my mother. We were eight days from an influx of new guests and five days from Mrs. Little's potential death.

"I *can* tell you what to do," Mom growled. She sat in her regular chair, a mug of coffee in front of her. I was convinced she'd taken to dosing her coffee to get through the day. I honestly didn't blame her. "I'm the boss in my house."

"This isn't your house." Aunt Tillie was beside herself. We'd managed to keep her from town for thirty-six hours, but she was raging. "I own the property."

"Technically you own half the property," Twila pointed out. "We own the other half." She immediately shrank in her chair when Aunt Tillie swiveled her murderous eyes toward her. "Or I'll just mind my own business."

"That would be best," Aunt Tillie agreed. It wasn't unusual for us to argue, but it seemed as if that was all we'd been doing for days. Everybody was chafing under the pressure of what was happening.

"You can't go to town." Mom was adamant. "We talked about this. You agreed."

"I agreed to stop cursing Margaret for the time being," Aunt Tillie clarified. "I did not agree to allow you to trap me here like a rabid animal."

"Well, maybe you are a rabid animal," Mom fired back.

"You're not the boss of me!"

I had a headache. I'd been buried in books for days, researching symbol after symbol, to the point everything hurt. My back hurt. My neck hurt. My stomach was in a constant knot. I needed something to ease the tension.

"How about we take a breath?" Landon unwisely injected himself into the conversation, waving a hand to draw attention. "This bickering isn't good for anybody."

"Who asked you, Sparky?" Aunt Tillie demanded.

Mom was more diplomatic. "Landon, you know you're one of the great loves of my life."

Landon shifted on his chair, uncomfortable. "Where is she going with this?" he whispered to me.

All I could do was hold out my hands before reaching for the tomato juice carafe. I couldn't quite reach it, so Chief Terry poured me a glass. He looked as conflicted as I felt.

"You're my daughter's soulmate," Mom continued, barely taking a breath. "You love her like she's supposed to be loved. You're a wonderful man."

"Thank you," he replied.

"You're still a royal pain," Mom roared. "Shut up. This has nothing to do with you."

I pressed my lips together when Landon shot me an incredulous look and fought the absurd urge to laugh.

"You're not to go into town," Mom ordered. "You're stuck here until we clear you. That's all there is to it."

Aunt Tillie's eyes narrowed to dangerous slits and her gaze bounced around the table, which was empty at the far end. To absolutely nobody's surprise, once Clove and Thistle realized we were waging war with Aunt Tillie they opted to refrain from joining us for meals. Clove blamed the baby and Thistle refused to engage.

That also wasn't going over well. Marnie didn't like being kept from her grandson.

"You're all on my list," Aunt Tillie growled. Then, rather than sit at the end of the table and glower as she normally would, she stalked to the kitchen. With a great amount of theatrical flair, she threw open the swinging door and disappeared. She hadn't as much as touched her breakfast.

"Well, that went well," Landon drawled as he munched a slice of bacon. He'd already eaten four, but I was beyond admonishing him.

"What did I say, Landon?" Mom demanded. She was huffy as she readjusted on her chair.

"I'm shutting up," he said with a devastating smile.

Even though she was clearly agitated, Mom couldn't completely avoid his charm. "Thank you."

"We're nowhere near figuring out what is happening, and things with Margaret are continuing to spiral," Chief Terry noted. "Yesterday she stepped on a rake on the way to the coffee shop and the handle hit her in the face. Mind you, nobody can figure out where the rake came from. Then, when she was at the coffee shop, her latte was full fat even though she ordered it otherwise, and she spilled it down the front of her silk shirt. She was a complaining mess."

"That doesn't sound so bad," Twila hedged.

"It will get worse," I said. "If she hasn't gotten letters from the bank on all the property she owns, it's only a matter of time. She'll start melting down in fantastic fashion."

"What else is new?" Marnie grumbled.

"It'll be ten times worse than we're used to," I warned. "This is only the start. Her mental state will start deteriorating."

"And again I say what else is new?" Marnie challenged.

I understood what she was getting at, but my temper was short. "We're running out of time."

"We still have five days," Chief Terry insisted. "I need you to not get worked up about something that is not coming to a head today. We can still solve this."

"Except I've gotten nowhere with the research," I grumbled, making an exaggerated slurp as I downed my juice.

"Bay, nobody needs that sound," Mom chided.

Now it was my turn to be crabby. "Is that bourbon or vodka in your coffee this morning, Mom?"

Next to me, Landon sat straighter in his chair, sensing trouble. "Bay ... ."

"Don't worry yourself with details that don't concern you," Mom shot back. "We have to do something. If I keep Aunt Tillie locked up here much longer, she'll lose her mind."

"What makes you think she hasn't already?" Marnie let loose a hysterical laugh.

"Fine. She'll lose it more than she already has," Mom corrected. "She's already driving us crazy. Things will get worse."

"How much worse can they get?" Landon complained. "Every woman in this house acts as if she's being haunted by the PMS fairy. It's not fun for anybody with a Y chromosome."

My eyes were slitted when they landed on him. "You think this is fun for us?"

"Oh, don't give me attitude, Bay," he warned. "I didn't cause this situation."

"Are you suggesting I did?"

"Not even a little."

"Okay, things are spiraling." Now it was Chief Terry trying to put an end to the verbal bloodshed. "I don't like that you guys are fighting. You never fight. I can't believe I'm saying this, but I prefer you go back to being mushy fools."

He wasn't the only one. Shame coursed through me as I gave Landon an apologetic smile. "I'm sorry."

He was rueful when his hand landed on the back of my neck. "Me too. You're just so tired, sweetie. You can't sit there and read those books until you go cross-eyed. You need to take a break."

"I don't know what else to do. I'm overwhelmed with fear."

"Fear?" He brushed my hair out of my face.

"If we fail and Mrs. Little dies, I'm afraid we won't be able to stop this. What if it just keeps spreading?"

"We won't let that happen." Landon's voice was soft. "It's going to be okay. Just ... take a breath."

"That's easy for you to say. I feel like I have an elephant sitting on my chest."

Landon's eyebrows slid toward one another. "You know, it's not like you to feel fear like this. It makes me uncomfortable to watch you struggle."

My anger returned with a vengeance. "Well, I'll do my best to make you freaking comfortable, Landon. It's all about you."

"Stop." His tone was pleading. "I just meant that you always push past the fear." He turned to Mom. "Is it possible the curse is doing something to us from afar? I mean ... couldn't it be winding you guys up because you're magical? It wouldn't be the first time some magical monster has marked you as a threat and tried to distract you."

Mom initially looked as if she was going to deny the possibility, but the tilt of her head told me she was considering it. "Twila, can you check on Aunt Tillie?" Her tone was grave. "Don't talk to her. Just make sure she's okay."

Twila nodded, wordlessly exiting toward the kitchen.

"I don't like to jump to conclusions, but now that you've brought it up, Landon, I can't help but wonder if you're on to something," Mom said.

"It's a possibility," Marnie added. "It would make a weird sort of sense. If somebody knows we're hip to the situation, they might be trying to fight us on a level we're not used to."

"I'm going to pretend you didn't say 'hip to the situation,'"

Landon grinned. "I'm just glad you guys aren't dismissing me outright." He slid his eyes to me. "What do you think?"

I didn't know what to think. "I feel off," I said. "I'm on edge. I assumed it was because I was tired and worried about Mrs. Little, but now that you've brought it up, I can't help but wonder if you're right."

"Would it have to be a witch?" Chief Terry asked. "These are two separate spells, so it would have to be a witch."

His knowledge of the paranormal world was vast thanks to his association with us, but it was still limited.

"Not necessarily," I replied as I rubbed my forehead. "It could be a demon ... or even some sort of energy vampire. We don't know enough."

"Here, baby." Landon unscrewed the top of an aspirin bottle — he must've been carrying it around in his pocket — and tipped two tablets into my hand. "Take that and then eat your breakfast. You need your strength if we're going to figure this out."

"Especially if we have some sort of behavior modification curse working against us," Mom said. "The more I think about it, the more I think Landon is right. There's more than one thing happening here."

I was right there with her. "We have to find a way to protect ourselves."

"Can't we put Aunt Tillie on that?" Landon asked. "It would give her something to do."

"That's a good idea," Mom concurred as she flicked her eyes to the swinging door to look at a returning Twila. "Anything that directs her attention elsewhere is welcome at this point. If she's going to be trapped here, she needs a project."

"Are you talking about Aunt Tillie?" Twila looked grave.

Mom nodded. "Who else? If we're cursed, we need her to work on a solution."

"Well, that's great in theory," Twila said. "Unfortunately, she's not here."

Mom blinked several times. "What do you mean she's not here?"

"She's not here," Twila repeated. "The family living quarters are empty. Peg is gone. The scooter is gone."

"Son of a ... !" Mom slapped her hand on the table and viciously swore before standing. "She clearly wants me to kill her. There can be no other explanation."

"Don't get worked up," Landon said. "We all know where she went. It won't be difficult to find her."

"Definitely not," I agreed. I moved to push myself to a standing position, but Landon grabbed the belt loop on my jeans and pulled me back down. "What?"

He shook his head. "Like you said, she won't be difficult to find. You need to eat your breakfast first. You barely ate anything yesterday. Now we believe we're up against a whole new sort of curse on top of the one we were already grappling with. You need food."

"He's right, Bay." Mom wearily took another sip of her doctored coffee. "Eat your breakfast and then find her. When you do, tell her I want to talk to her."

That sounded like an ugly conversation. "We need to figure out what's happening to us first. I know Mrs. Little is in danger, but I can barely think."

Mom was grave when she focused on Landon. "We need Aunt Tillie to solve this one. It's good you voiced your concerns."

Landon's expression was blank. "What else would I do?"

"You could've remained quiet and not said anything," Mom replied. "Things would've continued to fester. At least we know there's likely something wrong."

"We still have to convince Aunt Tillie she's been cursed. She won't readily believe it."

"Well, she doesn't have a choice. We need her help. She's our best option."

That was a frightening thought.

. . .

I RODE WITH LANDON TO TOWN AND we parked in front of the police station. Chief Terry, driving separately, had remained at the inn when we left. He said he would be a few minutes behind us, but I knew he was really trying to soothe my mother.

"I'm sorry if I've been hard to deal with," I offered to Landon as we stepped onto the sidewalk. "I don't ever want to be horrible to you, and I think maybe I have been the past twenty-four hours or so."

"You weren't horrible," he countered as he rubbed my back. "You were just ... not you. It's okay. I don't have delicate feelings. I can survive this. In fact, as long as I have you, I can survive anything."

It was a nice sentiment. We didn't have time for cuddle games, though. "Let's find Aunt Tillie." I slipped my hand into his and turned. We didn't have to look far. She was planted on a bench in front of the Unicorn Emporium, her gaze steady as she watched Mrs. Little through the window. "That was way too easy," I muttered.

Landon smirked as he gripped my hand. Concern lined his features, but he did his best to shutter it.

Aunt Tillie didn't look up when we crossed to her. I knew the moment she recognized my presence, however, and braced myself for a diatribe.

It never came.

"We're cursed," she said before I could speak.

I was taken aback. "You knew?"

"I just figured it out. I thought I was angry with your mother — and I am because she's a bossy know-it-all who believes she should have control over everything — but she's not acting any differently than she normally does. All of our emotions are heightened, which means someone has cast a spell ... or a curse."

"Any idea which we're dealing with?" Landon asked. "Is there any way to figure it out and get rid of it?"

"I have a few ideas." Aunt Tillie's lips twisted as she regarded Mrs. Little. "I don't like when other people mess with her. That's my job."

"So, let's get rid of whatever this thing is and then we can focus on saving Mrs. Little," I suggested. "The sooner we save her, the sooner you can go back to torturing her."

"That's the plan," Aunt Tillie agreed. "Besides, kicking somebody when they're already down is not my style. I like a level playing field."

"We've got to get what's happening to us under control. Do you have any ideas?"

"For starters, we need to erect a dampening field around all of us. That goes for Clove, Thistle, and that little boy baby. If they haven't been targeted already, it's only a matter of time."

I made a face. "His name is Calvin. He's your great-great-nephew ... and he was named in honor of your husband, who you loved very much."

"He was supposed to be a girl."

"Well, we know better than most that things don't always happen as they're supposed to. Get over it. He's Clove's baby, but you're the one acting like a baby where he's concerned."

"I'll consider it." Aunt Tillie tilted her head and rubbed her cheek. "At the very least, I can dampen the effects of the spell we're under. I expect whoever cast it to ramp up the power when he or she figures out it's not working. We have to be ready to counter that."

"How do we do that?" Landon asked.

"We mix potions in Hypnotic," Aunt Tillie replied. "Thistle should have all the herbs we need. We'll need a big batch so we can take regular doses. After that, when our heads are clear, we'll figure the rest of it out."

It was all we had. "Let's make the dampening potion. Maybe when we can think better we'll figure out a way to shut down the second curse entirely."

Aunt Tillie didn't look convinced. "It's far more likely we'll have to find whoever is casting these curses and shut him or her down, but I'm open for anything."

"Then let's do this."

Aunt Tillie let out a breath and then nodded. "Yeah. Nobody messes with Margaret but me. This means war."

II
ELEVEN

"Is this going to work?" Thistle was dubious as she leaned over the cauldron — which was supposed to be just for looks as far as tourists were concerned — and watched Aunt Tillie stir the potion.

"What do you think?" Aunt Tillie shot back. Thistle had been on her last nerve since we'd entered Hypnotic. Thankfully, because it was an off week, Thistle had no problem locking the door and closing the blinds. It was best nobody in town knew what we were doing.

"I don't know," Thistle replied in her Thistle way. "I believe that's why I asked."

"When have I ever made a potion that didn't work?"

I made a slashing motion across my throat to stop Thistle from answering but it was too late.

"Well, there was that time when we were kids and Bay had that crush on Tony Frogenstern. You made that love potion so he would get all hot to trot for her, but instead it made him break out in zits all over his body. And I mean *all over* his body. The guys who were in gym class with him weren't afraid to describe what his penis looked like, and it sounded terrifying. There were eruptions going on all over the place ... but apparently not the big one."

I was mortified.

Landon grabbed me around the waist and pulled me onto his lap on the couch. He'd insisted on sticking close until we'd imbibed the potions and he was convinced we were back to our old selves. There was no way he would separate from me until he was certain. His anxiety wouldn't allow it.

"Tell me about Tony Frogenstern," he prodded. "Do I need to track him down and smack him around?"

"You're fine." I patted his cheek, and because it felt good, nestled my face in the crook of his neck. "You smell good."

Landon's lips curved against my forehead. "Are you feeling cuddly?"

"I just ... you smell good. You're warm too."

Landon wrapped his arms around me. I couldn't see his face, but the way he shifted his shoulders told me he was concerned. "This isn't normal," he said to somebody other than me. It was obvious he'd decided to cut me out of the conversation.

"Are you saying she doesn't cuddle with you?" Aunt Tillie didn't sound worried. "Come on. I've spied on you through the windows of the guesthouse and know that's not true."

"That's in the privacy of our home," he shot back. "Also, stop spying on us. It's weird."

"Oh, whatever." Aunt Tillie dropped something else in the cauldron. I could see her out of the corner of my eye. "Five more minutes and we'll know if this works. Seriously, why do you think she's acting out of sorts?"

"Because she's doing this in public." Landon gripped me tighter. "She's not afraid to show affection, but she never curls up in my lap in public. I want that potion in her as soon as possible."

On a different day, his worry would've jarred me back to reality. I was floating now, though. "I'm so tired."

"It's not normal," he insisted to Aunt Tillie.

"No, it's not," she agreed as she moved over to stand in front of us. "Here." Her hand was cold when it landed on my forehead, which struck me as odd ... and kind of soothing. "She's warm."

"Like a fever?" Landon batted Aunt Tillie's hand away and touched my forehead. "She is warm. I don't like it."

"Okay, Esmerelda, take a breath." When I met Aunt Tillie's steady gaze, I saw she was worried. "It's possible Bay was infected with whatever this is before us. She was at the first suicide. Maybe whoever set this in motion saw her there and decided to move against her then."

"She wasn't acting out of sorts until two days ago," Landon insisted.

"Yes, but she's been acting more out of sorts than the rest of us," Aunt Tillie insisted. "It's the only thing I can think of."

"She is going downhill fast," Thistle noted. "What if ... what if it's like the bad luck curse? What if it increases in speed at the end?"

That was enough to fill Landon with panic. "Give it to her now!"

"Three more minutes," Aunt Tillie barked. "We have to make sure it's perfect. If we give it to her too early and it doesn't work ... ." She trailed off.

"It's okay," I reassured them in a dull voice. I recognized something was definitely wrong but couldn't seem to make myself care.

"It is okay," Landon reassured me. "You're going to be okay."

I closed my eyes and listened to the beat of his heart. It was faster than normal but soothed me ... right into sleep. The next thing I knew, Landon had me pinned to the couch. I was thrashing about, as if fighting him, and Aunt Tillie was pouring a foul liquid down my throat. "What are you doing?" I sputtered, while reflexively swallowing. "Are you trying to kill me?"

When Aunt Tillie responded, it wasn't to me. "That was a double dose. I think she was close to the edge."

"I told you," Landon snapped. He looked as if he was in meltdown mode. "Is she okay?"

"You tell me," Aunt Tillie shot back.

"No, I'm going to tell you both." Thistle used her hip to shove Aunt Tillie away and knelt beside my head. "How many fingers am I holding up?"

"She doesn't have a concussion," Landon whined.

Thistle ignored him. "How many?"

For some reason, her intensity made me laugh. "Three. You always hold up three."

She nodded. "I guess that was sort of a lame question." She smiled and then her concern returned with a vengeance. "How do you feel?"

"Pretty good. I ... um ... feel a little weak, but overall, I feel better than I have all day."

"That's good." Landon stopped holding me against the couch and slipped his arm under my waist, tugging me on top of him. He buried his face in my hair.

"How long was I out?" I asked as I awkwardly patted his arm.

"That depends. What do you remember?"

"I remember telling Landon he smelled good ... and then I knew something was wrong, but I couldn't make myself care."

"It's an offshoot of the bad luck spell," Aunt Tillie said. "It was definitely cast by the same person. I think ... I think when it gets to the end, it spirals fast. That's what happened with that Bill Blake guy."

"That means it's also going to happen with Mrs. Little," I said as Landon's lips brushed my forehead. "I'm okay. Aunt Tillie's potion worked."

"We need to make more at the inn," Aunt Tillie said. "I didn't break the curse. I merely staved off the side effects for now. We need to dose ourselves every eight hours or so. I have enough to get everyone through the next twenty-four hours, but we need to make more."

I thought about Mrs. Little, what she might be feeling. "Can we try to give Mrs. Little some? Even if we can't lift the curse right away, we might be able to hold off the symptoms."

Aunt Tillie shrugged. "It can't hurt to try, but she won't drink anything that we put in front of her. You know that as well as I do."

"What if we tell her the truth?" Landon interjected.

Thistle, Aunt Tillie, and I all swung dubious looks at him.

He didn't back down. "I'm serious. If we tell her what she's up against, at least then she won't think she's going crazy."

"No, she'll believe that she's been infected by a bad luck curse and not only are we not to blame but we also want to help her," Thistle drawled. "That sounds exactly like her."

Landon shot her a quelling look. "Do you have a better idea?"

"I just may." Thistle drew herself up to her full height, which wasn't saying much, and then frowned. "I'm sure I'll think of something."

"It might be our best option," I said. "We can invite her out to dinner and slip the potion into her drink. That will buy us some time. If she believes us, we might be able to do even more."

Aunt Tillie was incredulous. "Are you new or just stupid from almost dying?"

"You said she was nowhere near close to death," Landon railed.

"I lied. I didn't want you freaking out."

"Now you're on my list," he growled.

I gripped his hand to calm him. "Aunt Tillie, it's possible Mrs. Little will agree to work with us. I mean ... she is all about self-preservation."

"She doesn't trust us," Thistle pointed out. "She won't believe anything we tell her. She'll assume we're trying to mess with her."

"We have to take that chance."

"Well, awesome." Thistle threw her hands in the air. "Have fun with that."

"I take that to mean you don't want to come with me when I talk to her," I surmised.

"Definitely not."

"I'll go with you," Landon offered. "Maybe having me there will make things easier."

"You're married to a witch," Aunt Tillie pointed out.

"It's worth a shot," Landon insisted. "I'm with Bay on this. We should tell her."

Aunt Tillie remained dubious. "Give it a shot. When it blows up in your face, don't come whining to me."

I WAS STILL A BIT SHAKY WHEN LANDON and I left Hypnotic. I felt ten times better than I had but figured it would take hours to get my full strength back.

"You don't have to worry about me," I reiterated to Landon as we walked. "I'm well on my way back to one-hundred percent."

"Except you're not." He kept his arm around my waist, insisting on absorbing some of my weight for the walk. "Aunt Tillie's potion is a stopgap. We have to find who's behind this if we want to cure you for good."

"Aunt Tillie's potions pack a wallop. I'll be fine."

"You'd better be." He pressed a kiss to my forehead and then focused on the Unicorn Emporium. Mrs. Little was visible behind the counter. "How do you want to handle this?"

"I thought we would just vibe it."

"Vibe it?" A hint of a smile played around the corners of Landon's mouth when his eyebrows hiked. "Are you sure you don't want to put a little more thought into it?"

"It's best we just feel her out. She won't be open to anything we have to say. Thistle was right about that. We don't have a choice but to try."

"I guess." Landon let loose a heavy sigh. "Okay, let's give it a shot."

I waited for him to push open the door and entered before him with a great deal of trepidation. "Mrs. Little?"

She jerked up her head, dark clouds momentarily overtaking her features before she blanked her expression. "I don't have time for whatever games you want to play today, Bay." She went back to looking at what appeared to be a ledger book, her brow furrowed. With her luck – all of it bad these days – her books probably weren't balancing. That alone would be enough to drive her insane.

"I don't want to play games," I said. "In fact, there's nothing funny about any of this."

"Oh, don't even." Mrs. Little's eyes narrowed. "If you're here to pretend to play peacekeeper between Tillie and me, forget it. She's evil. I'm not going to kiss her wrinkled behind simply because she can ... do ... these horrible things." She gestured toward the unicorns, which had been silent since we entered the store.

"They haven't been doing anything the last forty hours or so, right?" I was almost afraid to ask. If Aunt Tillie had gone back on her word and kept the curse running it would end badly when my mother found out.

Mrs. Little's eyes lit with suspicion. "How can you know that?"

"Because Aunt Tillie promised to leave you alone — at least for now."

Mrs. Little's eye roll was pronounced. "That sounds just like her."

"Believe it or not, Aunt Tillie doesn't like going after someone who is already having a problem."

"What problem do you think I'm dealing with?" Mrs. Little demanded.

"Um ... I don't know." I licked my lips as I glanced at Landon for support. He was suddenly fascinated by the framed chalk drawing on the wall and refused to look at me. "It seems like you're having a run of bad luck," I hedged.

"All caused by Tillie. She stopped messing with the unicorns and now she's going after me directly. I know how she operates."

"But ... it's not her."

"Of course, it is. It couldn't be anybody else."

"But ... ."

Landon's hand landed on my arm, and he gave me an almost imperceptible shake of his head. Mrs. Little wasn't going to trust us no matter what. I'd known that coming in. We had to come up with another solution.

"Okay, well, I'm sorry things are going poorly for you right now," I said as I let Landon lead me to the door. "If you need anything, please don't hesitate to call."

"Right." Mrs. Little made a face not even a mother could love. "You'll be the first I call, Bay." She rolled her eyes.

I kept my mouth shut until we were on the sidewalk and then darted a worried look toward Landon. "She doesn't trust us."

"Not even a little," Landon agreed, rolling his neck. His eyes were on the voodoo store across the street. "You know, it hasn't escaped my attention that our problems started the same time she opened up shop here." He nodded toward the store.

"How many times do I have to tell you that just because she's a practitioner of voodoo doesn't make her evil. It's insulting that you believe that."

"I didn't say she was evil."

"You were thinking it."

"Actually, I was thinking that they use a lot of symbols and runes in voodoo. Well, at least if the things I've seen on television and in movies are to be believed. Have you considered asking your new friend to dinner? Mrs. Little obviously doesn't trust us, but she might. I mean ... if she isn't evil and all."

I chewed my bottom lip, debating. "I can't just walk up to her and ask about the symbol."

"You're a reporter, Bay," Landon pointed out. "You deal with people who don't want to tell their stories. Why not invite her to dinner at the inn, wait until everybody in the family is dosed with the potion, and then ease her into the idea that something horrible might be happening in town?"

"I don't think we should go exactly that route."

"I don't care what route you go." Landon was adamant. "I just want to get ahead of this. She might be able to help us."

It wasn't the worst suggestion I'd ever heard. I started across the road.

Landon raced to keep up. "Wait, don't you think you should plot out what you're going to say?"

"It's just a dinner invitation."

"Yeah, but ... she'll think you're weird."

I paused with my hand on the door. "What else is new?"

He pressed himself close to my back as we entered the voodoo shop. It was so dark it took my eyes a few moments to adjust.

I found Emori behind the counter. She looked surprised when she saw us.

"Is something wrong?" she asked when we didn't immediately speak.

I shook my head. "I wanted to apologize for the way I ran off the other day. I didn't even realize I left you mid-interview until earlier today. It was just such a shock."

"Totally," she agreed on a head bob. "It's okay. What happened on the street the other day takes precedence."

"I'm really sorry." My plan took form quickly. "I was hoping you could join us at the inn for dinner tonight and finish the interview out there. We don't have guests right now, and my mother and aunts are marvelous cooks. It would just be us and the rest of the family."

She paused, and I thought she was going to say no. Then she smiled. "I would love that. What time?"

"Does seven o'clock work?"

"Perfect. Consider it a date."

"Awesome. I can't wait to introduce you to everybody. They're going to love you." *And if you turn out to be evil after all, it will be easier to hide the body out there,* I silently added.

12
TWELVE

I met Emori in the lobby upon her arrival at the inn. I was all smiles. She smiled in return, but curiosity rolled off her in waves.

"I've heard a lot of things about this place," she noted as I led her through the hallway. "People in town spread a lot of gossip about your family."

I kept my voice neutral. "Oh? What sort of gossip?"

"Well, for starters, they say your great-aunt is a loon." She made the announcement just as we reached the dining room.

Aunt Tillie, who was in her usual spot, jerked her head in our direction. "Or maybe that's just what I want them to believe."

If Emori was embarrassed to be caught talking out of turn, she didn't show it. Instead, she grinned at Aunt Tillie and crossed her arms over her chest. "Funnily enough, that's what I said when Laura Bickerstaff brought it up."

My nose wrinkled. "Why were you hanging out with Laura Bickerstaff?" She was three years ahead of me in school and I didn't have fond memories of her.

"She stopped in to invite me to lunch." Emori moved away from me and scanned the antique framed photos on the wall. "I make it a point to get to know the people wherever I end up."

I pursed my lips and nodded. That made sense. "I don't want to color your opinion of her," I said. How was I supposed to phrase this?

"But she's a judgmental beast," Emori finished, amusement sparkling as we locked gazes. "Believe it or not, I'm good at reading people."

I believed it. Still, I was wary. "What do you think about us?"

The sigh Emori let loose was long and drawn out. "You're going to keep playing the game, aren't you?" The question was so quiet it was difficult to make out.

"What game?" Aunt Tillie asked. She seemed genuinely curious as she watched the voodoo maven wander around the room.

"You're magical." Emori blurted it out as if it was the most normal thing in the world. "You're not just humans pretending to be magical. You're the real deal."

"And you?" I asked, tamping down my anxiety. "You're clearly magical."

"What do you think?"

I licked my lips, debating. "I felt a spark that first day. I wanted to follow up on it, but I was distracted by what was happening outside the store."

"The curse."

"Um … ."

"She means the curse," Aunt Tillie confirmed. She rarely had trouble tackling problems head-on. She never tried to cover for what we were or what we could do. She was open about everything, which I was convinced had something to do with her age. She just didn't give a hemlock sprig about anything.

Emori's expression brightened considerably. "Well, at least you're admitting something is going on. I figured that was the case when that man tried to kill himself on Main Street. Your great-niece used magic to stop him from stabbing himself. I felt it ripple. When the car appeared, however, I knew we were dealing with something much bigger than a standard curse."

I didn't even realize I was holding my breath until it gushed out. "You knew it was a curse from the start and didn't say anything?" I couldn't stop myself from sounding accusatory.

"I'd like to point out that you didn't say anything either," Emori noted.

"Yeah, but ... ." I trailed off. She had a point.

"We should be honest with each other," she said as she eyed the chairs at our end of the table. To my utter surprise, she started pointing at chairs and ticking off names. "You. Father. Husband. Great-aunt." She pointed to the other side of the table. "Mother. Aunt. Aunt. Are any other members of your family coming for dinner?"

"How did you know?"

"You all have strong essences."

"It will just be us this evening," I replied. "We decided to leave my cousin Clove and her baby out of it in case you were evil."

Emori let loose a delighted laugh. "Do you think I'm evil?"

"Probably not. We've been bamboozled before, though, and we don't take chances."

"I'm not here to bamboozle you." Emori plopped down in one of the chairs usually reserved for guests. "I'm here because I wanted a change."

"But you're the real deal," I insisted, my eyes darting to the swinging doors that separated the dining room from the kitchen as Landon appeared, cookie in hand. "Don't ruin your dinner."

"Oh, there's plenty of room for dinner," he assured me, his eyes drifting to Emori. "We're so happy you could join us."

Emori's eyes flicked to the opposite door as Chief Terry entered. "You're the father."

Chief Terry looked surprised. "I'm not anybody's father."

"He's my father," I corrected quickly. "At least in my heart."

Emori's smile softened. "What you feel in your heart is most important. Let's not play the game. I know the Winchesters are real witches. They know I'm the real deal. We've moved past that."

Landon cocked an eyebrow as he munched his cookie. "I guess that's good." He crossed to me and kissed the top of my head as I sank into my chair. "How are you feeling?"

"I'm fine," I reassured him. "Don't fret."

"I can't help it. I'm king of the fretters."

"Or king of the apple fritters," Chief Terry muttered. His attention was for me. "I heard you were very sick earlier. Why didn't you call?"

"I didn't realize I was sick until it was too late to do anything about it," I replied. "I'm sorry. It just sort of happened."

"You're okay now?"

I hesitated. "Aunt Tillie brewed potions that keep the symptoms at bay. We have to take the potion every eight hours at this point to make sure we're in the clear. Until we find out exactly what we're dealing with, that's how it has to be."

"Well, I don't like that." Chief Terry planted his hands on his hips and turned his attention to Mom as she came through the swinging door with a huge platter of chicken breasts. "Make your daughter go to bed and rest."

Mom's eyebrows hopped as she regarded him. "And hello to you too."

"I'm sorry." He was instantly contrite. "Hello. I'm happy to see you. Make your daughter go to bed, and in one of the upstairs bedrooms so we can keep an eye on her."

Mom sighed. "Terry, she's okay. I'm not happy she was sick either. I would've preferred to have been there with her, but she's an adult. She gets to make her own decisions."

My forehead creased. "Since when?"

"Oh, don't be you, Bay." Mom placed the platter on the table and immediately headed to me. "Thistle called with a recap. You were very sick. I'm a little annoyed I didn't know either."

"Don't give her grief," Landon chided as he sat in the chair next to me. "She had no idea."

"Landon figured out there was something wrong with us," I said. "He said that we were acting out of sorts. I didn't realize it. We were much more combative than usual ... which is saying something."

"It really is." Mom looked briefly amused and then shook her head. "We're on a potion diet until we can end the curse. We have another batch — a much bigger batch — going in the greenhouse. We're going to keep everyone packed with potion. You have enough to get you through the night, but you need to come back for breakfast tomorrow to stock up."

"I don't like that she has to keep taking potions," Landon said. "I want her completely cured."

"We can't do that until we know what we're dealing with," I reminded him. "We're doing the best we can. You need to accept that."

"Yeah, yeah, yeah."

When I glanced at Emori, I found her watching me with unreadable eyes. "It's been a busy day," I offered lamely.

"It sounds so." She had her head cocked as she looked me up and down. "Are you suggesting you're cursed? I don't see any curse fragments in your aura."

"Something weird happened this afternoon." She was in on the secret, so I saw no reason to cut her out of the conversation. Part of me wondered if she was to blame for what was happening, but the odds of three store owners turning into murderous fiends in a few short months seemed long.

Plus, well, I liked her. I couldn't put my finger on exactly why, but I trusted her. I didn't want to cut her out when I felt she could help. "So, it went like this." I laid everything out for her.

"That definitely sounds like a curse," she acknowledged. "I don't see a curse anywhere on you though." Emori flicked her eyes to Mom and Aunt Tillie. "Nor on either of you."

"It's definitely there." I no longer had any doubt. "I was

somehow infected at the overpass suicide. That's why I was worse off than everybody else."

"It could be a byproduct of the curse," Emori mused. "It sounds like some intricate magic. What do you know?"

"A symbol appears on the palm of the hand when the victims are first infected, and when they're near death it returns. It fades quickly after the initial infection and then only reappears when death is close. We have no idea who is causing this or why. We also don't know if more than one person can be infected at a time."

"I can't be certain, but if this was a mass contagion we would see people killing themselves left and right," Emori said. "You're a police officer?" She focused on Landon.

"FBI agent," he replied.

"You would know if people across the region were killing themselves in large numbers."

He hesitated and then nodded. "I might not hear about the odd suicide, but if multiple people were killing themselves in public I would know."

"Which means we have two dead people and one infected person right now," Emori summed up. "I'm willing to bet that there was at least one more before Chester Hamilton. He was likely not the first. There might even have been two more."

"We need to find the source," I said. "It's a contagion curse, but not on a mass scale."

"Except that your entire family has been infected," Landon noted. "You might not have been infected with the same thing as our victims, but you're still sick. You almost died on me this afternoon, Bay."

I patted his hand. He didn't mean to sound so unhinged. "I know, and I'm sorry. I was unaware of what was happening. That's the insidious nature of what we're dealing with. It was only when I was starting to spiral that I realized something was wrong."

"How did you feel when you realized that?" Emori asked.

"Rationally, I knew I should be doing something. I understood that it was necessary. But I couldn't make myself react. It was very odd. I've never come into contact with a curse like that. It didn't feel like it was cast by a witch."

"Hmm." Emori pursed her lips as her eyes drifted back to the photographs. "Your line has been magical from the start?"

Mom nodded. "Pretty much. All the women in the family are born magical. The degree of magic fluctuates. Aunt Tillie, for example, is very powerful. Our mother, her sister, was happy being a kitchen witch."

"Mom and her sisters are all kitchen witches too," I explained. "They're powerful but ... well ... not as powerful as Aunt Tillie."

"I'm the most powerful witch in the Midwest," Aunt Tillie readily agreed. "People should fear me."

Emori chuckled. "You're humble, too."

"Totally," Aunt Tillie agreed.

"She's not humble," Landon countered. "And she's not the most powerful witch in the Midwest. She might've been at one time, but Bay is the most powerful now."

His vehemence surprised me. "I don't know that I believe that," I hedged.

"You are." He was adamant. "I saw what you did to Minerva. You're a badass."

"I'm a badass," I agreed. There seemed to be no point in denying it. "There are a lot of badasses around here. Scout ... and Stormy ... and a few others."

"You are strong," Emori said, drawing my attention. Her expression was serious. "I knew it the minute we met. You're unbelievably strong. It doesn't matter who the strongest witch in the Midwest is."

"It's me," Aunt Tillie muttered petulantly.

"Your family as a whole is unstoppable," Emori agreed. "You complement one another. It's a good mix."

"That doesn't change the fact that they're all cursed," Landon muttered. "We need to fix this situation ... fast."

"Like your wife, I'm not sure we can fix it until we have a better understanding of what's going on." Emori was matter-of-fact now. "It's possible she was infected that first day. Maybe whoever cast the curse on Chester Hamilton saw her because she was close, recognized what she was, and decided to infect her. It's also possible the curse was a byproduct of the original curse. She could've brought it home to all of you. She also could've gotten a double dose because she was present at the two deaths."

"So we still don't know anything," Landon grumbled, his hand landing on my back.

I leaned close, brushing my lips against his cheek. "It's going to be okay," I reassured him.

"Isn't that supposed to be my line?"

"Yes, but you need to hear it. For now, I'm okay. You saved me today when you recognized something was wrong."

"I think I only managed it because I have no magical abilities. Everybody else was fighting to the point where they didn't notice something was wrong. I'm not special, so I wasn't affected."

"You're special." I gripped his knee under the table. Hard. "Don't sell yourself short."

"Definitely not," Mom agreed. "You saved Bay. We're safe for now. It's the best we can hope for until we learn more."

"We do know one thing of importance," Emori added as she leaned back in her chair. She seemed to be contemplative. "The symbol Bay saw is specific. I've heard of similar signs. Not a bad luck curse, or a suicide curse, but I've heard of symbols appearing at the beginning and end of a curse cycle."

"What do you know about how that works?" Mom asked. "Can you help us end this cycle?"

Emori held out her hands as her shoulders hopped. "I can try. I think we're looking for a talisman. The original victim, whoever he or she may be, came into contact with the talisman and set things in motion. We need to find the talisman. It will likely have the symbol on it."

"How do we do that?" Landon asked. "I'm willing to head out and find it right now if you tell me how."

Emori flashed a sad smile at him. "I don't have an answer. We need to track back from the victims. If Chester Hamilton was first, then he somehow managed to trigger the talisman. If it was somebody before him, we need to figure out who ... and then track the talisman from there."

"That sounds like a lot of work when we have nothing to go on," Chief Terry noted. "We're also on a timetable. Margaret Little only has five days left before she's supposed to kill herself in spectacular fashion."

"We can only do what we can do," Emori said. "We have to take it one step at a time. Let's break down everything again during dinner. I need to know the specifics. I have access to different research books that might provide help."

I was hopeful she was right, but it didn't seem enough. "How do we protect Mrs. Little from herself while we search for answers?"

"It's possible we can't protect her," Emori replied. "You can't save everyone, Bay. You can only do your best."

That was so not what I wanted to hear.

13
THIRTEEN

Emori gushed over the food. She promised to delve hard into the research. It was something, but it didn't feel like nearly enough as Landon and I meandered along the path from the inn to the guesthouse.

"Tell me what you're thinking," Landon prodded as he readjusted the bag of potions he was carrying with his left hand. The fingers of his right were entwined with mine. "Are you feeling okay?"

I had to bite back a sigh. "Landon, it's going to be a very long few days if you keep asking me that."

"I don't care. You're my wife. I'm going to ask how you feel. I'm also going to pick fights. If you're quick to anger, that's a sign you're feeling sick. I won't let anything happen to you, Bay. I'll do whatever it takes to keep you safe."

"Ugh. It's hard to be angry when you say things like that," I muttered.

He grinned. "That's what I'm going for." He leaned in and pressed a quick kiss to my lips. "Come on." He tugged on my hand. "Let's get home. I want to spend some quality time with you."

"You always want to spend quality time with me."

"Is that a complaint?"

"No." I shook my head. "I like spending quality time with you too."

"I know." He rested the side of his head against mine. "That's not the type of quality time I was referring to, though."

"You're not going to drag me under a blanket so we can say mushy stuff to one another again, like before the wedding."

"And if I am?" There was a challenge to his tone.

"I guess I'm okay with that too."

"Good."

The crisp night air made for a quiet trek. My mind was busy, to the point I couldn't stop some of my concerns from spilling out. "It's just us."

"Hmm." He dragged his eyes to me. "What's just us?" he asked after a beat when I didn't continue.

"You and me. Right now. It's just us."

"Do you have a problem with that?"

"No. But there are a few things we need to talk about."

"If you're going to start being depressive about this curse, I'm going to call foul and say it's time to move on to a different topic."

"I'm not going to be depressive. I'm never depressive."

He made a 'Yeah, right' face.

"I'm an optimist," I argued.

"Bay, I love you more than anything, but you are not an optimist. You're a glass half empty girl. It's okay. You switch to a glass half full girl with some regularity, and I love you the way you are, but you always look on the dark side of things. I'm used to it."

Was he right? Was I depressive? I frowned as I thought about it. "We need to talk about Mrs. Little." I would be proving him right with this conversation, but I didn't see a way out of it. "We have five days to cure her."

"That's plenty of time."

"Maybe, but we need to talk about what happens if we don't."

Landon scowled. "Don't let defeatist thinking get you down, sweetie."

"It's not defeatist thinking. We need to be real about what's going to happen. We're going to help her to the best of our ability, but if we fail ... ." I trailed off. Saying the next part out loud would be difficult. "If we get to the final day and haven't figured out a way to save her, we have to isolate her."

Landon slowed his pace. "You're afraid she will infect someone else."

"What Emori said makes sense. I think the contagion only moves from person to person at the end. Otherwise, we would be swimming in suicides."

"That's good for us, right?"

"It's better," I agreed. "If we can't remove the curse from Mrs. Little, though, we have to let her die in such a way that she can't touch anyone else. It's the only thing we'll be able to do to end this."

Landon was so quiet that I had to look to see if he was still monitoring the conversation. His expression told me he hated the idea.

"I don't like it either," I insisted, "but we can't let her infect someone else at the end. We'll just be dragging things out if she touches someone else. We have to end it one way or another."

He looked pained as he squeezed my hand. "Bay, I'm going to be honest here, and I don't want you arguing with me. Not this time."

I had no idea where he was going, so I simply waited.

"If Mrs. Little dies, you'll blame yourself. This isn't your fault."

"I knew something was wrong when Chester Hamilton died," I argued. "If I'd chased it then, at the very least I could've isolated Bill Blake at the time of his death. Mrs. Little wouldn't be infected."

"It's not your fault." Landon was adamant. "We didn't know. There's no way we could've known."

"I felt something was terribly wrong from the start."

"And I told you that you were seeing things that weren't there. If you have to blame someone, blame me."

I shook my head. "It's not your fault."

"And it's not your fault." His expression was grave. "I believe we can save Mrs. Little. But if we can't, I do not want you wallowing in guilt. We're doing the best we can. That's *all* of us. Just ... don't pull a you and take the weight of the world on your shoulders. We're doing the very best that we can. That has to be enough."

His words made sense. They weren't easy to hear, but they made sense. "I'll try to keep the guilt at bay if you do the same."

"That's the plan."

"And you have to stop asking me if I feel okay every three minutes. It's going to drive me insane."

"I can't agree to that." He shot me a rueful smile. "I have to push you occasionally to check your responses. If all goes as planned, you won't be in danger any longer when the curse dies. Either you guys will save Mrs. Little and end it that way, or we'll stop it from spreading when she dies. I'm hoping that means you'll be free."

I hoped so too. "We still don't know how I was infected."

"I have faith we'll figure it out. Until then, you have to drink potions every eight hours. I plan on setting the alerts on both our phones to make sure you're safe ... and I will be there when you drink your potion each and every time."

"That sounds like a bit too much active husbanding," I groused.

He grinned. "It will make me feel better. It's good to have checks and balances in place in case you lose your head again. Sam and Marcus are doing the same with Thistle and Clove."

It did make sense, but I didn't have to like it. "Do you think I infected the rest of the family?" I'd been dwelling on that since Emori mentioned it as a possibility.

"You didn't know it was a possibility."

"That doesn't change the fact that I likely brought it home."

"Everyone is safe." Landon was firm. "Chief Terry is watching your mother and aunts to make sure they take their potions. We'll all keep an eye on Aunt Tillie. Sooner or later, we'll come up with a solution."

Landon slung an arm around my shoulder and tugged me to his

side. "We're going to figure this out, Bay. I know it seems overwhelming right now, but we're okay. We have the potions. We have five days to save Mrs. Little. I have faith it's all going to work out."

What if it didn't work out? I was a bold talker when it came to letting Mrs. Little die, but when the moment came, would I be able to follow through?

He was right for now. We were doing everything we could. That had to be enough.

I WAS EXHAUSTED WHEN WE FINALLY tumbled into bed after an hour-long cuddle session on the couch. He seemed to need it as much as me. His promised playtime never came to fruition, but neither of us minded. I took my potion before getting under the covers, watched as he set the alarm on his phone for eight hours, and then let him pull me against him.

I was out within seconds of closing my eyes.

I'd become accustomed to weird dreams since fully embracing my witch destiny. I'd been an ambivalent witch as a kid, uncertain if I wanted to be like my mother or Aunt Tillie. When I moved to Detroit to pursue my dream of being a big city reporter, I'd been convinced I was ready to leave my witch legacy behind. That never happened, and by the time I returned home I was ready to shift my thinking. It wasn't until meeting Landon and fully embracing what I could do that things truly started to make sense. The dreams, sometimes prophetic, were part of that.

The dreamscape I woke in was hazy. I registered several things in rapid succession, the first of which was that we seemed to be on a bluff. It wasn't the bluff behind The Overlook, though there were similarities. The sun was high in the sky, but it was as if somebody had slapped a murky filter over it in a photography app. I stared at it for a long beat, frowning, and then shook my head.

"Great," I muttered to nobody in particular. "What am I doing here?"

The only response was a hiss. When I jerked my eyes toward the sound, I found a shrouded figure.

"Oh, well good." I wasn't nearly as excited about this development as I would've been a year ago. My dreams rarely gave me answers outright. They were a way for my subconscious to work things out. In fact, it was likely I would find more questions. "I'm guessing you're the enemy."

The figure laughed. It was impossible to tell if the voice was male or female. "Perhaps you're the enemy."

"I'm not the one infecting people with a bad luck curse."

"Bad luck isn't the ultimate goal."

"No, death is," I said. I gave the figure a wide berth as I glanced around the bluff. Upon second inspection, there was more here than I initially realized. "There are runes here." I moved toward them and knelt, my eyebrows drawing together as I absorbed the figures. "They're not the same as the one I saw on Chester Hamilton's hand."

"There are many different types of runes," the figure noted. I was thankful it seemed to be purposeful in keeping its distance.

"What are these runes for?"

"It's not your concern."

"I beg to differ." I fixed the dark figure with a pointed look. "You came after my family. I'm pretty sure anything you do from here on out is my business."

"We didn't come after your family. Nobody knew you would be there. It was an accident."

"Something tells me you don't deal in accidents." I traced the runes, desperately trying to commit them to memory. I didn't often remember dream details well. "Everything you've done here is on purpose."

"Everything we've done here has been for the greater good," the shade countered. "You're interfering in things that don't concern you."

That was interesting. "We?" Whether the shade had meant to acknowledge it wasn't working alone, I couldn't say. It had confirmed there was more than one entity, and now I had a string to tug. "How many people are with you?"

"It doesn't matter." The figure hissed. "This doesn't concern you."

"I almost died today because you were wreaking havoc in my playground," I shot back. "It does concern me."

The shade stood there a moment, still, and then slowly started shaking its head. "You don't know what you're talking about. You're a witch. You're not involved in what's to come. We don't have time for witches."

Well, that was also interesting. "You cursed me because you thought it would keep me out of whatever you have planned. You saw me by the bridge when Chester Hamilton died. I'm guessing that you either marked me then or when Bill Blake infected Mrs. Little. I was definitely the first one you saw. You infected me first. I brought the infection home to my family." Becoming a vessel that could kill my family was too much. "You almost carried out your plan."

"We only wanted you to stay away." Now the shade was blasé. "You and your sister witches are known for sticking your noses where they don't belong. This is our game. You need to play your own."

"I think we'll just win your game instead."

"Or you could take a deal," the shadow countered.

It wasn't the tack I expected, so I remained where I was and waited.

"You could take a deal," it insisted. "If you agree to back away and let this game play out as it was always meant to, we'll remove the curse on your family. You can live your lives free from potions and upheaval, and we'll live ours. We can be separate. There is no need for our lives to cross."

It was an interesting offer, but one I had no intention of taking. "No. We'll handle both curses. Thanks for the suggestion, though."

Irritation radiated outward from the ethereal figure. "You won't like what happens if you don't maintain distance. This doesn't concern you."

"Yeah, you sound like a broken record. I get it. You don't want us interrupting your plan. If you didn't want us getting involved, you should've stayed out of our territory. You didn't, so that's on you."

The figure huffed, hands clenched into fists at its side. "We don't have to explain ourselves to you. We've made a perfectly reasonable offer. We can free you from the plague threatening your family."

"I find it interesting that you're only offering this deal after we found a way to handle the problem ourselves this afternoon," I said. "I'm guessing that if we hadn't come up with a solution you would've let us die."

"Witches are abominations."

"I've heard that before," I said. "I've heard it from those trying to hurt people, like you. Why is it you're never the abomination?"

"Stay out of our business." The shadow's appearance briefly wavered before solidifying. "We don't have to be enemies. We can never be friends, but we don't have to go to war."

"That's where you're wrong." My tone was icy. "You came to our town. You targeted our people. We're already at war."

"It's a war you can't win."

"If you believed that you wouldn't be here trying to broker a deal. It doesn't matter what you say. We're going to end this ... and you. If you want to survive, you'll stop what you're doing and run before we find you. That's the only offer you'll get from us."

"And if we refuse?"

"Then we'll end you."

"What if we end you?"

"We're willing to take that chance, because it's the right thing to do."

"And if you fail?"

"Then we fail. We won't cede the fight before it truly starts."

"You'll regret this route. Mark my words."

"Funny, I was just going to say the same to you."

14
FOURTEEN

We had five days ... and we made it through the entire five days without answers. We pored through books, cast locator spells for outsiders who could be causing our problems, and all the while kept taking our potions so we wouldn't succumb to the secondary spell.

We had nothing, and Mrs. Little's death date was upon us.

"What's the plan?" Mom asked over breakfast.

I didn't have an appetite and turned up my nose at the pancakes and bacon. "We have to isolate her." Saying it out loud was difficult, but we were out of options. "We have to make sure she's not around anybody all day."

"How are you going to do that?" Mom was grim, but above all else she enjoyed having a plan of action. As the days ticked by and we hadn't found a solution, things became tense in the Winchester family. This time it wasn't a curse fueling us, it was despair.

"We've been talking, and we think we've come up with a plan," Landon replied, his hand on the back of my neck. I hadn't slept the previous night. He had, at least some. I'd remained perfectly still so as not to wake him and yet he opened his eyes every hour, on the hour, to check on me. He did his best to lull me, but in the end, I managed a grand total of two hours in dreamland. I was ragged and dragging.

I wasn't the only one.

"Who is we?" Mom prodded.

"The three of us," Chief Terry replied. He had a mug of coffee in front of him but was also ignoring the pancakes. "We think we know what to do."

"You need to eat," Mom snapped, taking me by surprise with her vehemence. "That's the first thing you need to do. You can't tackle this day if you're running on fumes."

Chief Terry gave Mom a weak smile. "I'm not all that hungry. I don't think I'm up for pancakes."

Mom worked her jaw. "Then I'll make eggs."

It was such a Mom thing to say. She wanted to solve all of our problems with food.

"Mom." I drew her attention to me. "You can't force feed us and expect everything to be okay. Mrs. Little is going to die today. We haven't found a single thing to help her. We're out of time." It was difficult to get out. I hated Mrs. Little. I mean, downright despised her, but I didn't want her to die, especially this way.

"Bay, we're not out of time yet," Mom argued. "We can still come up with something."

I was open for any and all suggestions. "What have you got?"

"I ... don't know." Mom swallowed hard. "I've never known you to accept defeat like this, though. It's not you."

"I'm not accepting defeat." I darted my eyes to Aunt Tillie's empty chair. I hadn't seen her in almost twenty-four hours. The last time I'd laid eyes on her she'd been almost manic. "We have to mitigate the problem. We can't save Mrs. Little, so we have to stop her from infecting anyone else. Our best hope is to end the curse here."

"That won't be easy," Landon added. "Bay's being taunted in her dreams, and if the people she's talking to are to be believed, the curse will work overtime to get Mrs. Little near someone in the minutes before her death."

I murdered him with a death glare. I hadn't told anybody but him about my dreams. "Big mouth," I grumbled, shifting my shoulder away from him. "I told you that as my husband, not so you could share it with everybody."

"I am acting as your husband." Landon refused to stop touching me. "You're driving yourself insane with this, Bay. You've done all that can be expected of you. This is not your fault."

He could say it as many times as he liked — and he had — but that didn't change the fact that I believed otherwise. "It doesn't matter. We can't save her." I'd resigned myself to that fact around four in the morning. That's when I'd finally managed to close my eyes. "We have to save everybody else in town now. That's all we can do." My voice cracked as I finished.

"Oh, Bay." Landon tugged me close and hugged me even though I fought the effort. He stroked my hair. "Baby, I'm so sorry, but you can't let this break you. There was nothing else you could've done."

I was never going to believe that. During the past week I'd watched from across the street as Mrs. Little descended into madness. She'd hurt herself on numerous occasions, been threatened by the bank when it presented her with a delinquent mortgage that shouldn't have existed and started ranting about bad luck. It had been two days since anybody entered her store because word had spread quickly. It was the one stroke of luck we'd managed.

"We need to go ahead with the plan," I pressed. "We need Aunt Tillie." I looked at her empty chair again. "Where is she?"

"She's not hungry either," Marnie volunteered. "She's been quiet the past two days. I think this is hitting her harder than any of us expected."

"She just doesn't want Margaret to suffer at the hands of anybody but herself," Mom noted. "She'll be okay."

I wasn't so sure. "I need to talk to her." I pushed myself to my feet and found myself on shaky legs. "She's part of the plan to isolate Mrs. Little. We need her powers of mayhem."

"You still haven't told us the plan," Twila said. "Shouldn't we know? I mean ... we can't help, but we should know."

"We're going to flood the unicorn store," Chief Terry explained. "A burst pipe will allow us to put up crime tape to keep people out of the store. Then the three of us — Landon, Bay and I — will be with her when she ... goes." He choked on the last word. He was as tortured by this as the rest of us.

"That's horrible." Mom made a clucking sound. "It will ruin all the unicorns."

"Do you have a better idea?" Landon challenged, an edge to his voice.

Mom arched an eyebrow. "Nobody needs your attitude," she snapped. "I was just saying ... ." She trailed off and immediately adjusted her tone. "It's horrible the three of you have to do this. I'm sorry."

Landon waved off her apology. "No, I'm sorry. I didn't mean to yell at you. It's just ... it's hard." His eyes found mine. "It's so hard."

Tears pricked the back of my eyes, but I refused to give in to them. "I'll grab Aunt Tillie. I think we'll drive separately downtown. I might want a bit of alone time later."

Landon looked pained but nodded. "Meet us in front of the police department in thirty minutes. We can't afford to leave her alone long. We need to get everything in place, and the sooner the better."

I was stiff when I nodded. "Sooner is better." I wanted to get it over with. It was horrible to admit, even to myself, but the longer this dragged out, the more difficult it would be.

AUNT TILLIE WAS QUIET DURING THE RIDE to town. She was listless as she tapped on the window, her eyes focused on the blurring foliage as we moved toward an ending nobody expected. I wanted to engage her in conversation, but I honestly didn't know what to say.

"We just need you to handle the pipe bursting," I said as I parked in front of The Whistler. We could walk to the police station in a few minutes. "We want it to be bad, but if you could refrain from taking out the whole block that would be great."

"I've got it." There was no life in Aunt Tillie's voice as she trudged next to me, scraping her shoes against the pavement. "I want to be there when it happens."

I wasn't surprised. I also wasn't ready to acquiesce. "It's not necessary."

"It is to me."

"You're not friends," I pointed out. "Why do you want to be there?"

"Because it's the right thing to do. I know her best. Besides, you never know. Her need to best me might mean that she somehow overcomes the curse."

It was something I hadn't considered. "Wait ... you think it's possible that the only way to beat the curse is to overcome it yourself."

"I don't *know* that," she warned. "I just think ... maybe ... ."

Maybe we'd been looking in the wrong place after all. I licked my lips and looked up, locking gazes with Landon as we closed the distance. "It's not out of the realm of possibility," I said finally.

"Definitely not," she agreed.

"Aunt Tillie is coming inside with us," I announced when we reached Landon and Chief Terry.

"I thought we agreed that wasn't a good idea," Chief Terry hedged. He looked genuinely uncomfortable.

"It's possible that Mrs. Little might be able to fight off the curse herself," I explained. "It's a small possibility, so I don't want you getting your hopes up. If we want to manipulate her into doing what we want, Aunt Tillie must be there to goad her."

"I don't understand," Landon said.

"I'll tell her to kill herself," Aunt Tillie replied simply. "When it's time, when she's ready to end it, I'll tell her to do it. If there's any part of Margaret still there in that moment, she'll want to fight me."

"It's our only chance." The small bit of hope Aunt Tillie had kindled inside me was serving as an adrenaline boost. "It probably won't work."

"But maybe," Landon said, his lips curving. "Maybe her hatred for Aunt Tillie is stronger than the curse."

"It's all we have."

He gripped my hand. "Then we'll play it out. If it doesn't work, though, I want you two to let it go. You can't blame yourselves."

"I don't blame myself for anything," Aunt Tillie replied. "This is going to work. I have faith."

Landon held her gaze for an extended moment and then nodded. "Okay. It's worth a shot."

AUNT TILLIE WAS SUDDENLY SPRYER THAN she had been in days when it came time to flood the Unicorn Emporium. She was almost gleeful — or as close as she could get given the circumstances — when she started waving her hands.

Chief Terry and I flanked her so nobody on the sidewalk could see her. Thankfully nobody was out because it was a blustery day. Landon was across the street watching Mrs. Little through the store window. When the pipe burst, it made a deafening racket. The next thing I knew, water was flooding the street like a hurricane surge.

"Is there supposed to be so much water?" I asked as I hopped up on the curb to avoid the initial flood.

"It's a water main break," Chief Terry replied grimly. He seemed fascinated by the swirling water. "We needed it to be big." He looked up and down the road, a muscle working in his jaw when two people exited the bakery and immediately stopped when they saw what was happening. "Here we go." He prodded me forward. "I'm calling my men to shut down the area. Go inside to check on Mrs. Little."

I nodded. "We've got this." Even as I said it, I recognized it likely wasn't true, but I needed hope. Without it, I would be nothing but an empty shell. "This is going to work." *Please work,* I fervently wished as we started across the street.

Aunt Tillie splashed her feet hard in the water, and when we joined Landon on the opposite side of the street our pants and shoes were soaking.

"Maybe we should've thought this through more," he noted. "You're going to get a chill."

"It's fine," I reassured him. "There are more important things to worry about." I inclined my head toward the store. "Chief Terry should have the building completely roped off in fifteen minutes. It's up to us now."

"It's up to the two of you," Landon countered. "I'm just here for emotional backup ... and maybe as an official presence if somebody else tries to enter the building. I have no true power here."

"I think Aunt Tillie is the only one with power here," I admitted.

I craned my neck as we entered the store. I heard cursing somewhere in the back but had yet to lay eyes on Mrs. Little. I gestured to the door and Landon nodded as he locked it. Whatever happened, we were in it now.

"Mrs. Little?" I called out in a shaky voice, cringing when the noise in the storage room ceased. "There's a water main break. It appears to be right under your store. Are you okay?"

I openly gasped when she appeared in the doorway. She looked nothing like herself. The hair that was always perfectly coiffed hadn't been washed in days. She wore no makeup, and her eyes were red-rimmed. Her cheeks were sallow. On top of that, I was fairly certain she was wearing pajamas.

"What are you doing here?" she demanded. "I don't want you here."

"We're here to check on you." I kept my tone neutral. "We're ... worried."

"It's a water main break," Landon added. "Your store is in danger of flooding."

"Of course, it is." Mrs. Little threw her hands in the air, giving us a clear view of the symbol etched on her palm. "My whole life is in danger of flooding. Do you have any idea what I've been through this week?"

I had some idea. I'd been spying on her for days. "It's been an interesting week," I said.

"Interesting? Good grief, girl, it's been an outright disaster. And I know what's causing it." She seemed more together than Bill Blake. Sure, she was a ranting maniac, but there was still some semblance of the real her beneath the surface. I chose to take that as a good sign, even if I would ultimately end up with a broken heart.

"You know what's causing it?" Landon leaned against the glass door, his arms crossed over his chest. "Have you been hearing voices or something?"

Mrs. Little wrinkled her nose. "Voices? Are you kidding me? I don't hear voices." She straightened her small frame and smoothed the front of her pajama top. "Only crazy people hear voices."

"I believe that's why he asked," Aunt Tillie replied as she cocked her head and looked Mrs. Little up and down. "She has a shimmer."

I nodded. It was rude to talk about people as if they weren't there, but we were working on a timetable. "I see it. Chester Hamilton had it too."

"What about Bill Blake?"

I shook my head. "I know this is going to sound weird, but he seemed worse. There was no shimmer. Mrs. Little almost seems normal."

"As compared to what?" Mrs. Little demanded, clearly not realizing she was insulting herself.

"Yeah, as compared to what, Bay?" Aunt Tillie drawled. She didn't look at me, however. She was far too focused on Mrs. Little. "I think ... I think I can remove the shimmer."

I didn't know if that was smart or stupid. "How?"

"How do you think?"

"Magic," Mrs. Little hissed. "This is happening because you've been casting spells. I know it ... and I've reported you to the FBI. You're all going to jail."

I flicked my eyes to Landon, my question evident.

"Don't worry," he said. "Nobody is going to believe anything she has to say."

"Everybody will believe me," she barked. "Everybody knows."

"There is it is again!" Aunt Tillie jabbed her finger toward Mrs. Little. "That's definitely a shimmer, and it seems to be wrapped around her and trying to press inward. It hasn't overcome her yet."

"Is that why she's more cognizant of what's going on?" Landon demanded. "She does seem better than Chester Hamilton. I can't speak to Bill Blake, but she's better than Chester."

"I don't think the magic has fully penetrated Margaret's shell," Aunt Tillie replied. "It's possible she wasn't fully infected. You said she swatted Bill's hand away, that there was very little contact. That could play into this. It could be that Margaret's lack of imagination makes her a harder nut to crack."

"What are you doing?" I asked when Aunt Tillie raised her hands.

"I'm getting rid of the shimmer. If I do that, I think Margaret will be free of the curse."

"You're the curse," Mrs. Little snapped. "You've been a plague on my life for decades. The FBI is going to make sure that you pay for it."

"We're all looking forward to that," I replied as Aunt Tillie's fingers began to glow. Under different circumstances I would've admonished her to hide her actions. There was no sense doing that right now. Mrs. Little knew the truth about us, and she was already bordering the town limits of Crazyville, clearly determined to be mayor.

I sucked in a breath when Aunt Tillie's magic collided with Mrs. Little. The unicorn store owner began flailing her arms to hold off the magic. She was furious, and I didn't blame her, but she went rigid when the shimmer began to detach from her body.

"What's happening?" Landon asked as he pushed himself away from the door. "Is it working?"

"Can you see anything?" I asked.

"I see a glow. In fact ... wait ... what's she doing?"

When I looked back to gauge the progress of the spell, Aunt Tillie was no longer winning the battle against the shimmer. In fact, now that it was free of Mrs. Little, it appeared to be gaining power ... and heading straight for Aunt Tillie.

"No!" I lashed out with my magic before I could think, determined to stop the cloud of bad luck in its tracks. I was too late.

The shimmer slid over Aunt Tillie like the green ooze that we used to play with as kids. My heart ceased beating as I tried to figure out what to do. Aunt Tillie looked resigned as the ooze settled over her.

"What is that?" Landon demanded as he appeared at my side. "What did you do?"

"What *did* you do?" I growled at my great-aunt. I was in the dark as to what had happened.

"I think ... I think ... ." Aunt Tillie seemed distracted as she raised her hand to stare at her fingers. "I think Margaret is free of the curse."

I forced myself to look at Mrs. Little. She almost looked normal again. Well, except for the filthy hair and pajamas. The manic look in her eyes had fled.

"That's good, right?" Landon prodded. "That's what we wanted. You didn't even have to taunt her."

"I didn't," Aunt Tillie agreed, "but I don't know how good it is." She swallowed hard before flipping her hand over so I could look at the palm. The symbol was there, glowing red and bright. It was like a bloody warning that our lives were about to tumble out of control. "I'm pretty sure I'm cursed now."

Oh, well, great. I lashed out with my foot and kicked the nearest porcelain unicorn display, sending ten creatures tumbling to the floor where they shattered.

"You're paying for those," Mrs. Little snapped. "I'll have you arrested if you don't."

I pressed my lips together as I regarded Aunt Tillie. If Mrs. Little was no longer in danger, she was no longer my concern. It was a relief ... mostly. "Mom is going to kill you," I said. I didn't add that she was likely to kill me too. That was a given.

"We bought ourselves some time," Aunt Tillie insisted. "That's good."

Was it? It felt as if we'd given ourselves a whole new set of problems.

15
FIFTEEN

Mrs. Little had gaps in her memory, a concern that caused Chief Terry to order her transported to the hospital. She put up a fight — was spitting mad — but when I pointed out she'd come to work in her pajamas and the water main break would keep people from her store anyway, she seemed embarrassed and acquiesced.

Once it was just us inside the store, I started stalking Aunt Tillie through the aisles.

"What were you thinking?" I hissed.

She didn't answer. She seemed lost in thought. Or maybe she just wanted me to think that because she didn't have the answers I needed.

"What are we going to do?" I felt sick to my stomach when I turned to Landon, who had his head bent together with Chief Terry in the corner. When he met my gaze, there was worry there ... and something else I couldn't identify.

"It's going to be okay," he reassured me in a wooden tone. "Just ... let's not freak out, okay?"

"Let's not freak out? Let's not freak out!?" My voice was unnaturally shrill. "Oh, right. What's there to freak out about? Aunt Tillie is doubly cursed now and has a week to live." My voice cracked.

Landon wordlessly detached from Chief Terry and headed to me. "Come here," he whispered as he pulled me to him and pressed my face into the hollow between his neck and shoulder. "It's okay, Bay."

It didn't feel okay. In fact, nothing felt okay. "Landon ... ."

"Shh." He swayed back and forth, his hand warm as it moved up and down my back. "We're going to figure it out. The important thing is that we saved Mrs. Little."

"I would rather keep Aunt Tillie than save Mrs. Little." Part of me thought I should be ashamed of saying something like that out loud, but I meant it.

"We're going to save them both." He held me tight a beat longer and then pulled back, his eyes conflicted as he searched my face. "Let's take it one step at a time." He pressed a soothing kiss to my forehead and then turned to face Aunt Tillie. "We need a breakdown of what you did."

"Hmm?" Slowly, Aunt Tillie tracked her eyes to Landon. "What I did?"

"With the spell. I heard you say you were going to try to detach the shimmer. I don't know what that means, but I'll bet whatever you did put us in this predicament."

"*We're* not in this predicament," Aunt Tillie countered. She was surprisingly calm given the circumstances. "I did this. I'm the one who has to deal with the fallout."

That snapped me out of my funk. "We have to figure out a way to save you," I insisted. "The whole family is in this together."

"Maybe that's not the way it's supposed to play out, Bay."

I had no idea what to make of her attitude. I expected her to melt down, get dramatic, throw a couple people on her list for good measure.

The sound of footsteps near the door drew my attention and I let out a breath when I saw Thistle. She looked confused — had someone called her? — but she walked into the store as if she owned it. "Mrs. Little is still alive?" She looked dumbfounded. "I thought there was no way to save her."

"It seems Aunt Tillie found a way," Landon replied as he leaned against the counter and watched Aunt Tillie pick her way through the store.

Thistle looked between Aunt Tillie and me. "Something obviously happened. Clove texted that I should get over here, that the baby showed her images of Bay and Aunt Tillie here, and she knew something important had happened."

I straightened, surprised. "The baby showed her what happened?"

Thistle shrugged. "That's what she said. She was upset, told me to get over here and check on you guys and then call her back. She thought something really bad had happened."

Calvin could control emotions and pick up on the emotions of others. The fact that he could register the severity of a situation at such a young age was astounding. "Well, that's something to explore," I said.

"Later," Landon said. "We can focus on the baby later. We need to focus on our current problem."

"I'm still not sure what our current problem is," Thistle said. "It would be great if you explained."

"Aunt Tillie is now infected," Landon blurted.

Thistle's sharp intake of breath made me press my eyes shut. "What? How? I thought the only way to pass the curse was right before death. Mrs. Little is still alive. I saw her leave in an ambulance."

"The transfer didn't happen in a normal manner," Landon explained. "I'm not an expert, obviously, but Aunt Tillie said she saw a shimmer and attacked it. She wasn't strong enough and the shimmer moved from Mrs. Little to her. Now Aunt Tillie is infected. That's it in a nutshell."

"Well, great," Thistle drawled. Her eyes were accusatory when they landed on me. "How could you let this happen?"

"Hey!" Landon bristled as he pushed away from the counter and stepped between Thistle and me. "Don't blame this on her."

"It's okay," I said. "She has a right to be angry. I was supposed to be in charge." *And I failed miserably at my job*, I silently added.

"It's not okay," Landon argued. "You didn't make the decision to do ... whatever was done. It was Aunt Tillie."

"Yeah, but everybody knows that Aunt Tillie can't be trusted to cast a spell without supervision," Thistle argued. "Bay was supposed to make sure the curse died here. Now we have to keep taking the potions to keep our moods in check, just to be on the safe side, and also figure out a way to keep Aunt Tillie from dying in a week."

"We'll figure it out," Landon growled.

"I'm glad you have so much faith in us, but we'll have to mitigate all the bad luck Aunt Tillie is about to incur while we fight the curses," Thistle argued. "Do you have any idea what form this bad luck is going to take with a powerful witch?"

"No." Landon blinked several times. "Do you?"

"No, but it won't be good."

I pressed the heel of my hand to my forehead. Thistle was right. This was not going to end well. In fact, it was going to be a disaster of epic proportions.

"Sweetheart, let's not panic," Chief Terry said as he moved to my side. He'd always been in tune with my moods. He was terrified but refused to show fear in front of me. He was determined to be my rock. "Tillie, how do you feel?"

"I'm fine," Aunt Tillie replied automatically. "Don't worry about me."

Frustration bubbled up and grabbed me by the throat. "No? We don't have to worry about you? You can set fires with your mind and call tornados from nowhere and you're about to get hit by a string of bad luck so severe it could cripple everybody in this town. If that's not something to worry about, I don't know what is."

"Calm down, Bay," Landon admonished. "There's no reason to panic just yet."

I turned my back to him. The sympathy in his eyes made me angry. None of this was his fault but I needed someone to blame. I refused to let it be him when I obviously dropped the ball.

Then something occurred to me.

"I have to go to the inn." I gripped my hands into fists at my sides as I headed to the door. "I have to tell Mom what happened."

Landon's eyebrows hopped and he immediately started shaking his head. "Let's not be hasty."

"I can't keep this from her," I argued. "She needs to be involved. We have to come up with a plan."

Landon looked anguished. "Bay ... ."

"I have to go right now." I headed for the door, only focusing on Thistle when I was almost through it. "Keep an eye on Aunt Tillie. She seems weird, even for her. I'll let you know when the coast is clear. Mom is going to blow up, but she'll settle eventually."

"She's definitely going to blow up," Thistle agreed. She looked torn. "Do you want me to go with you? You shouldn't be alone when Aunt Winnie goes nuclear. I can absorb some of the anger."

"She won't be alone," Landon replied as he came to my side. "I'll go with her."

"You don't have to," I countered hollowly. "This is on me."

"It's not on anybody, Bay," Landon snapped. "It just happened. Your mother will understand."

He had much more faith in her powers of acceptance than I did. "We have to tell her now. She needs time to absorb it if we're going to fix this."

"Then we'll go." Landon turned to Chief Terry. "You can handle the water main break?"

Chief Terry nodded. He looked tortured. "Bay, maybe I should go with you to talk to your mother."

It was a nice offer, but I couldn't accept it. "This is my responsibility."

"It's nobody's responsibility, Bay. It just happened."

"Oh, we both know that's not true."

. . .

I FELT LIKE I WAS TRUDGING TO MY death when Landon and I got to the inn. Landon offered to take me somewhere else, back to the guesthouse, so I could collect my thoughts. Dragging things out would only make them worse.

"I have to do this." I squeezed his hand and then trudged across the parking lot. Each step felt heavier than the previous, and by the time I entered the inn, I felt sick to my stomach.

Mom was at the front desk sorting through the mail. When she looked up, I saw sympathy waiting for me in her blue eyes.

"Is Margaret dead?" she asked.

I shook my head.

"No?" Hope flared fast and hot. "Then you managed to save her."

"Apparently so," I acknowledged. "I'm still not sure what happened. I only know that when we got to town, Aunt Tillie had an idea. She thought if we could make Mrs. Little fight her own condition, we might be able to break the spell."

"I don't understand." Mom's expression was neutral. "How would that work?"

"Aunt Tillie suggested that we needed to dangle something strong in front of Mrs. Little, like her hatred for Aunt Tillie. Aunt Tillie suggested she tell Mrs. Little to kill herself so she would want to do the opposite."

"Huh." Mom rubbed her cheek, seemingly taking it in. "I know it's weird to say, but it makes sense. If there's one thing that fuels Margaret above all else, it's her hatred of Aunt Tillie."

"Yeah." I bobbed my head. I could feel Landon behind me but dared not look at him. I would start crying if I did. "We never really got to embrace that plan. When we were inside the store, Aunt Tillie noticed a magical shimmer around Mrs. Little."

Mom's forehead wrinkled in concentration. "A magical shimmer?"

"I saw it that first day at the overpass but didn't know what to make of it. I didn't notice it with Bill Blake, but that doesn't necessarily mean anything. I wasn't that near him when he died and there was a lot going on."

"Hmm." Mom nodded in understanding. She was engaged in the conversation but she'd yet to glom on to the fact that things were about to take a turn.

"Mom ... ." I trailed off and swallowed around the lump in my throat.

Landon's hand landed on my shoulder in that moment. He was lending me strength. He was also about to shift into protective mode. Before I could stop him, he took control of the conversation.

"We had Mrs. Little isolated in her store," he said in a dull voice. "She was ... spiraling. She was talking nonsense and bad luck. She blamed Aunt Tillie for her predicament."

"I'm not one to make excuses for Margaret, but she was out of her mind," Mom argued. "I can see why she would think that."

"I'm not blaming Mrs. Little," Landon reassured her. "I'm just trying to set the scene."

It was only then that Mom realized we were about to drop a bomb on her. The way she lifted her head told me that she'd finally grasped what was about to happen ... and things were going to be even uglier than I initially anticipated. "Just tell me," she gritted out.

I took over. "Aunt Tillie thought she could remove the shimmer. She believed that if she could destroy that magical layer, she would save Mrs. Little. She managed to separate the layer from Mrs. Little just fine. When it came time to destroy it, though ... ." I licked my lips, my mouth suddenly dry.

"Aunt Tillie couldn't control the shimmer," Landon explained. He was pressed tightly against me now. If there was going to be an emotional explosion, which was likely, we would absorb it together. "She tried to fight it, but it attached to her."

"To who?" Mom asked blankly.

"Aunt Tillie."

There was no initial explosion. Instead, Mom stood there, pen poised in her hand over the ledger book. When she finally did speak, her tone was icy. "If I understand what you're saying, Margaret is no longer cursed and is fine, but now Aunt Tillie is cursed. I believe that's what the two of you are trying to tell me."

I cringed against Landon but nodded. "That's exactly what we're telling you."

Mom dropped the pen and rested her palms on the ledger. "How did this happen, Bay?"

"I don't know. It just ... happened so fast."

"I trusted you with Aunt Tillie's safety."

"Hey, now," Landon blurted. "You cannot blame her for this."

"Can't I?" Mom raised a challenging eyebrow. "Bay had two jobs. She was supposed to make sure Margaret didn't infect anybody else and make sure Aunt Tillie didn't find trouble. She seems to have fallen down on both jobs."

"Hey!" Landon exploded.

"Don't bother." I wrapped my fingers around Landon's wrist and tried to tug him away. "She's just upset."

"Yes, Bay, I'm upset," Mom shouted. "You were supposed to protect her."

"You cannot blame this on Bay," Landon roared. "This is not her fault. She was trying to control the situation. Aunt Tillie is a grown woman. She made the decision, she's responsible for the fallout."

"Oh, don't even," Mom hissed, her eyes slits of disappointment. "Everybody knows Aunt Tillie can't control herself in the heat of battle. She's incapable of thinking clearly under certain circumstances. Bay knows that better than anybody. She was supposed to protect her."

"Bay is not Aunt Tillie's guardian," Landon growled. "I cannot believe you're blaming this on her."

"Who else, Landon?" Mom's annoyance was clear. "Bay was in charge. This is her responsibility."

"Un-freaking-believable." Landon moved his arm around my back and tugged me to his side. "You know, I've heard a lot of wacky stuff from this family over the years. A lot of wacky stuff. This is the absolute worst thing I've heard.

"Bay is not to blame for everything that happens that you don't like," he continued. "She did her best today. Aunt Tillie made the decision to do what she did. Blaming Bay is the most ridiculous thing I've ever heard."

Mom looked momentarily chastised, and then regrouped. "Aunt Tillie could die." Mom's voice cracked. "We could lose her. She's the only mother I have left."

I thought my heart might shred. "She's the only grandmother I have," I said. "I don't want anything to happen to her. It just ... went down so fast. I didn't realize what was happening until it was too late."

"That doesn't help us now, does it, Bay?"

I swallowed hard. "No." There was nothing else to say, so I turned to leave. I was hoping Landon would exit with me, but he couldn't let it go.

"You act disappointed in her," he snapped at Mom.

"I am," Mom replied. "We're in big trouble now, Landon."

"It's not her fault. You weren't there. You didn't see. You left the heavy-lifting to her and now want to give her grief about how things went down." Landon practically spit out the words. "I'm disappointed in you. I just ... can't believe this."

He stood behind me. "Come on, baby. Let's get out of here."

That's what I wanted more than anything, and I simply nodded.

"We need to talk about how to fix this," Mom argued. "We have a lot to deal with."

"Maybe you should fix it," Landon shot back. "You know everything, right? You know better than anybody even though you weren't there. You left Bay to watch Mrs. Little die and handle Aunt Tillie. If you think it's all so easy, maybe you should be in charge."

With that, he ushered me out of the inn. We didn't stop until we were near my car, at which point he cupped my chin and stared into my eyes.

"She didn't mean what she said," he whispered. "She's just upset."

"She is," I agreed. I refused to cry. "She's afraid Aunt Tillie is going to die, and we'll all be forced to do nothing but watch."

"We won't let that happen."

I wished for his faith, but I felt defeated. "I need to get out of here. Can we take a drive?"

He nodded. "Yup. Let's get out of here. Some space from your mother will do us both some good."

16
SIXTEEN

Landon drove around for fifteen minutes before heading to the bluff. He parked at the top and then drew me outside, settling me on his lap as he got comfortable on the ground.

"It's okay, Bay." His voice was low. "We're going to figure this out."

The fact that he was determined to protect me had tears threatening to surface. "I know it's going to be okay."

"You do?" His surprise was obvious as he brushed my hair from my neck and rubbed his cheek against mine. "How do you know that?"

"Because we don't have a choice. We can't survive losing Aunt Tillie."

"You know that eventually we're going to lose her. Nobody lives forever."

"That's not what she thinks."

He chuckled. "We still have a lot of years left with her. I'm sure of that. You can't take this all on yourself. You need to let others in to help."

"Mom?" Even saying that one word made me bitter.

"Don't get me started on your mother."

Despite my anger, loyalty had me straightening on his lap. "She didn't mean it. She's just upset. You heard her. Aunt Tillie may not be the only mother she's ever had but she's the one left, the one everyone loves despite her antics."

"Your mother is afraid." Landon was matter-of-fact. "She shouldn't have said what she did to you. It's not your fault."

"It feels like my fault."

Landon growled. "Stop whipping yourself. You always blame yourself. It's the one thing about you that drives me crazy."

"I think it's because I'm the oldest. I was always in charge, always responsible."

"Well, you're not responsible for this. Aunt Tillie did what she did."

I let loose a sigh. "We can't eat at the inn tonight. Mom needs space. Do you want to order takeout and spend the night in bed?"

I thought he would readily agree. Instead, he shook his head.

"No?" I arched a surprised eyebrow.

"They'll come looking for us there. Thistle. Your mother. Marnie and Twila. I thought we'd go someplace they'd be less likely to find us."

"And where is that?"

He grinned. "We haven't seen your father since we came back from our honeymoon. They always have good food out there."

"You willingly want to spend time with my father?" That wasn't like him, and I was dumbfounded.

He nodded. "Your father and I are making inroads. He was surprisingly open when I approached him about Chief Terry walking you down the aisle. When I explained it was the best thing for you, he jumped at the chance to help me. Like everybody else, he wants what's best for you."

I was silent a moment, considering, and then I nodded. "That sounds like a good idea. I definitely don't have to worry about Mom looking for me there."

"That's what I was thinking." He brushed his lips against my cheek. "I love you, Bay. We're going to figure this out. You have my word."

We both knew he couldn't make that promise and keep it. Still, I needed to hear it. "Ten more minutes here, huh? I like when it's just us."

"Ten more minutes," he agreed. "You'll have me forever, though. There will be plenty of time for just us. I'm going to demand it."

"You don't have to demand it. I'll willingly give it."

"I know. That's why we're such a good match."

"Now and forever."

"Oh, sweetie, you're never getting rid of me. In this world and the next, you're stuck with me."

It wasn't exactly a hardship.

LANDON TEXTED TO TELL DAD WE were coming for dinner. He didn't request that they make room for us. He simply told him we were coming. Dad was waiting for us in the lobby of the Dragonfly.

"There they are." Dad beamed as he emerged from behind the front counter and gave me a hug. "I've been wondering when I was going to see you. How was your honeymoon?"

"It was good," I replied automatically.

"It was great," Landon countered as he shook Dad's hand. "Other than Aunt Tillie crashing the festivities, it was downright perfect."

Dad's eyes widened in surprise. "Are you kidding me? Tillie went on your honeymoon?"

Landon shook his head and frowned at the memory. "She just showed up."

"It turned out she always wanted to see Moonstone Bay," I explained. "She said it was on her bucket list." As soon as I said it, I regretted it. My throat tightened and tears flowed from my eyes.

"Hey, what's this?" Dad moved closer and used his thumb to swipe at the tears. "What's wrong? I knew something was up when

Landon said you were coming for dinner. I thought I was going to have to browbeat you to get you out here."

"It's nothing," I replied automatically. There was no sense dragging him into our problems. It wasn't as if he could help.

"Bay and Winnie got into a fight," Landon replied, his hand solid and warm on my back. "Winnie said some horrible things and Bay is trying to be stoic."

"Ah." Dad nodded. "I'm sorry about that." He studied my face. "Do you want to tell me what's going on?"

"There's no point," I replied as my voice cracked. "I made a mistake and now we're in trouble. There's nothing you can do."

Landon was exasperated. "Bay, we've been over this. You didn't make a mistake. Aunt Tillie is responsible for her own actions."

Dad, ever calm, smiled. "Let's get some tea and settle in the parlor. We still have thirty minutes until dinner is ready. We don't have guests this week, so Teddy and Warren can finish dinner prep without me."

"That sounds good," Landon replied before I could.

Sincerity shone through Dad's eyes. "Head into the parlor. I'll be along in a few minutes." He squeezed my shoulder. "Whatever it is, Bay, I'm sure it will be okay."

I could only hope he was right. Despair was my companion right now, and I didn't like it.

DAD BROUGHT OUT A VARIETY OF TEAS. Landon sorted through them, and when he handed me a mug, I wasn't surprised to find that he'd picked one that was supposed to promote relaxation and serenity.

"So, tell me what's going on," Dad prodded.

Landon related the tale. He was getting good at explaining the magical occurrences that regularly upended our lives. When he finished, Dad looked perplexed.

"So ... Tillie is going to die?" He didn't look nearly as happy about that prospect as I thought he would.

"She's not going to die," I argued, vehemently shaking my head. "She's just ... in a lot of danger."

Dad leaned back in his chair and looked at the fire. "If you would've asked me a year ago how I felt about this situation, I would've felt differently. I never want anyone to die," he added hurriedly when I shot him a dark look. "I just wouldn't have thought I'd be upset at the prospect of losing Tillie. She's never been warm to me."

"She's been good to me," I argued.

Dad held up his hand to quiet me. "Bay, you're not listening. I don't want anything to happen to Tillie. She's a pain but she's a decent person. Do you know she helped us plant a garden this year?"

I was taken aback. "No. I ... no. She never mentioned that." I looked to Landon for confirmation.

"She didn't," Landon agreed. "I can't believe she would keep that secret. Are you certain she's not using your garden to hide the pot she's growing?"

Dad let out a warm chuckle. "We haven't found any pot."

"You don't get the runs when you think about pot, do you?" I asked. Aunt Tillie had warded her own pot field with a curse that struck any law enforcement representative who tried to find the field with a severe case of the trots.

"Not that I'm aware of. She likes growing things, and we were having trouble with our vegetable garden. She had fixes for everything, and after she intervened, the garden flourished."

"Huh." I had no idea what to make of that. "She's always so full of surprises." The words were barely out of my mouth before I burst into tears. I could no longer contain them despite my best efforts.

"Here we go." Landon didn't sound upset when he slid his arms around my legs and lifted me out of the chair before settling me on his lap in the same chair. "I knew this was coming. Bay, you need to let it out. The sooner you let these emotions run their course, the more focused you'll be."

I couldn't respond. I was too busy sobbing.

"Landon is right, Bay," Dad said in a soothing voice. "You've always kept your emotions in check, and often to your detriment. Crying doesn't make you weak."

It felt the opposite to me. "I have to pull it together. Aunt Tillie needs me."

"We all need you, Bay." Landon's voice was soft. "It's okay to cry. You've needed to let loose since it happened. Just ... let it out. We can't fix what's been broken until you let it out."

He rubbed my back as I cried. It took me five minutes to pull myself back together. In truth, the notion of losing Aunt Tillie frightened me more than I envisioned. I knew she would die eventually, but I wasn't ready for it now. Maybe I never would be.

When I finally sniffled for the last time and raised my eyes, I found my father watching me with an unreadable expression. I felt like an idiot falling apart in front of him. Landon was a different story; he'd slapped me back together a few times. "I'm sorry," I offered. "That was a weak moment."

"No, Bay." Dad shook his head. "You're the strongest person I know. You don't always have to take the weight of the world onto your shoulders alone."

"I've been telling her the same thing," Landon noted, offering me a cheeky grin. "See, your father and I have been bonding."

That elicited a laugh, as I'm sure he intended. "I'm sorry for falling apart."

"Don't do that," Landon chided, shaking his head. "You didn't fall apart. You regrouped. I need you to be open to that occasionally. When we do have a kid of our own — one that isn't boring — are you going to call the kid weak for crying?"

"Of course not, but I'm an adult."

"And your mother slapped you like you were a child, and it hurt."

Landon's expression darkened. "I never thought I would be this angry with her, but I'm furious."

Dad cleared his throat. "You're not going to want to hear this, but you need to let Winnie off the hook."

It was odd to hear that coming from him, but I was intrigued. "Since when are you on Mom's side?"

"I'm not on her side. I just ... understand her in a way you likely can't. She was always strong for you guys, something I'm guessing you got from her." He smiled. "You probably don't want to hear it, especially right now, but you two are more alike than you realize."

"I definitely don't want to hear that," I muttered darkly under my breath.

"But it's true. She was the oldest and she sacrificed herself to take care of her sisters. You've been expected to do the same with Clove and Thistle. Tillie is always the wild card. She's a mother one moment and the worst behaved child who ever existed the next."

"She's ... something," I agreed on a glare. "She's in danger. We have to do something."

"You will." Dad's smile was warm this time. "Your mother already regrets what she said, Bay. I know her. Just because we couldn't stay married doesn't mean I don't still love and respect her. We simply weren't a proper fit. But she's a good person.

"Right now, in this very moment, I bet she's sitting in that huge kitchen baking something decadent," he continued. "She's whipping the batter into submission and running every moment of the conversation with you through her mind. She regrets it. She wants to apologize but doesn't think she's worthy of forgiveness.

"You have to understand," he said as he shifted to stare directly into my eyes. "When Ginger died, those girls were terrified. They'd never considered a world without their mother. Then Tillie became their mother and things shifted again. Despite her many faults — many, many faults — Tillie was the best second mother they could've asked for. The prospect of losing her ... well ... it's too much. Your mother doesn't mean to hurt you. She's just hurting herself."

Deep down, I knew that. Before I could respond, a noise at the edge of the room drew my attention.

"He's right," Mom said as she wrung her hands together. She looked wrecked. I couldn't believe she was actually here. Other than my wedding and a few other instances in which she'd had no choice, she'd done her best to avoid my father since his return. "I am sorry."

"How did you know we were here?" Landon demanded as he moved me to the chair cushion and stood. "I wanted Bay to get some peace. If you're here to yell ... ."

Mom held up her hand to silence Landon. "I'm not here to yell. I promise. Jack was right. I regretted what I said as soon as I said it. I just ... needed a little time. The women in this family always need a bit of time to collect themselves."

"If this is you apologizing, you suck at it," Landon complained.

"I'm sorry," Mom said. "I didn't mean to hurt Bay. I don't believe what I said to her. I just ... what are we going to do?" She looked momentarily helpless, something I wasn't used to seeing. "We can't lose Aunt Tillie."

"Where is she?" I asked.

"She's at the inn ... and it has started." Mom swallowed hard. "She's already crashed the scooter twice and Peg bit her."

"Not my Peg." Landon adamantly shook his head. "There's no way."

"It's not the pig, it's the curse," I said. "Things will start falling apart fast." Something occurred to me. "Her magic is going to start faltering. We can't let her cast spells."

"I'm already ahead of you," Mom said. "Thistle is making the next batch of the emotion potion. We need that now more than ever. She'll have enough finished tonight to get us through several days. We have time," Mom insisted. "We'll pool our resources and figure out a way to fix this. At the very least, we can do what Aunt Tillie did to extend things. I can remove the shimmer from her when it's time and then we'll have another week with me being cursed."

I shook my head. "We can't let it jump again."

"Then we have to find a solution, because I'm not going to let Aunt Tillie die." Mom turned fierce. "Bay, you're the strongest witch in the family. I know what I said to you earlier was wrong, but we need you to help fix this. You're the only one who can. I don't want to put unnecessary pressure on you, but you need to figure a way out of this."

"Not to put too much pressure on her," Landon growled. "Seriously, we need to talk about your method of apology."

Mom shot him a fond grin. "I'm not at my best. You'll have to excuse me. This has ... shaken ... me. I know I'm an adult, but losing my second mother ... I just can't."

Landon took pity on her and accepted her outstretched hand. "We're going to fix this. I promise. I need you not to cripple Bay emotionally in the process. It's going to take all of us working together to get through this."

"I'll do my best," Mom reassured him.

Landon flicked his eyes to Dad. "So, you have room for one extra at dinner?" He inclined his head toward Mom. "Winnie could use a breather. Once we're back at The Overlook, things are going to be tense. One last fresh breath before the storm can only benefit us all."

Dad's smile was warm and welcoming. "That's a fine idea. We can't help much because we're non-magical, but we want to do what we can. You're our family too." He pinned Mom with a serious look. "Whatever you need."

"Well, we might need some babysitters at some point," Mom said. "Aunt Tillie can't be left alone if she's a walking calamity."

A muscle worked in Dad's jaw. "This is your way of punishing me." He was grim. "After all these years, you're finally getting your revenge."

Mom let loose a hollow laugh. "You're family, Jack. You said it yourself. You have to suffer right along with us."

"The horror." Despite his words, Dad smiled. "Come on. Dinner is ready. Let's eat, and then we'll start hashing things out."

17
SEVENTEEN

Although I would never admit it to him, Landon was right. The tears had done me some good. I was emotionally wrung out and needed to vent. After dinner at the Dragonfly, I crawled into bed at home and slept like the dead. When I woke the next morning, after a full ten hours of sleep, I was ready to go.

Unfortunately, I had no idea where to focus my energy. I stewed about it during family breakfast, a meal fraught with furtive energy. The only conversations that bubbled up were of the mundane variety. Calvin was sleeping a solid five hours in one shot. That was good for Clove and Sam. Thistle was adorable with Calvin. Blah, blah, blah.

I mean, I loved the baby as much as everybody else, but I didn't care that he was having regular bowel movements. Apparently, Aunt Tillie didn't care either, because she jumped in during a conversational lull to take control.

"I want to have a funeral for myself," she announced.

I choked on my toast and Landon had to thump my back.

"What?" Chief Terry asked when everybody else at the table was rendered mute.

"A funeral." Aunt Tillie had been uncharacteristically quiet throughout the meal. She pushed the food around her plate, making everybody all the more uncomfortable.

"You're not dead," Twila pointed out.

"Thank you, Twila, I never would've figured that out on my own," Aunt Tillie said dryly as she rolled her eyes. "I don't know what I did before you were here to tell me the obvious."

Mom shot her a quelling look. "Why would you want to have a funeral before you die?"

"And you're not going to die," I added. "We're going to stop ... whatever this is."

Aunt Tillie graced me with a sympathetic look. "This isn't your fault. I should've told you that yesterday. You were gone when I wanted to talk to you about my wishes."

Her wishes? This conversation was weird, even by Winchester standards. "We're not talking about your wishes." I didn't care if everybody at the table thought I was in denial, I wouldn't allow Aunt Tillie to be taken by a curse. "We're going to fix this."

"Bay, let's hear her out," Landon countered. "She has a right to tell us what she wants."

I murdered him with a glare. "I'll take your bacon away forever," I warned. "Keep pushing me and you won't like what happens."

"You're on your own," he said to Aunt Tillie.

Laughter broke out at the table, and for the first time since Aunt Tillie had been infected, it appeared to be genuine.

"I'm glad to see your priorities are still intact," Aunt Tillie drawled. "At least you're not treating me like some fragile china teacup."

"I would never do that," Landon agreed. "I am curious about how you feel about all this. Bay and Winnie got their feelings out last night. You've been an enigma."

"I've just ... been thinking." Aunt Tillie held out her hands.

"Knowing there's an expiration date on your life forces things into focus."

"Stop saying that," I growled.

"Bay, I don't want to die, but I want to be realistic." Aunt Tillie was firm. "There are some things I want do before ... the end comes. Like holding my own funeral."

"It's a waste of time." Was she trying to kill me? "Funerals are for when you die. You're not going to die for a long time."

"It's my life, Bay. A funeral is necessary. I want to see all the people I love before I die. That's why I want to host it now."

"But ... ." I looked to my mother for help and found her eyeing Aunt Tillie with so much love it caused my heart to squeeze.

"That's a fine idea," Mom said with a serene smile. "I can help you plan it, come up with a menu and guest list."

"Oh, I've already come up with a guest list." Aunt Tillie whipped a sheet of paper out from under the table, indicating she had planned to drop this funeral idea on everybody all along. "Here you go."

Mom took the list, frowning after she got through several names. "Why do you have jobs listed next to the people you're inviting?"

"It's going to be a theme funeral."

I was instantly alert. "What sort of jobs?"

"Well, for example, she has Margaret listed as a VIP attendant and expects her to dress like a court jester and dance," Mom replied primly.

"It's a circus theme," Aunt Tillie explained. "In fact, I want you to call those circus people who were here last year so they can come. I want to see Nellie again. That's also one of my dying wishes."

"How many dying wishes do you have?" Landon asked as he bit into a slice of bacon. All thought of curbing his gluttonous ways had fallen by the wayside given our new predicament. He wasn't the only one who would be stress-eating this week.

"Fifty." Aunt Tillie procured another sheet of paper from under the table and handed it to me. "I expect everybody to pitch in and help with these."

Now it was my turn to frown. "How do you expect us to get the dictator of North Korea here so you can kick him in the nuts?" I demanded.

She shrugged. "That's for you to figure out."

Landon shot me a smile as he snagged the list from me. He seemed fairly relaxed for a guy who was going to have to deal with a ridiculous amount of family drama the next few days. "You want to marry Paul Rudd? I didn't know he was on your crush list."

"He never ages," Aunt Tillie replied simply. "I want to bottle whatever he has going on. Marrying him will make it easy to conduct laboratory experiments on him. He can't have me arrested if we're married."

"Yeah, I don't think that's how it works," Landon said dryly.

"What would you know?" Aunt Tillie demanded.

"Call it a wild guess." He kept perusing the list. "You want to ride a dinosaur into battle? Don't you think a few of these — just a few, mind you — might be impossible to carry out?"

"Nope." Aunt Tillie shook her head. "We're going to do all of them. I have faith."

Mom shook her list of funeral attendees and cleared her throat to get Aunt Tillie's attention. "I very much doubt Elton John is going to come up with a new version of *Candle in the Wind* and come here to play it," she argued.

"He did it for that British chick," Aunt Tillie shot back.

"Princess Diana was his friend."

"How do you know we're not friends? He could be on my *Call of Duty* team. You don't know."

"Well, we'll definitely get on ... some of this." Mom placed the sheet of paper on the table. "Would you like us to write eulogies?"

What strange version of Hell had I wandered into? "We're not writing her eulogies," I snapped. "She's not dying."

"I would love eulogies," Aunt Tillie replied as if I hadn't spoken.

"I'll write them for you so you don't have to take time away from my lists, but I trust you'll feel what I write ... and practice how to deliver them correctly in front of a mirror before the big day."

This was too much. "May I speak to you?" I asked my mother pointedly.

Mom briefly looked up. "I'm busy right now. Eat your breakfast."

"We need to talk."

"Eat your breakfast, Bay." Mom was firm. "If your aunt wants to throw her own funeral, where she can say goodbye to people on her terms, what does it matter to you?"

"She's not going to die!" I didn't mean to yell as loudly as I did, or slam my hands on the table, but I did both.

"Here we go." Landon pulled a bottle out of his pocket, sparing a brief glance at the clock on the wall. "We're twenty minutes late getting you your potion this morning. I'm sorry everybody." He looked genuinely contrite. "That won't happen again." He opened the bottle and handed it to me. "Down the hatch."

I glared at him. "It's not the curse. I won't let her die."

"Drink that," Landon ordered, his eyes fierce.

"Yes, Bay," Mom said pointedly. "Drink it."

I was sullen when I tipped up the bottle and pounded the contents. The potion tasted like Aunt Tillie's wine after it had been left out in the elements for a week, but there was nothing I could do about that. Landon was right again. I was feeling wild. It was time to take control.

"Let's talk about our plans for containing the curse," I said. "I was thinking that maybe we could cast a containment spell. Do you remember that time we got into the poison ivy when we were kids? You guys made that ointment so the rash would be contained even if we scratched. We could modify that spell."

Mom looked intrigued at the prospect. "Do you think that's possible?"

"It's somewhere to start," I replied, my eyes drifting to the dining room doorway when the scuff of shoes got my attention. I was surprised to find Emori standing there. I hadn't seen her since the uncomfortable meal several nights ago. "Hey." I was taken aback so I just stared. Emori was clearly uncomfortable as she shifted back and forth and let her gaze bounce between faces. "Um ... hey."

"I believe what Bay meant to say was sit down," Mom offered graciously. "We have more than enough."

"Are you sure?" Emori looked distinctly uncomfortable. "I don't want to interrupt. I heard what happened yesterday afternoon and wanted to offer my help."

"How did you hear?" I asked as I snagged a slice of bacon from Landon's plate. The potion was already working, the erupting emotions spewing out of me like hot lava were already being tempered, and now I had nothing but an empty hole inside of me that needed to be filled.

"There's a whole platter of bacon," Landon complained when he realized I was mowing through his stash. "Why do you have to eat mine?"

"Married people share," I replied sweetly. "I believe you told me that when you ate my half of the red velvet cake we smuggled home four days ago."

"I knew you stole that cake!" Aunt Tillie jabbed her finger in my direction. "You guys lied and stole it when you knew I was saving it for myself. You're so on my list."

I would've rolled my eyes any other time she issued the threat, but this time I merely nodded.

"Bacon curse," Landon begged.

Aunt Tillie shook her head. "I'm not rewarding you jerkwads. Don't even think about it."

"Have I come at a bad time?" Emori looked as if she would rather be anywhere but in the middle of our drama.

"Sit down." I waved at a chair. "We're spiraling and it's not going to get any better."

"Ain't that the truth." Landon gave me a friendly pat under the table. "We're going to talk about the bacon thievery later," he added in a low voice.

I ignored him and focused on Emori. "How did you find out what happened?"

"I stopped in to see Thistle yesterday afternoon." Emori eyed the huge spread. "Do you guys eat like this all the time? You'll have heart attacks if you're not careful."

Landon wrinkled his nose. "And I was really starting to like you."

"Ignore him," I said when Emori shot him a puzzled look. "He's in a mood."

"Okay, Hulk girl." Landon shook his head. "I'm not the only one in a mood, Emori. Prepare yourself for mayhem."

"That's why I'm here." Emori was calm. I'd yet to see her otherwise. "Thistle explained how Tillie absorbed the curse. It was difficult to understand through all the tears, but I got the gist of it."

I jerked up my head. "Tears?"

Emori nodded. "She was wrecked."

I slid my eyes to Aunt Tillie, who didn't look surprised in the least. "Are you going to make Thistle dress up for your funeral?" I don't know why that was the question that popped into my head.

Aunt Tillie nodded. "Of course. She's going to be the bearded lady. I even have a spell so she doesn't have to fake a beard."

I pressed my lips together to keep from laughing. "What a marvelous parting gift."

"I thought so." When Aunt Tillie met my gaze there was nothing diabolical lurking there. She was just a woman facing mortality ... and it hurt to see her stripped bare.

"Anyway, I've been searching for the symbol in my books because it seemed familiar," Emori continued. She took one tiny scoop of eggs, and one minuscule serving of hash browns. She only bothered with one slice of toast. She didn't go for any of the breakfast meats. "I can't find the exact symbol, but I have found a few similar ones. I think I know where we can find answers on this specific symbol."

That information was enough to drag my eyes from her sparse plate to her face. "What is it?"

"I'm not sure, but I'm fairly certain it's an old curse. I think it's Greek in origin."

"Greek?" I focused on Aunt Tillie. "Does that mean anything to you?"

She shook her head. "No, but a lot of curses originated in Greece."

"Where can we find answers?" I pressed. I would take anything at this point.

"Detroit. Greektown to be exact. I know two women who own a store there. I think they can help us."

"Detroit?" My anxiety spiked. "That's a long drive. Can't we just email the photo of the symbol?"

"They eschew technology. They don't have cell phones ... or email. I've been trying to get them to establish an online store because they could clean up, but they're reticent. We have to go down there."

I darted my eyes to Landon to gauge his opinion.

"I think it's our best shot for now," he said. "I know it's a haul — and I don't relish you being that far away — but it can't hurt to ask."

I nodded. I was already figuring out the logistics in my head. "I need to take a couple potions with me, just to be on the safe side. If something happens and we need to spend the night down there ... ."

"We have extra in the fridge," Mom offered. "You can take some of ours and if we need extra, we'll get it from your fridge."

I nodded. "Okay, well ... then I guess I should finish up and we can go." I flashed a smile for Emori's benefit. "These women, are you certain they can help?"

"Am I one-hundred percent certain? No." Emori wagged her head. "But I trust them implicitly and I think they're our best bet."

"Then that's good enough for me." I snagged another slice of bacon from Landon's plate, relishing the way he growled. "My car is in the lot and has a full tank of gas. We can leave as soon as you're finished."

"I'm going with you," Aunt Tillie announced, causing my stomach to sink.

"Um ... I don't think that's a good idea," I said. "You're a trouble magnet right now."

"The answers might be there," Aunt Tillie pointed out. "If these women know what the symbol means, they might have a fix, even if it's only temporary. It's better I go just in case."

I opened my mouth to argue further and then thought better of it. "You have to do what I say, and take your potions regularly," I warned. "We have to be really careful."

"We both know I won't agree to do what you say," Aunt Tillie shot back. "But I will agree to be a good little girl."

"What about your funeral preparations?" Mom asked. "Do you want to put those on hold?" She looked hopeful.

"Of course not." Aunt Tillie shook her head. "You keep plugging away on the preparations."

"I thought you wanted to be in charge," Mom prodded.

"I am in charge. I'm delegating. You can do all the things I don't want to do, and I'll enjoy the funeral. I can't wait to hear your speech about me. I spent hours writing it last night. It's going to be beautiful."

Mom frowned. "Don't you think people should be able to write their own eulogies?"

"What fun would that be? I want to hear how wonderful I am. If I let people choose what they want to say I'll come off looking like a ninny."

"She has a point," Landon noted as he grabbed the bacon platter and settled it between us. Apparently, we were going to be gluttons together.

"You really are just all sorts of helpful today," Mom drawled, shaking her head. "Fine. We'll continue with the funeral preparations. Bay, watch your great-aunt." She hesitated, likely remembering our blow-up from the previous day. "I know you'll take care of her."

"I'll do my best," I agreed. "I wouldn't consider taking her if I didn't think she was right. If there's a solution down there, we want to get to it soon."

"That's the only reason I'm agreeing," Mom said. "Keep in touch. I want to know what's happening."

"Oh, don't worry." I slid my eyes to Aunt Tillie, who was already making a list of the things she wanted to change into for the trip. "I have a feeling you'll be hearing from us often enough that you'll get tired of your ring tone."

"Probably." Mom bobbed her head. "I still want to be kept informed. We finally have a thread to chase. We need it to turn into something good."

18
EIGHTEEN

Aunt Tillie yelled "shotgun" in the parking lot, but for safety's sake we made her sit in the rear. I checked to make sure there was nothing back there that could possibly hurt her and buckled her in myself, a great insult to her.

"I can buckle my own seatbelt," she groused.

"You're cursed," I reminded her. "I'm just trying to be safe."

"The curse won't claim me for six more days. I want to live my life on my terms. Don't turn into your mother."

I held her gaze for what felt like forever and then finally nodded. I wanted to point out that was the meanest thing she'd ever said to me, but I didn't. "Okay."

"Oh, don't make that face," she sneered. "I'm not dying yet."

"Just out of curiosity, what do you hope to gain from this funeral? I mean ... what do you want to happen?" I was asking for myself. If she needed something specific and we weren't capable of saving her — a fear I wouldn't voice aloud — I wanted to make sure she got everything she wanted.

"I want to hear how much I'm loved."

I waited.

"And maybe a few laughs," she conceded. "You know, one last win over my enemies. I figure Margaret owes me. I did save her, after all."

"She might not realize she owes you," I said.

"Something tells me she knows."

"If she doesn't, we'll make sure she knows before ... ." I didn't finish the statement. I couldn't.

"Before I kick the bucket?" Aunt Tillie's eyes danced with mirth.

"I'd appreciate it if you didn't say things like that." I shut her door and then climbed into the driver's seat. "I won't let this curse take you." I fastened my own seatbelt and started the car. "We're going to end this on our terms, like we always do."

"I know." Aunt Tillie sounded as if she didn't have a care in the world. "I do need one thing from you just in case, though."

I felt itchy all over. "What?"

"I want you and Landon to take Peg."

My stomach constricted at what she wasn't saying. "We'll make sure Peg is taken care of," I said.

"No, I want you guys to take her." Aunt Tillie was firm. "She loves Landon. I know he'll keep her with him until her dying breath. I want her to be with people who love her. Your mother, while a wonderful witch, wouldn't give her the love she needs."

I merely nodded as I slid my sunglasses into place. "We'll take her."

"Awesome. Now, crank up the Led Zeppelin. Let's make this a proper road trip."

IT TOOK FOUR HOURS TO drive to Detroit. I was familiar with the freeways and traffic patterns and had no problem navigating to Greektown. Emori and I were careful to keep Aunt Tillie between us as we walked across the uneven sidewalk to the store.

"Are you sure this is it?" I asked when we arrived. It looked like a random door in a wall. There was no awning. No name on the window. It almost looked like an abandoned building.

"I'm sure." Emori flashed a smile that was likely meant to soothe me. "Like I said, Carol and Sheryl are unique. They manage a thriving business ... and they do it all under the radar."

"Carol and Sheryl?" I asked.

"Sisters." Her grin widened. "You're going to love them."

We followed her into the store, keeping Aunt Tillie between us. Once we were inside, my eyes went wide. We were in a voodoo shop, the sort I'd only ever seen in movies. I was barely inside before I heard the kibitzing.

"You cut the osha root wrong," a female voice complained. "You were supposed to cut it crosswise, not in squares."

"What does it matter?" another female voice replied. "It crushes the same."

"It matters because crosswise is correct and square is wrong."

"Oh, whatever. You really need to pull that stick out of your ... oh, hello."

I slid around one of the display stands so I could see the women behind the voices. Carol and Sheryl were not what I was expecting. "Hello."

They were both in their sixties, maybe older. Both boasted hair that was sort of blond but shot through with gray. They looked almost identical except one had blue eyes and the other green. "You're the voodoo queens?" I blurted.

The women laughed in tandem.

"I don't ever remember claiming to be a voodoo queen," one of them replied. "You might have me mistaken for somebody else."

"She's confused," Emori volunteered, stepping to my right and grinning. "She assumed when I said I knew people who could help that they would be like me."

"Ah." One of the women nodded. "That explains it." She moved out from behind the counter. "Emori, I thought you'd moved up north. What are you doing down here?" She embraced Emori strongly. "I know it's only been a few weeks, but I've missed you."

"I've missed you too, Sheryl."

Sheryl had the blue eyes. I looked to the woman who remained behind the counter. She seemed shyer than her sister.

"So, introductions are in order." Emori rubbed her hands together. "Sheryl and Carol Coronado, this is Bay and Tillie Winchester. They're ... ."

"Witches," Carol interjected before Emori could finish. "They're witches."

I squared my shoulders. "We didn't say that."

Carol laughed. "Oh, dear, you don't have to. Your very being says it ... as does your strange aura. I've never seen one quite that color. It's opal. Seriously, how can you have an opal aura?"

"Not opal," Sheryl corrected. "Moonstone. She's very powerful."

I ran my tongue over my teeth, discomfort running roughshod over my emotions. "Maybe this was a mistake," I hedged.

"No." Emori held out her hand. "You can trust them. I promise. I've known them my entire life ... or at least since I was a young girl. They can help."

"Help with what?" Carol asked.

"I'm guessing it's the curse on this one." Sheryl pointed at Aunt Tillie, who had been careful not to touch anything. She talked big about being ready for death, but her actions said otherwise. This level of caution was completely unlike her ... and a smart move. There were dangers in every corner of this store. "You've got the mark on you."

"I've got several marks on me," Aunt Tillie confirmed. "If you believe the stories, I was born with a tail ... it was forked, but I never wagged it."

Sheryl belted out a gregarious laugh. "I like you. Too bad you're cursed."

"That's why we're here," I said. "We stumbled across a curse chain of some sort. When trying to break it, we altered the trajectory. We need to know how to end it completely."

"I see." Sheryl's eyes narrowed as she looked Aunt Tillie up and down. "We'll need information if you expect us to help. How about you come to our snug in the back of the store, have a cup of tea, and catch us up?"

I nodded. I trusted them, even though that wasn't my way. Aunt Tillie had embedded a healthy sense of skepticism in us from a young age. When I glanced at her, I found her readying to follow. She met my gaze and smiled.

"It's okay," she reassured me. "They can help."

"How can you be sure?"

"Sometimes you have to chuck caution to the wind and have faith, Bay. I think that was the one lesson I fell down on the job with when you were a kid. I made you hypervigilant, but you're not always a believer."

"I believe in you."

"And I believe in you," Aunt Tillie said. "Sometimes you have to believe in others."

"Wise words," Sheryl offered. "Wise words indeed. Now, come on. We'll have some tea and see what we can figure out."

THE SNUG TURNED OUT TO BE A cozy room complete with a fireplace, small sofa, and two easy chairs. Sheryl and Carol took the chairs, leaving us the sofa.

"Was this some sort of business during Prohibition?" I asked once everybody was comfortable.

"Actually, it was built during the Civil War," Sheryl replied. "It's one of the historic landmarks for the Underground Railroad. Slaves stayed in this room, out of sight from the public, until they could be transported safely to Canada."

The Underground Railroad was fruitful in Detroit thanks to the proximity to the border. I managed a smile as I settled in next to

Aunt Tillie, who was waiting until it cooled to drink her tea. She wanted to avoid burning her mouth. I had to hand it to her, she was taking the curse seriously.

"Tell us what happened," Carol prodded.

Emori took the lead on the story. She knew all the important bits. When it came to relating how Aunt Tillie had been infected, I took over. When we finished, Sheryl and Carol were both contemplative.

"This symbol you saw, can you describe it?" Sheryl finally asked.

"I have a photo." I pulled up my phone and found the photograph I was looking for before handing it over. The sisters leaned close to study it.

"Was this man living or dead when this photo was taken?" Carol asked.

"Dead."

"How long?"

"Twenty minutes or so."

"Hmm." Carol pursed her lips for a moment and then rose from her chair. She headed for the bookshelf, tracing her fingertips over the spines until she found the tome she sought. When she returned to her chair, she was intent.

"It's a Greek curse symbol. I've seen it before."

"I didn't know the Greeks cursed people," I admitted.

"Curses have been a part of *all* religions at one time or another." Carol's smile was enigmatic. "Witchcraft does not hold the patent on them."

"I know. I just ... guess I never really thought about it."

"The Greeks were famous for cursing objects," Carol explained. "Those objects were often used to call ghosts from the underworld to bring suffering on one's enemies. Then the objects were buried with the dead."

"I would imagine, back when knowledge was limited, that curses were used to explain bad luck ... whether the curse was real or not."

"Oh, most assuredly." Carol nodded. "Not all curses were created equal. Some were just assumed. Others, like this one, were real." She turned the book so I could see the page. There, chiseled on a stone tablet, was the symbol.

"That's it!" My excitement got the better of me and when I hopped to my feet, I landed on top of Aunt Tillie's foot.

"Ow!" She screeched so loudly I thought she might wake the dead Carol mentioned. "You broke my foot!"

Horror washed over me as I swung back around, my hands extending in supplication. "I'm so sorry! Do I need to take you to the hospital? Don't move. I don't want any bones to shift. You could be permanently hobbled."

Aunt Tillie's response was a dramatic eye roll. "Oh, you are the absolute worst. Who raised you?"

I blinked several times. "You."

She laughed. "Look at my shoes, dingleberry," she admonished. "These are steel-toed boots. Nothing is breaking this foot."

I relaxed, if only marginally, and narrowed my eyes. "Then why did you yell like that?"

"I already told you. I'm a dying woman. I need to get my jollies somewhere."

If she weren't cursed, I would've hit her hard with something horrible. Instead, I reined in my temper. "Let's get back to the symbol. What can you tell us?" I sat down again because I figured that was safer for Aunt Tillie.

"There aren't many specifics," Carol replied as she focused on the text. "There's no one god associated with it, at least according to this book. We can keep looking."

"How are we supposed to get the information if you don't have a phone? We have to go back. Tonight."

"We can find a phone," Carol said. "Just because we choose to not be tethered to an inanimate object, we can contact you. We're not barbarians. Just leave us a number."

I pulled out one of my business cards and turned it over. "I'm going to put the number for the inn on here ... and my husband. If you can't get me, don't stop trying."

"Husband." Carol's fingers moved over my left hand, causing my diamond engagement ring to momentarily glow. "Ah. True love."

I lifted my eyes to study her. "Exactly what are you?"

"Not everything needs to be defined," Carol replied with a grin. "Yes, there are witches, warlocks, and demons. There are vampires and fairies. Sometimes there's just magic. It's not necessary to be one thing."

I thought of my friend Scout, who was part fairy and part witch. Then I thought of the Romani circus woman who had no idea what she was. My mind briefly touched on Stormy, a hellcat who was still figuring things out. "I get it."

"You're more than one thing, Bay." Carol patted my hand again. "You're one of the most powerful witches I've crossed paths with. Your strength is not in being a witch, it's in being a wife, daughter, and cousin. Never forget that."

For the second time in as many days, I found my eyes burning with unshed tears. "You're pretty good at getting to the heart of matters," I said.

"You're stronger than you think," Carol said. "You're off your game. You're cursed, too ... but it's a weak curse."

"It doesn't feel weak when we don't drink our potions," I countered. "When that happens, we lose our minds and almost die."

"Die?" Carol cocked her head. "I don't think so. It might make you think that, but I doubt it's powerful enough for that. A coma is far more likely."

I made a face. "I'm not sure that's better."

She laughed and then sobered. "I can get rid of the secondary curse. The first will take more magic than I'm capable of mustering, however."

"You can get rid of the one that's causing our emotions to go haywire?"

"Of course. We can concoct a potion."

"We need enough for the entire family," I said. "I'll pay, of course."

"Don't worry about that." Carol inclined her head toward her sister. "I'll put you in charge of the potion while I keep reading about the symbol."

"Of course," Sheryl said. "I'll do the work while you sit and read. That's how it always goes."

"Oh, stop whining." Carol didn't look particularly bothered as she went back to reading. "There are a few interesting tidbits about this symbol, but I can't find a name for it."

"I'll take anything you can give me."

"Well, for starters, it was adopted by a cult about five-hundred years ago."

"I can't say I'm surprised. Cults always come out of the woodwork and adopt symbols that might've meant something entirely different to someone else."

"True. This cult, however, believed that if you killed enough people, you would gain perpetual luck."

I froze with my hand halfway to my tea mug. "There it is again. It keeps coming back to luck."

"Doesn't it?" Carol looked equally intrigued. "I've never come across a luck spell, and I've been in the game for a long time. I guess I shouldn't be surprised that it exists. What's interesting is why it popped up now ... and where. Emori told us a bit about Hemlock Cove before she decided to set up shop there. You must know more."

I nodded. "I do."

"Is Hemlock Cove a magical nexus?"

It wasn't the first time I'd heard the term. "Yes. We have many magical nexuses up there. I know there's another in Hawthorne Hollow, only twenty minutes away."

"Your nexus, is it close to your home?"

"Yes. Is that important?"

"It's ... interesting." Carol's forehead wrinkled as she went back to studying the book. "Bay, your enemy is in Hemlock Cove. I don't think it's a coincidence this curse found you. It was likely always meant to. The secondary curse proves that."

"You're saying that whoever is behind this is one of us," I said. "A local, I mean."

"It's likely someone you already know or have at least crossed paths with. It's definitely someone who knows who and what you are. You need to track the origin of the curse. That's where you'll find your overlap. Somewhere in the tangled webs of a person's life — maybe the first man you saw die, maybe someone before him — is your answer. You'll know when you hit on the right thread."

"So, we chase Chester's past to figure out if he was the source or if he was infected by someone else." I slid my eyes to Aunt Tillie. "And we do it quickly because we only have so much time."

"Unfortunately, that's the best advice I can give." Carol looked sad. "I wish I could do more."

"You've done plenty," I reassured her. "Lifting the secondary curse is big. It takes some of the pressure off. You also identified the symbol. At the very least, we know where to look."

"I still wish it was more."

"We can only do what we can do. That goes for all of us. We'll figure it out."

"We will," Aunt Tillie agreed. "I'm not ready to go yet. I'm only middle aged."

Sheryl smirked. "You could be one of us."

"Oh, she's one of a kind," I countered. "That's why we're keeping her — no matter what."

19
Nineteen

Landon was waiting in the parking lot when I returned to the inn. I was exhausted after eight hours on the road — and what felt like twenty straight hours of Aunt Tillie — but I was also exhilarated.

"Hey." I opened my arms and went in for a hug, which he gladly accepted.

"Hey." He rested his cheek against the top of my head. "I missed you today."

"You saw me this morning."

"Yes, but I'm used to being able to stop in your office to see you whenever I want. We normally get lunch together. I only got texts today."

He wasn't trying to be funny, but I laughed all the same. "I think you're saying that you had plans for a little afternoon delight that were derailed."

He was sheepish when he pulled back. "I don't need afternoon delight. I do like my afternoon nap with my wife, though."

"You have a key. You could've taken a nap without me."

"I did. It wasn't the same. Thankfully you left that hoodie draped over your office chair, so I had something to hold."

I was absurdly touched. "You cuddled my hoodie like a stuffed animal?"

He shrugged. "I pretended it was you."

"So cute." I poked his cheek and did my best to ignore the fake retching Aunt Tillie made from the other side of the car. Emori had helped her out — we were diligent when watching her at rest areas on the way home — and they watched us with overt amusement. "We need to get Aunt Tillie inside. We're surrounding her like bodyguards to get her from point A to point B."

"Good idea." Landon ran his hand over my back before focusing on Aunt Tillie. "How are you feeling?"

Aunt Tillie shrugged. "I'm not raving yet. I consider that a good day."

"You idle at raving," he pointed out.

"That is a gross exaggeration," she sniffed, her lower lip jutted out. Her eyes twinkled with mirth. "What's for dinner? I'm starving. These two nervous nellies wouldn't let me eat on the way home because they were afraid I'd choke."

"We might've been a little overzealous," I confirmed when Landon slid his eyes to me. "We couldn't help ourselves."

"Well, there are worse things," Landon said. "At least everybody made it home in one piece. No car trouble either?"

"Actually, the car wouldn't start at one of the rest areas," I replied. "It was fine before, so I used my magic to get it going. I'm guessing that when it's time to leave and I'm alone the car will be fine."

Landon looked at the vehicle. "I'll be the one to start it — just in case."

I thought about arguing, but there was no reason. "We need to get some stuff out of the back." I walked around to the hatchback and used my fob to pop it. "Can you grab that crate for me?" I pointed to the potions Carol and Sheryl had provided. "Emori and I can flank Aunt Tillie as we go inside, but that's heavy."

"Sure." Landon's forehead creased with confusion as he lifted the crate, a grunt escaping. "Um ... geez. What is this?"

"A cure for the secondary curse. Emori's friends had all the ingredients in their store. Aunt Tillie and I already took our cures, and it appears to have worked. We have enough for everybody and a second dose in case something happens and we somehow get reinfected."

"Are you sure it worked?" Landon's eyes widened as he looked me up and down.

"I'm pretty sure," I confirmed. "I haven't felt this good in days. Even with the potions we were already taking, I think we were being affected. We'll see with the others. I didn't take my afternoon dose of the other stuff, so if I wasn't cured, I'd be spiraling right now."

"Well, that's just great." Landon made a face. "I'm glad you risked having a meltdown while driving. Makes perfect sense."

"Don't go there," I warned as I fell into step next to Aunt Tillie and trailed him to the inn. "It's been a long day, but we have hope."

"You said you identified the symbol," he said as he used his hip to prop open the door for us.

"That's the most important thing. I ... ." I wasn't watching closely enough and missed the fact that Landon's foot was in our path. Normally that wouldn't be a problem, but with Aunt Tillie's curse, everything had become a danger.

She tripped over his foot as she entered the inn and pitched forward, careening to the floor. I jerked forward to grab her but wasn't fast enough. She was flying through the air, the wall and floor offering twin dangers, when Chief Terry appeared.

He was a big guy, tall and solid. He absorbed Aunt Tillie's slight frame without pitching backward and hurting himself. His eyes went wide as he steadied her.

"What's this?" he demanded as he pressed Aunt Tillie against him. Apparently, news that she was cursed had spread and even he was worried. "Who tripped her?"

Landon was sheepish. "I didn't mean to. I just ... didn't think."

I gave him a reassuring smile. "It's okay. You just have to wrap your head around the mindset that everything is a danger to her."

"Especially myself," Aunt Tillie said with a grin as she pulled back from Chief Terry. She looked none the worse for wear. "How was it for you, big guy? Ready to trade Winnie in for the more seasoned model?"

Chief Terry looked scandalized. "Why would you even say that?"

"Apparently having an expiration date has made Aunt Tillie's tongue bold," I replied. "Well, bolder than usual."

"Yes, I've decided that if I'm going to die, I'm going to say whatever I want," Aunt Tillie announced. "No more holding back so as not to hurt anyone's feelings."

"You held back?" Chief Terry looked dubious. "Exactly when did you do that?"

"All the time." Aunt Tillie patted his shoulder. "But I'm over it. Speaking of that, where are my nieces? I have some things I want to say to them."

I cringed at the prospect. "Aunt Tillie ... ."

"Shut it." She jabbed a finger at me. "It's my life. I'm going to live it to the fullest."

I was chagrined as I watched her disappear inside the inn.

"She'll be fine," Landon reassured me as he shifted the crate. "You have a lead?"

"We have a place to look," I corrected as I dragged my hand through my hair. I didn't realize I was feeling sorry for myself until I looked up and found twin expressions of sympathy on Landon's and Chief Terry's faces. "I'm fine. We're better off than we were. Let's get these potions to the others and then I'll fill you in."

. . .

ONCE MOM, MARNIE, AND TWILA DOWNED their potions, we left them to deal with Aunt Tillie. She would never admit it, but the trip had taken a lot out of her. She made a big show of settling in her easy chair in the kitchen to bark orders at Mom and the aunts, but I knew she was exhausted.

"Dinner is in an hour," Mom admonished as I moved toward the swinging doors. "We'll want to know what you learned."

I nodded.

"Is it okay if I stay and help with dinner preparations?" Emori asked. "I'm fascinated with your cooking process."

Mom beamed at her. "Of course."

I had no idea if Emori was really fascinated or if she simply wanted to give Landon and me some time to ourselves. Either way, I took advantage of her offer and led Landon into the library. The second the door was closed, I threw my arms around his neck.

"What's this?" He rubbed his hands up and down my back. "You really did miss me, huh?"

"So much," I agreed, briefly pressing my eyes shut. "It was a long day."

"But you got answers." He kept circling back to that. "You know what to do."

"We got direction," I clarified as I pulled back.

He traced his fingers under my eyes. "You look exhausted."

"It was eight hours of driving. Somehow Aunt Tillie managed to fill twenty hours with being Aunt Tillie. But we're okay. I'll get a good night's sleep tonight."

He prodded me toward the couch. "Tell me what happened."

I filled him in as he massaged away the long hours on the freeway. He was perplexed.

"What do you think we're dealing with?"

"I don't know."

"I have to be honest, my knowledge of Greek curses is even more minuscule than that of my knowledge of witch curses."

I laughed and leaned into him, groaning when he hit a particularly tender spot in my lower back. "Oh, right there."

He brushed his lips against the ridge of my ear. "I'll rub you all night, Bay. Just tell me what to do."

We didn't know which enemy we were supposed to be fighting, so we couldn't fix what was broken. "I need information on Chester Hamilton. He's the first victim we know who was infected. He could've inherited the curse from someone else."

"Okay." Landon kissed my cheek and pulled away, causing me to groan. "I'll massage you again later. Promise. I have a whole file on Chester. I spent the better part of the day going through it."

I couldn't contain my surprise. "Why?"

"I had to do something. Being stuck here when you were gone, well, let's just say it didn't make for a productive day."

I smiled as he grabbed the folder from a bag on the floor and then leaned in at his side as he opened it. "It's good to know you missed me."

His lips quirked. "I always miss you when I'm not with you, Bay."

"Always?"

"Yup. If I could spend every moment of every day with you, I totally would."

"Even if I get my way and limit your daily fat intake?"

He glowered. "What did we talk about?"

"Yeah, yeah." I rolled my eyes. "You want a heart attack prevention spell. Something tells me if that was really an option someone would've already perfected it."

"You're the most powerful witch in the world," he countered. "You haven't tried yet."

"Let's not get ahead of ourselves. I'm not even the most powerful witch in Michigan. As long as Scout is running around, that title isn't up for grabs."

"Scout is enhanced with fairy blood. You're a pure-blood witch."

"Good point." I kissed his cheek. "Let's argue about this later. Tell me what you have on Chester."

"Most of this you already know," he prefaced as he flipped open the file. "He and his ex-wife divorced because he thought she was having an affair. That was all over their social media."

"Did you talk to the ex-wife?" I asked.

He nodded. "Trina. She's dating a UPS driver."

I raised my eyebrows, causing Landon to smirk.

"She claims it's not the same UPS driver Chester was obsessed with. She said it was just a fluke."

"Do you believe her?"

Landon shrugged. "I don't know what I believe," he admitted. "I didn't particularly like her. The remorse she showed for what happened to Chester was ... brief. The first thing she asked about was his life insurance policy."

I sat straighter. "Maybe she's a witch. Did she feel like a witch to you?"

"Baby, I am the last person who should answer that question. If you remember correctly, I didn't pick up the signs you were a witch when we first met, and I was obsessed with watching you."

"You were a novice back then. Now you're an expert."

"I'm an expert on Bay," he clarified. "I don't know if she's a witch. She seemed cold, but that doesn't make her a witch."

I nodded in agreement. "I'll see if I can get close. If she's magical, I should be able to pick up on it."

"We'll *talk* about you doing that later," he hedged. "We need to tackle this together going forward."

"Fine. Tell me about the daughter."

"She was a harder read," Landon said. "She was upset when we told her about her father. She said she didn't believe he would kill himself and initially said she thought it was murder. When I asked how his jump from a freeway overpass could be blamed on anybody else, she clammed up."

"That probably wasn't the best way to approach her," I noted.

"I agree now. She was a typical teenager. Stoic one minute and wrecked the next."

My mind was busy. "Did you check into the life insurance?"

"See, I knew you would circle back to that." He grinned before leaning in to give me a kiss. "You have a mind like a shark. You're always thinking."

"Is the life insurance a lead?"

"I don't know. Chester changed the beneficiary months after his divorce, something that did not sit well with Trina. She was furious when she found out."

"The daughter is the beneficiary."

Landon nodded. "The sole beneficiary. And the money is in a trust until she's twenty-two. If she wants to go to college, an account manager with access to the fund will pay her tuition. Otherwise, there's no touching that money for six years."

"Hmm." I tapped my bottom lip. "How did Daisy react to the news?"

"She didn't say much. In fact, I'm not sure how interested she was in the money. Trina, on the other hand, was furious. She has no claim to the money. She raged about Chester cutting her off."

"If she didn't know, she could be a suspect," I mused. "I need to get a read on her."

"I can arrange that."

"What else is in there?" I inclined my chin toward the file.

"Some background on Chester's parents, Fred and Astrid. His father died about three years ago. Colon cancer. His mother has been out of contact for about fifteen years. It's hard to track the exact dates."

"Out of contact?" That was a weird way of phrasing it. "Does that mean she's dead?"

"I don't know. We didn't chase the information that hard. She divorced the father shortly before taking off."

"But ... people don't leave without a reason."

"All I could find was a notation about a cult. Brotherhood of the Eternal Soul, I believe.

I was taken aback. "A cult?" I thought back to what Carol had mentioned in her shop.

"Does that mean something to you?"

"I ... don't ... know." That was the truth. "Carol said the symbol was tied to luck. It was carved into items and people used it to curse their enemies. Then they would bury them with the item."

"And it caused bad luck?"

"Yeah. She mentioned an obscure cult that used the symbol to cast bad luck spells. They believed if they cursed enough people, they would be able to build up good luck for themselves."

Now Landon looked intrigued. "That sounds ... convenient."

"Right? Does it say anything about the mother's curse?"

Landon turned back to the file. "There's no name. We could ask around. Somebody must know the backstory, an old neighbor or acquaintance."

I nodded. "Can you track that down for me? I'd like to head out after dinner if we can arrange it."

"Oh, Bay, you're so tired," Landon protested. "Can't it wait until tomorrow?"

I shook my head. "Being with her today, having to spend all that time with Aunt Tillie, was painful. I was grateful, though, because part of me believes that we'll be out of time in a few days. We need to chase this tonight."

Landon chewed his bottom lip and then nodded. "Let me do some digging. We can go to Grayling after dinner. That's where the parents lived."

"Thank you." I meant it. "Just one more thing."

"With you, there's always one more thing." Despite the words, Landon smiled. "What do you need, light of my life?"

"Don't tell anyone what we're doing. I want it to be just us. Aunt Tillie will want to go if she knows. She's safer staying here."

"You're my favorite partner." He kissed my forehead. "What are you going to do if you get a lead on this cult? Will you keep the information from her?"

It was a fair question. "Let's figure that out later. Tonight, I want it to be just us."

"I can live with that, but I need one thing from you." His eyes were earnest. "No matter what, going forward, we need to be in lock-step. I know I let you down when I didn't act fast enough on Chester Hamilton. That won't happen again. I promise. I need you to have faith in me."

"I always have faith in you," I promised. "I understand why you didn't believe me."

"I don't. I should've followed your instincts. Part of me knew that was the right move, but I went against my better judgment. From here on out, you call the shots. I just want to be included."

Hope welled in my chest as I gripped his hand. "This feels right. I think we're actually on the right track."

20
TWENTY

Everybody was present for dinner and potions were doled out speedily. I wasn't the only one who immediately felt better. Backup potions were served, and I left the recipe with Mom so she and the aunts could make more the following day.

Landon packed up dessert to take home. He explained to Mom that I was exhausted after the drive and we wanted to hash things out before we enacted a new plan the following day. Mom was shrewd, and the way she looked at Landon told me she didn't completely buy his story. One look at Aunt Tillie had her nodding. She likely figured whatever we had planned, it was better if it was just us.

"We'll see you for breakfast." She patted my shoulder. "I'll make the chocolate chip pancakes you love so much."

"That sounds great."

We left my car in the inn parking lot and then we set out for Grayling.

"Did you tell Chief Terry what we were doing?" I asked when we exited the highway on the Grayling exit.

"Yeah. I thought it was best he knows. He's in this as deep as we are. He might tell your mother, but only in private. She'll understand why we hid what we were doing."

"She already knows we're doing something. Packing dessert was a dead giveaway."

"I didn't want to risk dropping in too late. The woman who lives next door to the house where the Hamilton family resided before Chester moved out is in her seventies."

Landon followed his GPS until we arrived at the house in question. I studied the house next door — there was only one to choose from on the dead-end street — and then joined him at the front door.

"You do the talking," I supplied before he could. "I know how this works."

He smirked and pinched my flank before ringing the doorbell. "You're a smartass when you want to be."

"It's a Winchester family trait. I learned it from Aunt Tillie."

"Who is going to be fine," Landon said.

"She's going to be fine," I agreed. "One way or another."

Landon looked as if he wanted to question me on the second part, but he kept his mouth shut and plastered a warm smile on his face as the door opened. The woman on the other side was dressed in comfortable jogging pants and an oversized T-shirt, perhaps getting ready for bed. Her eyes were full of suspicion.

"I don't need any Essential Oils," she said.

I tried not to be insulted.

"We're not selling Essential Oils," Landon assured her as he held up his badge. "We have questions about your former neighbors."

"The Dorchesters?" The woman made a face. "There's no way they did anything illegal. They were boring as all get out. They didn't even have any dandelions in their yard they were so dedicated to keeping up appearances. You must have the wrong people."

"We're not here to ask about the Dorchesters," Landon replied. "We're here to talk about the Hamiltons."

"Oh, really?" The woman's demeanor shifted in an instant. "I figured this day would come eventually." She unlocked the screen and ushered us inside. "You might as well come in."

I exchanged a surprised look with Landon but quickly shuttered it as we followed the woman into the house. She led us to the kitchen, put a kettle on the stove, and then fixed us with a serious expression.

"I'm Theresa Logan," she said. "You probably already know that."

"Yes, Ms. Logan, we do." Landon shook her hand and then stepped back so I could do the same. "I discovered your name when I was running a check on the Hamiltons' old house. You were here when they lived here, correct?"

"I've been here forty years," Theresa confirmed. "I was here when they moved in, and still here when they moved out. I'm never leaving this place. It's my home."

"Home is a good thing," Landon reassured her. "We have some questions about the Hamiltons."

"I'm sure you do." Theresa made a tsking sound with her tongue. "What did Astrid do?"

My shoulders hopped but I managed to keep my expression neutral. The fact that she'd immediately glommed onto the notion that we were here about Astrid Hamilton was telling.

"How do you know we're here about Astrid?" Landon asked.

"Because she was a freaking nut and I'm not stupid," Theresa replied. "I might be old, but I'm certainly not slow on the uptake. It's best you don't play games and just tell me what you're after."

"Fair enough." Landon steepled his hands on the table. "Chester Hamilton jumped from the Au Sable freeway overpass about a week and a half ago," he started. "Do you remember him?"

Theresa's eyes went wide. "The boy? You're here about the boy?"

"We're here for answers on the family," Landon hedged. "Chester's suicide is the basis for our investigation."

"Well, isn't that just a kick in the pants?" Theresa shook her head and let out a sigh. "I was kind of hoping he would escape. He was always a good kid. You say he jumped? I don't understand why he would do that. He was never a depressed kid, despite the weird crap Astrid used to pull."

"Why don't you tell us what you remember about the family?" Landon prodded.

"Sure." Theresa didn't look bothered by Landon's tone as she got up to collect the kettle. "At first I thought they were a normal family. They seemed normal enough. They had just the one kid, and I assumed that was by design. Back then, once a family had a boy, that was often enough ... especially if there was only so much money to go around."

"Were the Hamiltons strapped for cash?" Landon had his notebook out.

"They did okay," Theresa replied. "The father, Fred, worked for the railroad. The mother was a homemaker, or so I thought at first. She was way more than that."

"How so?"

"She left the house a lot for a homemaker," Theresa explained. "I'm not some busybody who always spies on the neighbors, so get that notion out of your head. But I broke my ankle once and was laid up here for six weeks. I had nothing to do but stare out the windows ... and I saw a lot during that stretch."

"Like what?"

"Well, like across the road, Mindy Newman was having an affair with a local plumber. I didn't see them doing it, but nobody has a clogged pipe at noon every single day."

Landon smiled. "Ma'am, we don't care about Mindy."

"No, you've got something specific on your mind," Theresa agreed. "That much is obvious. As for Astrid, I don't know what to tell you. I thought she was hanging around with the other women in town. You know, they all had those social clubs they loved. I figured out I was wrong when the weirdos showed up."

"I'm going to need more information than that," Landon prodded. "Who were the weirdos?"

"Those freaky robed people who hang out in the woods by the river."

"Can you tell me more?" Landon asked.

"You're not local, are you?" Theresa sighed. "I should've guessed that."

"I'm from Hemlock Cove," I volunteered. "I'm not all that familiar with Grayling, but I know weird."

"If you live in Hemlock Cove you definitely know weird," Theresa agreed. "You all think you're witches. I think I read that. I don't like witches."

I had to bite the inside of my cheek to keep from reacting.

"Anyway, from what I hear, those robed freaks moved to Hemlock Cove. I think they fit in better with the crowd over there, and I'm not sorry to see them go."

"We still don't know who the robed freaks are," Landon pointed out.

"I don't know the name of their group. I only know that they appeared out of nowhere and purported to be some sort of religious group." Theresa took on a far-off expression. "Now, I'm not one to judge, but some religions are better than others."

I wasn't in the mood for a philosophical debate. "What religion were they?" I asked.

"I can't rightly recall. It was one of those cult-y names."

"Brotherhood of the Eternal Soul?" Landon prodded.

Theresa snapped her fingers and pointed. "Yup. That's it. How did you know?"

"Call it a lucky guess," Landon replied. "I've never heard of that cult, and I've been working in this area for years. They can't be very big."

"That I don't know. I only know they wore robes around town when they tried to recruit — they even stopped here a time or two before I threatened them with a shotgun. They preached a bunch of nonsense about liberty and light."

"Do you remember the specifics?" I asked.

Theresa shook her head. "I didn't want to know what they were talking about. I have my own religion, and I don't want anybody trying to take it from me. Those freaks wanted me to give up everything I'd ever believed."

"But Astrid was open to their teachings?" Landon asked.

Theresa nodded as she placed mugs of steaming tea before us. She didn't offer sugar or cream. "I don't know when they got her. I don't know if she was always part of their group and initially tried to hide it. At some point she was simply one of them."

"What about her husband?"

"I don't think so, but obviously I wasn't privy to the inner workings of their marriage. They didn't get along all that well anyway. If you asked me, all they had in common was the boy."

"Was Chester part of the cult?" I asked.

"I don't think so," Theresa replied. "I never saw any children going door to door with them. I never saw Astrid take Chester when she left with the group. As time went on, it seemed that Astrid became more estranged from her family. She rarely did anything with her husband or son.

"Then, when Chester packed up for college, Astrid and her husband were rarely in the house together," she continued. "He spent his nights carousing at the bar. Sometimes he didn't come home. She didn't seem to care. She was always busy with them."

"Our records show that the Hamiltons divorced ten years ago," Landon prodded.

"That's all?" Theresa made a face. "Astrid moved out of the house a good seven or eight years before that. I assumed they divorced then."

"It's possible Fred didn't care enough to divorce her," Landon mused. "If he was carrying on with other women at the bar, being tethered to a wife he didn't live with might've made for a convenient excuse as to why he couldn't truly be with anybody else."

"Possible," Theresa agreed. "I didn't know they weren't divorced. Chester never came home after moving away to college. He married right after he graduated and started his own family. He'd visit his father occasionally. I have no idea what sort of relationship he had with Astrid."

"Do you know where Astrid moved to when she left?" Landon asked.

"I only know that one day a truck showed up. People in robes went in. They came out with a few suitcases and boxes. She got in the truck with them and that was it."

I couldn't help being disappointed. "You never saw her again?"

"Oh, I wouldn't say that." Theresa chuckled. "I saw her at the river exchange downtown one day, that place where they rent canoes and kayaks. She was wearing a robe, and it took me a few minutes to recognize her. She was with the freaks trying to recruit people."

"Do you know where they set up home base?" Landon asked.

"I heard they were living at the old camp, out by Haggard Road," Theresa replied.

"That was a summer camp," I said. "It shut down operations about thirty years ago."

"It was just a bunch of old cabins and a dining area with an industrial kitchen," Theresa confirmed. "I heard they fixed it up nice, but they didn't own the property. Eventually the county came calling and took the land. That's when I heard they moved to Hemlock Cove, or thereabouts."

"That doesn't make sense." I shook my head. "If a cult moved into town, I would've heard about it."

"Maybe they didn't move into Hemlock Cove," Theresa said. "Now that I think about it, I believe they moved to Greater Lodge North."

My heart skipped a beat. "Are you sure?"

"What's Greater Lodge North?" Landon asked me.

"An old summer camp," I replied.

"Like our property?"

We'd purchased the land the old camp I frequented as a child sat on several months ago. We were cleaning it up with an eye on building a house there eventually. It would take several years to come to fruition, but we enjoyed spending time there and planning for a beautiful future next to the lake.

"Not like our camp," I replied. "It was a different camp. It was for teenagers."

"Bad teenagers," Theresa said.

"Troubled teenagers," I clarified at Landon's confused expression. "Kids recovering from addiction spent summers there."

"And the ones who liked to sleep around," Theresa added.

"Troubled kids." I was firm as I shot Theresa a quelling look. I didn't need to deal with her judgement on top of everything else. "It would be similar to the camp they were previously living at. Multiple cabins. One big building with an industrial kitchen. They had a church if I remember correctly."

"Chapel," Theresa corrected. "You have a chapel at camp, not a church."

Landon ignored the correction. "Is this campground in Hemlock Cove?"

"Between Hemlock Cove and Gaylord," I replied. "I'm not sure who owns the land now."

"They moved to Hemlock Cove because the town is full of freaks — witchy freaks, for crying out loud. They fit right in." Theresa shook her head. "Better there than here."

I was about at the end of my rope with her. "Just out of curiosity, did you ever see any symbols on the robes?"

"Symbols?" Theresa's expression was momentarily blank. "Can't say that I did. Sorry."

"That's okay." I forced a smile that I didn't feel and pushed myself to a standing position. "You've helped us a great deal. We appreciate your time."

If Landon was annoyed that I'd taken over the interview, he didn't show it. He followed me out to his Explorer. He didn't say anything until the doors were shut and the blowers were pointed at us to chase away the cold.

"What do you think?" he finally asked.

"We're getting somewhere." I tried for a smile and failed. "If this cult co-opted the symbol from earlier times, then it makes sense."

"Why would Astrid target her son?"

"I guess we'll get our chance to ask questions tomorrow and find out."

"You want to talk to the cult first thing in the morning," Landon surmised. "How did I know that was going to happen?"

"You're a smart guy ... with a genius for a wife."

"She is a genius." He kissed my cheek. His expression was grave when he pulled back. "Could this be a magical cult?"

"I think at least one member has access to magic. Otherwise, there would be no cult. We need to find out who and shut it down fast. We only have a few days."

He rubbed his thumb under my left eye. "You need sleep."

"That's a fabulous idea. We can have dessert in bed as a reward for a job well done and then crash."

He beamed at me. "Now you're thinking. That was going to be my suggestion."

"Ah, it must be fate."

"I knew that a long time ago. There was never going to be anybody else for me. It was always going to be you."

"Right back at you."

21
TWENTY-ONE

I slept like the dead and when I woke, I had red velvet cake crumbs in my tank top cleavage. That's where I found Landon looking when I turned to see if he was awake.

"Do I even want to know what you're thinking?" I asked.

He grinned. "I was thinking, 'Yum, leftovers.'"

I chuckled as I rolled to cuddle with him. "I don't want to give you grief about your eating habits."

"I feel as if you're trapping me," he admitted. "I mean ... you lured me in with that face and hair, so much like an angel, and then you closed the deal with your mother's cooking. You can't take the food away from me now. It's cruel."

I arched a speculative eyebrow. "Do you love me or the food?"

"I love you both. My day is perfect when I can combine my two loves."

"You're not eating the crumbs out of my cleavage," I warned. "Besides, Mom is making chocolate chip pancakes."

"Why don't you have to watch what you eat?" He sounded petulant. "Why is it just me?"

"Because I love you more than anything."

He made an exasperated face. "It's hard for me to stay angry when you say things like that."

"Why do you think I say them?"

"We can talk about moderation when this is over," he finally conceded, although he said "moderation" as though it was a dirty word. "I'm not going to kowtow to you just because we're married. I get the final say."

"Okay. Just out of curiosity, why are you suddenly agreeing?"

"Because seeing you with that baby makes me want to live a really long time. I want to see you with our babies — and our grandchildren. Also, I'm not afraid to die. I know there's something else out there and we'll have forever together. It's just ... the idea of leaving you alone here bothers me."

"Like Uncle Calvin left Aunt Tillie," I mused. "I don't think she's ever gotten over it. She's dated a few times since then — like Kenneth — but it never sticks. She fell in love for life, like me."

"It's not just that, although that's a big part of it. It's the other thing, too."

"What other thing?" I asked.

"I don't want to leave so early that you find someone else. I can't share you on the other side. Like ... it's not going to be you, me, and some random dude who starts chasing you after I'm gone. You're a catch. Those guys will be salivating over you. I want us to be together for as long as possible."

I went warm all over. "That's what I want." I held him tight. "You can still have your bacon. You just need to cut it in half."

"I was thinking of starting slow. Like, I'll cut out one slice a day and we'll go from there."

I smiled into his shoulder. He was making an effort. "I believe I can make that work."

"Good." He kissed my forehead and checked the clock on the nightstand. "We should get ready. We have to explain where we were last night, and what we have planned for today."

I rubbed my cheek against his chest. "Five more minutes."

. . .

WE DROVE TO THE INN BECAUSE WE WOULD be leaving right after breakfast. It seemed quiet when we let ourselves in through the front door, but when we reached the hallway, we found utter chaos.

"What happened here?" Landon's eyes went wide as he took in the mess on the floor. The shelves Mom had so tirelessly decorated over the years, frequenting random estate sales whenever she had the time, were on the floor, their contents shattered.

"Be careful," Chief Terry called out when he appeared at the other end of the hallway. "There's glass everywhere. Your mother wants everybody to avoid the area until she can get in here and clean it up."

"What happened?" I demanded as I moved closer to him. "What did this?"

"That would be Tillie ... and Peg ... and her scooter." Chief Terry shrugged. "By the way, her scooter motor burned up. It set the hem of her cape on fire. That's that smell you're probably picking up."

I made a face. "The cape and the scooter are both gone?" For some reason, I felt sad at the thought. "She loved that cape and scooter."

"We'll get her a new one," Landon promised, his hand landing on my shoulder. "They're not that expensive. We'll have a cape made, too."

I swallowed the lump in my throat.

"Sweetheart, don't start crying," Chief Terry pleaded. "You know I don't like when you cry."

"I'm not going to cry." Just saying the words wasn't enough to make them true. "At least not in front of the two of you. I'm totally put together."

"Those are pretty bold words for a woman who woke up with red velvet cake in her cleavage," Landon countered.

"I don't want to hear this," Chief Terry complained. "Aren't we dealing with enough?"

Landon grinned as he put his hand to the small of my back. "Your little sweetheart likes to eat cake in bed, and she doesn't always eat daintily," Landon replied. "It's fine. I cleaned her up."

"Is that supposed to make me feel better?" Chief Terry demanded.

Landon shrugged. "It made me feel better."

Chief Terry was still rolling his eyes when we reached the dining room.

"Did you see the mess?" Mom asked. Her eyes — and hair, for that matter — looked wild. "Things are getting out of hand."

I had news for her; things were going to get worse before they got better. "You have to keep an eye on her," I insisted. "The curse won't kill her. That's not how it works. It needs her to kill herself."

"You found something out." Mom looked hopeful. "That's why you left the way you did last night. You know what we're up against."

"We have a lead," Landon countered, smiling for Aunt Tillie's benefit when she emerged from the kitchen. She was decked out in her usual fashion — combat helmet firmly affixed to her head — but today it felt like a necessity rather than a way to drive my mother insane. "Everyone should sit down."

We waited until the food was on the table and everyone was elbow deep in pancakes to tell them what we'd found. Nobody jumped for joy, but the relief pooling from my mother and aunts was palpable.

"At least that's something," Mom said. "Cults are never good, but we have a place to look."

"We do," I agreed. "The thing is, I've never heard of this cult. I didn't even know we had one."

"I didn't either," Mom admitted. "You would think news like that would spread, especially with Margaret. She wouldn't be happy about a cult."

"Definitely not," I agreed. "I don't know why we haven't heard about it. I just know they're likely there. Carol told me a cult had co-opted the symbol before. Given that Chester is dead, and his mother was part of the cult, we have to chase this lead."

"I agree." Mom was solemn as she sipped her coffee. "I just don't understand why we didn't know about them."

"I knew about them," Twila volunteered.

Slowly, multiple heads tracked in her direction.

"You did?" Landon prodded when nobody else said anything.

"I ran into them when I was getting groceries this summer. They invited me out to see their set-up."

"Why is this the first I'm hearing about this?" Mom demanded.

Twila shrugged. She was the most scatterbrained member of the family. That was saying something when you took Aunt Tillie's antics into account. Oh, and Clove's fear of ... well, just about everything. "It didn't seem important."

I held up a hand to still my mother. Fury was evident on her face, and if she started yelling at Twila the conversation would be derailed. We needed to be careful how we approached this. Landon was the best choice to cajole information out of her.

"How many people did you see?" Landon feigned polite interest as he sipped his coffee.

"Um, I think there were four of them." Twila was focused on her plate. If she realized that she was suddenly the center of attention she would start milking it, and nobody had time for that.

"How did they approach you?"

"They just walked up to me in the grocery store parking lot," Twila replied. "They asked if I was open to seeking enlightenment. You know me, I love enlightenment." Her eyes sparkled as she grinned. "We talked for a bit, exchanged philosophies, and then they invited me out to their camp."

"Their camp." I dragged a hand through my hair in an effort to tamp down my frustration. "That would be Greater Lodge North camp?"

"Um, yeah." Twila nodded. "I was out there once, years ago, when their normal caterer flaked on them. They had a camp full of kids. Remember, Marnie? We filled in because we thought they were doing good work."

"I do remember," Marnie confirmed. "It was a nice camp."

"Do you remember who owned the property then?" Landon asked. "Was it a church? Was it the town?"

"It was a charity," Chief Terry replied. "They were a multi-denominational charity. Sid Unger ran it. He was about eight years older than Bay. He had a rough childhood, turned to drugs, and when he cleaned himself up, he wanted to give back to the community. I'm pretty sure Walkerville cut them a deal on the property."

"What happened to Sid?" Landon asked.

"He died about four years ago." Chief Terry rolled his neck. He obviously didn't like talking about Sid. "He was a good guy, but he did a lot of damage to his heart when he was using. He had a heart attack. He was sick before then. The camp hadn't been used for years because he was sick."

I pursed my lips, considering. "Is it possible the cult managed to buy that property?"

"I think we all would've heard about that," Chief Terry countered. "Besides, if that property had come up for sale or auction, Margaret would've snapped it up. She's been buying property for years."

"And there's no way she bought it and let a cult move in," I mused. "It must still be in Sid's name."

"Which means the cult is squatting," Aunt Tillie said. "You can kick them off if they're squatting," she said to Chief Terry.

He nodded. "In theory."

"We're not doing anything until we know more," I stressed. "Right now, we know where they are. I want to keep it that way. If they're responsible for what's happening, knowing where they are can only benefit us."

"Bay is right," Chief Terry said. "For now, it's best to leave them where they are. After this is handled, when everybody is safe, we'll worry about who is squatting where."

"So what's the plan?" Mom asked. "I assume you're going out there." She looked between Landon and Chief Terry. "How will you know if they're involved?"

"Because they're not going alone," I replied before either of them could. "I'm going with them."

Mom blinked several times and then nodded. "Don't put yourself at risk on your first visit. If you determine they're involved, you come back here and put together a team before declaring war."

It wasn't a question.

"I don't foresee going to war today," I hedged. "But if I see an opening ... ."

"Don't worry about her," Aunt Tillie interjected, her mouth full of food. If she was bothered about taking out Mom's antiques — and her scooter — she didn't show it. "Everything will be fine."

"Bay is capable of taking care of herself," Mom agreed. "But we're dealing with a lot. I don't want her getting hurt on top of everything else."

"That's not what I meant." Aunt Tillie shook her head. "I'm going with her."

Everybody started speaking at the same time.

"I don't think that's a good idea," Twila hedged.

"You should probably stay here, just to be on the safe side," Marnie offered.

"Over my dead body," Mom roared.

"No, you're not," Landon countered.

I pressed the heel of my hand to my forehead and waited as Aunt Tillie eyed each speaker in turn. The set of her jaw told me she was annoyed, and yet she didn't explode.

Slowly, Aunt Tillie tracked her eyes to me. "You're going to need my help. You've never dealt with an evil cult."

I chose my words carefully. "And you have?"

"Of course. What self-respecting witch hasn't taken on an evil cult?"

I made an attempt at being blasé but fell flat. "I don't want to tell you your business, but you're a walking calamity right now. How is a hike through the woods and a confrontation with potential evil going to help?"

"I'm a badass."

"I know but ... ."

"I could be a badass professionally," she pressed.

"I'm not denying that, Aunt Tillie. But it's not safe for you to be out there."

"Aren't you the one who just said I was safe until the final day?" she challenged. "This curse won't kill me."

"That doesn't mean it won't maim you." I wasn't in the mood to argue with her, but I refused to back down. "What happens if you trip and break an ankle? Or a hip. We're going to stop the curse, but how will you feel if you're permanently hobbled? At your age ... ."

Aunt Tillie jabbed a finger in my face. "Be very careful how you finish that sentence," she warned.

Landon put his hand on my wrist to still me and forced a smile for Aunt Tillie's benefit. "Bay is already dealing with a lot. Taking you into the woods with us is a problem. She won't be able to focus on our potential enemy if she's worried about you."

"It's my life." Aunt Tillie folded her arms across her chest. "I want to fight to save myself. You can't take that from me."

I hated that she had a point, but I wasn't done arguing. "But ... ."

"No." She fervently shook her head. "You're not stopping me, Bay. I'm going, and there's not a thing you can do about it. It's my right and this is my fight too."

And that was the final word, I realized. We couldn't stop her. She would go out there alone if we tried.

"You're going," Mom said finally, bobbing her head.

Aunt Tillie was suddenly suspicious. "Wait ... you're the one agreeing with me? I must already be dead because hell just froze over."

Mom made a face. "I don't find that funny."

"You weren't supposed to."

"I am agreeing with you, Aunt Tillie. You have a right to fight this on your terms. You're going, and I'm going with you."

My mouth fell open. "Oh, no."

"Do you have a problem, Bay?" Mom challenged darkly.

"Yes."

"She doesn't." Landon squeezed my knee under the table, sending me an admonishing look. "She's hungry. She hasn't eaten her pancakes." He nodded to my plate. "The team is set. Winnie and Aunt Tillie are coming with us. It's good to have backup."

Was he kidding? There was nothing good about this situation. "Landon ... ."

He shook his head, a muscle working in his jaw. "It's done. We're all going." His expression told me he wasn't going to back down.

"Well, great," I said when I'd recovered enough to find my voice. "This doesn't have disaster written all over it."

"It will be a nice outing," Mom agreed primly. "It's a lovely fall day. Who doesn't love a walk through the woods on a lovely fall day?"

My hand shot in the air.

"Eat your breakfast, Bay," Mom ordered. "Leave the rest of the logistics to me."

Ugh, and I thought this day couldn't possibly get worse. I was wrong. So, so wrong.

22
TWENTY-TWO

"Bay, you should sit in the back with us." Mom fixed me with a prim look as everybody grouped outside Chief Terry's truck. We decided as a group – meaning Landon and Chief Terry decided and we nodded in agreement – it was best to signify our official presence with an official vehicle. That way there would be no confusion when we arrived.

"Why do I have to sit in the back?" I'd been planning to sit in the back but now that she'd told me it was necessary, I was agitated. "Maybe I don't want to sit in the back. Maybe Landon is going to sit in the back with you."

A presence moved in at my back and I didn't have to look to know who it was.

"Landon is sitting in the passenger seat to navigate," he corrected as his hand landed on my shoulder. "You can either sit on my lap so we can be mushy … ."

"Not going to happen," Chief Terry growled from the other side of the vehicle.

"Or you can sit in the back with your mother and Aunt Tillie," Landon finished.

I glanced over my shoulder and gave him a dirty look. "Thanks for backing me up."

His lips twitched. "Always." He kissed my temple and then prodded me toward the truck. "Everybody in."

THE RIDE TO THE OLD CAMPGROUND TOOK thirty minutes. Chief Terry carefully navigated the rutted dirt road that led to the property.

"They really should do something with this road," Mom noted. She was always excited when included in our adventures and today was no exception. "It's very bumpy."

"They're a cult, Mom," I noted. "I don't think that's the sort of stuff they care about."

"Well, they should." Mom made a tsking sound. Even cults need to worry about shocks."

"Good thinking." I held back a sigh — although just barely — and narrowed my eyes when Chief Terry made the final turn. "Look at that."

I'd visited the campground when I was a kid but hadn't been back in almost twenty years. In that time, the landscape had radically changed.

"What is that?" Landon leaned forward as Chief Terry parked — there were no other vehicles in the lot — and focused on a wooden structure shaped like a teepee.

"I'm sure it's their meeting space, the focal point of their faith," I replied. "It's their version of a temple."

He looked back to me. "That doesn't fill me with joy."

"No," I agreed. "I can't wait to hear what sort of cult they are."

"They'll couch it in obscure language," Chief Terry said as he pocketed his keys. His gaze was also on the teepee … if that's what it was supposed to be called. It was the best word I could muster. "They'll say they're worried about the planet, or they'll say they're trying to distance themselves from technology to purify their souls. They won't admit to being a cult."

"Yeah, speaking of that, we need to talk." Landon unfastened his seatbelt and turned to face us. "It's best we don't use the C-word in their presence."

"Cookie?" Aunt Tillie asked, faux sweetness dripping from her.

"Yes." Landon's expression didn't change. "Don't say 'cookie' or 'cult.' They'll be suspicious the moment we step onto the property."

"I'm sure they already are," I noted, inclining my head to two men who had appeared on the path to the campground. "What's the plan here?"

"I thought we would play it by ear." Chief Terry was stern as his gaze bounced between Mom, Aunt Tillie, and me. "Don't do anything weird."

"I never do anything weird," Mom shot back.

Chief Terry snorted. "I'm serious. Don't do anything weird ... and that goes double for you." He was firm as he fixed Aunt Tillie with a 'Don't mess with me' look. "We're here for you. Don't run your mouth."

"I didn't agree to that." Aunt Tillie shook her head. "I'll say what I want to say when I want to say it."

"We know the drill," I interjected, shooting Aunt Tillie a quelling look. "We're not going to do anything, at least right out of the gate. We need to get a feel for them. We have no idea what they're doing here. This is a fact-finding mission, nothing more."

Chief Terry didn't look convinced but nodded. "Let's do this."

Landon helped Aunt Tillie and me out of the rear seat, Chief Terry doing the same for Mom, and then he took up a protective stance by my great-aunt. It was a subtle shift, but I knew what he was doing. He trusted me to take care of myself. Aunt Tillie was the vulnerable one. I'd never loved him more.

"May we help you?" One of the men moved forward. He was armed with a stick — much like the one Aunt Tillie carried, although there looked to be carvings on the one clutched in his right hand.

"We're here to check out your operation," Chief Terry replied as he flashed his badge. His "official" voice made me grin. Underneath it all, he was a big marshmallow. He didn't show that side of himself to many people, however. "I also have some questions. Are you in charge?"

The man stepped forward to study the badge. "What jurisdiction do you feel you have here?" he asked.

"The campground is located within the boundaries of Hemlock Cove," Chief Terry replied. "That's all the jurisdiction I need."

"I believe if you want to enter our sacred lands you need a warrant," the man replied.

"Oh, yeah?" Chief Terry's expression didn't change. "Well, here's the thing; I called the deeds office, and this property belongs to Sid Unger. He died four years ago. Unless you know something I don't, this isn't your property."

The man blinked but didn't immediately respond. He was clearly thrown by the news.

"Yeah, that's what I thought." Chief Terry forced a tight smile. "Take me to your leader."

I had to bite the inside of my cheek to keep from laughing, and when I turned to my left, I saw a sign, one you can buy at novelty stores. It declared the area a Bigfoot safe zone.

"I'm not sure I'm supposed to take you back," the man hedged, shifting from one foot to the other. "Outsiders aren't allowed on our sacred land."

"It's not your land," Chief Terry reminded him. "You don't have any options here, son. If you want to make things difficult, I'll call the state police and we'll remove you from the property."

"But ... ." The man broke off, licking his lips. He looked caught, and then his eyes drifted to me. "I understand that you're a police officer," he started.

"Police chief," Chief Terry corrected.

"Police chief," the man readily acknowledged. "There is no reason for the rest of them to be here. They're not police officers."

"They're consultants," Chief Terry said.

"I go where I want," Landon added as he retrieved his badge.

"FBI." The man, who had yet to identify himself, visibly blanched. "I don't understand. Why are you here?"

"You don't need to understand why I'm here," Landon replied evenly. "We want to talk to the individual in charge."

"We'd also like to talk to Astrid Hamilton," Chief Terry added. "We're not particular about the order in which we speak to them."

"Astrid?" The man's eyebrows collided. "I don't ... ."

"It's okay, Brother Cedric," a male voice intoned from the trees to our right.

I tracked my eyes in that direction and found a slim man stepping into the parking lot. He looked to be in his late thirties, maybe early forties at the most, and he was dressed in nondescript dungarees and a flannel shirt. "These people don't understand about enlightenment. Nothing you say to them will matter. They're already biased against our way of life."

"I wouldn't say that," Chief Terry countered. He squared his shoulders as he regarded the newcomer. "I'm guessing you're in charge."

The man's smile was easy and fast. "My name is Eric Cadogen. I'm the supreme ruler of the Brotherhood of the Eternal Soul."

"Supreme ruler?" I sputtered.

"Some titles are better than others." Eric's smirk made me uncomfortable. "And who are you?"

Chief Terry took it upon himself to make the introductions. "I'm Terry Davenport, chief of police in Hemlock Cove. This is Landon Michaels. He's an FBI agent who covers this region."

Eric nodded at both of them in turn, but he didn't extend his hand in greeting.

"This is Winnie, Tillie and Bay Winchester," Chief Terry continued, barely taking a breath. "They work as consultants for my department." He delivered the lie without a stammer.

"Consultants?" Eric was dubious. "That's ... interesting."

"We're interesting individuals," Landon confirmed. "We have some questions."

"And we need to speak to Astrid Hamilton," Chief Terry added. "Her name came up in conjunction with an investigation we've been running. We need to talk to her."

"Sister Astrid is no longer part of our group," Eric replied.

"She left?"

"She departed this earthly plane and moved on to the next rung of transcendence," Eric replied. "Her journey is far from complete, but she's no longer needed here."

I slid my eyes to Landon for his reaction. He was uncomfortable with how this was playing out, but he kept his cop face firmly in place. "She died," he said.

"You would call it death," Eric confirmed. "We don't believe in death of the soul. There are merely rungs on a ladder to achieve ultimate ascension. She is now on a different rung."

"Well, here on Earth we like a record of our deaths," Landon said. "We don't have a record of Astrid Hamilton's death."

"It's hell to be a slave to mundane details like that, isn't it?" Eric drawled. He was being openly condescending now and didn't seem worried in the least that he was coming across as obnoxious.

"How did Astrid Hamilton die?" Chief Terry demanded.

Eric held Landon's gaze a moment longer — a silent challenge flowing between them — and then slowly turned his attention to Chief Terry. "She died in her sleep. It would've been almost a month ago. It was a tragedy, but she's no longer suffering in this world. She's moved on to the next."

"Where is her body?" I asked.

"It has been returned to the earth."

"Out here?"

Eric folded his arms across his chest and regarded me as one might a flea under a microscope. "And what sort of consultant are you, Miss Winchester?"

There was that condescension again.

"She does multiple things for the department," Landon replied.

"As well as for you, I'm sure," Eric said.

A muscle worked in Landon's jaw as he struggled to contain himself. "You want to be careful," he said.

"Very careful," Chief Terry agreed.

Eric's expression changed in an instant. "No insult intended."

"Right." Landon shook his head. "We need to know where Astrid Hamilton is buried."

"So you can dig her up?" Eric looked mournful. "Why would you want to do something so hateful?"

"Because unattended deaths are the bane of my existence," Chief Terry replied. "We need to see her body. Her son recently died — we came here to inform her of his passing — and we need to make sure that her death isn't connected to his."

"I don't see how it could be," Eric countered. "If you wish to exhume her body, there's nothing I can do about it. If we take you to the burial site, will you leave?"

"No," Chief Terry countered. "We just got here. We were under the impression this property was vacant. Imagine our surprise when we found out there were new residents."

"This is our sacred land." Eric insisted. "I secured this land myself after the passing of my father. He started our group."

"Brotherhood of the Eternal Soul," I said.

Eric's eyes were back on me within a split second. "I see you're familiar with our work. That's good. You could definitely use some enlightenment."

"You know, I don't like your tone," Landon snapped, forcing Eric to focus on him yet again. "You should know, in addition to being a trusted consultant, Bay is my wife. Show her some respect."

"He knows who I am," I offered softly. I hadn't meant to speak out loud. "He knows who we all are. He's playing a game."

"Oh, that's not true." Eric made a tsking sound. "Yes, I know who you are, but we're focused on enlightenment here. Your path leads in the opposite direction. We make it a point to know those who might threaten our way of life."

"How would she do that?" Landon demanded.

"She's simply incapable of being enlightened," Eric said evasively. "Don't be alarmed. Most people can't be enlightened. Given your relationship with her, I wouldn't be surprised you're on that rather long list."

"Is that supposed to be an insult?" Aunt Tillie asked, speaking for the first time.

"Yes." I flashed a smile for Eric's benefit but kept my temper in check. Something was clearly going on here. "May we look around?"

"No," Eric replied.

"Show me a deed with your name on it and we'll leave," Chief Terry said. "Otherwise, you can't keep us from this property."

"Even with a deed, you're not keeping me out," Landon said. "We need to see Astrid Hamilton's grave. We need to talk to your other members. We need some questions answered. We're not leaving until we do that."

Eric's left eye twitched. "What do you need to know?"

"How did Astrid Hamilton die?" Landon asked.

"I told you. She moved on to another life. We don't believe in death."

Landon snapped. "Stop playing games."

"I don't believe any of this is a game," Eric countered. "As for Sister Astrid ... she struggled at the end. She ran into a bit of bad luck, and it pushed her over the edge."

"She killed herself," I said, my eyes going to Landon. "She had a run of bad luck a week before her son died and then killed herself."

"Which means Chester Hamilton was here," Landon surmised. "Can you tell me when that was?"

Eric blinked. "I ... don't ... ."

Slowly, Landon extended a warning finger. "If you want to keep your little brotherhood together, you'll stop playing games with us. You have no right to this property. You're squatting. Luckily for you, the person who owned this land died and nobody is claiming it right now. You can stay for now ... unless you continue to push me."

"You need us to be magnanimous to you," Chief Terry added. "If you want us to go that route, then start answering questions."

The sigh Eric let loose was long suffering, but when he spoke again, it was with resignation. "What do you want?"

"We want to know everything," Landon replied. "And I mean absolutely everything."

"You're already biased against us," Eric argued. "There's very little to be gained from allowing you access to our inner sanctum."

"Again, you don't have a choice." Landon was having none of it. "You might be the supreme leader, but you have no true power here. You might as well at least pretend this is your idea."

There was a defiant tilt to Eric's chin as he regarded Landon. Then he slowly nodded. "Fine. I guess a tour is in order."

The man who had been talking to us before Eric's arrival — Cedric, if I remembered correctly — looked as if he was going to protest. A quick look from Eric had him snapping his mouth shut.

"Let's take a look around, shall we?" Eric's smile was tight and forced, and when his eyes met mine, there was a challenge there. "I think you'll be pleasantly surprised by what you find. We're not what you think."

"What is that?" I asked. "What do we think?"

"Nothing good. Come along. We've done a lot of work on the property."

23
TWENTY-THREE

Landon brushed my fingers as we started the walk to the campground. He didn't hold my hand — it would be a sign of weakness in Eric's eyes — but he likely wanted the moment of contact. I sent him a reassuring smile and then moved in closer to Aunt Tillie. Mom and I walked shoulder-to-shoulder with her to make sure she didn't fall ... and serve as a magical buffer should a tree suddenly uproot and fall toward us.

I noticed another Bigfoot sign as we closed in on the campground.

"What's the deal with Bigfoot?" I asked, breaking the silence that had descended over us. "Are you guys fans?"

Eric glanced over his shoulder, a gleam in his eye. "We love all of Mother Nature's creatures, big and small."

It wasn't really an answer, and I wasn't ready to let it go. "I don't think I understand what your group is trying to accomplish."

"Who says we're trying to accomplish anything?" Eric challenged. "Perhaps we're just trying to live our lives in a specific way."

"And what way is that?"

"We're simple people, Miss Winchester. We want to live simple lives, free of outside ... influences."

"So, no electronics?" I asked, refusing to let it go.

"We don't fear electronics. Some of them serve a purpose. We don't feel the need to let them take over our everyday lives. When my father started the Brotherhood, we lived in a vastly different world. He wanted to preserve it because he saw the dangers that were heading our way."

Well, that was interesting. "Your father?"

Cedric spoke up quickly. "All hail the father."

Eric sent him an indulgent smile but there was a hint of annoyance in his eyes. "My father was a great man."

"What was his name?" Landon asked. He'd taken up position behind us — thus buffering our group between him and Chief Terry — but he remained close enough to listen to the conversation.

"Jasper Cadogen."

The name meant nothing to me, but it obviously meant something to Aunt Tillie because she jerked up her head. She'd been intent on the ground for the walk, likely worried about the same things Mom and I were, but now she was focused on Eric.

"I knew your father," she said.

"Did you?" Eric seemed surprised. "How did you meet?"

"He ran a produce stand out on the highway," Aunt Tillie replied. She looked lost in thought. "He had a farm at one time. I think it was where the manufacturing plant was built. I seem to remember some sort of kerfuffle when that happened."

"Oh, I remember that." Mom bobbed her head. "There was some sort of fight regarding ownership of the farm."

A muscle worked in Eric's jaw as he flicked his eyes to Mom. "The farm was stolen from my family. Those thirty acres had been in my family for three generations, and Dunham Plastics swooped in and stole it."

"That's not exactly how I remember it," Mom said. "If I recall the story correctly, your family had taken over land from a neighbor. It was never yours, and yet you planted it."

"Then you're remembering the story wrong," Eric replied curtly.

I glanced over my shoulder and found Landon watching me. Mom had clearly touched a nerve and Landon had noticed. He sent me a reassuring smile. It was something we would have to follow up on later. Eric wasn't going to tell us the truth.

"So you owned that property and the plastics family swooped in and bought it," Chief Terry noted.

"For a fraction of what it was worth," Eric replied. "We had no say in the matter. It was stolen from us thanks to a greedy corporation."

I pursed my lips, searching my memory. "There was something about the factory," I said. "It was only in business a few years before it failed."

"It was karma." Eric was grim. "When you steal from those who have right on their side, karma always rears her pretty head."

I'd never quite heard it phrased that way. "The property was beset by a series of issues. There was a fire ... and a worker lost a hand." I rolled my neck as I desperately tried to remember the whole story. "The owner of the company jumped to his death from the roof of the building."

Landon said from behind us, "That was some bad luck."

The chuckle Eric let loose was light. "Do you believe in luck, Agent Michaels?"

"Of course," Landon replied. "You've seen my wife. I consider myself the luckiest man in the world."

My cheeks heated but I refrained from saying anything. Landon was trying to push Eric's buttons. I might've been mortified by the manner in which he did it, but I understood his aim.

"So, it's true love," Eric mused. "You're indeed a lucky man to find true love. So few do."

"So very few," Landon agreed. "If your father started this ... group ... what happened to him?"

"He moved to the next rung," Eric replied simply.

"When was that?"

"Several years ago."

"It will be ten years in the spring," Cedric volunteered, earning another glare from Eric. "We'll all reach the pinnacle then."

My heart skipped. I had no idea what the pinnacle was, but I'd read enough regarding cults to allow the fear a momentary foothold.

"Is there an official record of your father's death?" Chief Terry asked pointedly.

"I have no idea." Eric held out his hands. "I've never given much thought to official death records."

Chief Terry was unruffled. "I can look it up easily enough when I get back to town."

"What happens if you don't find the proper records?" Eric asked.

"Then I think you're going to be missing your next rung." Chief Terry showed off his teeth in a grim smile when Eric jerked his head to look at him.

"I see." Eric didn't look happy.

"I certainly hope so." Chief Terry inclined his head toward the teepee. Up close, it was even more impressive. It towered a good fifty feet into the sky. built completely of branches. It had taken a long time — and a lot of manpower — to construct. "What's that thing?"

This time when Eric looked back, he was testy. "That is our temple. Outsiders are not allowed inside. If you try to enter, I will lodge a complaint."

"Who with?" Landon asked. "He's the chief of police."

"I will find someone."

"It's fine," Chief Terry said. "I don't need to go inside the temple today." There was a veiled threat left hanging. "Tomorrow is another story, of course."

"Of course," Eric agreed. His feral smile was back. "Where would you like to look first?"

Chief Terry deferred to me. "I'll let Bay lead the charge on this one."

"Your consultant," Eric said blankly. "Fine." Eric sounded as if he was talking around a mouthful of broken glass when he focused on me. "Where would you like to look first?"

The campground was quiet. I thought it would be bustling with activity. Two large bonfires burned on either side of the temple, but nobody was around to monitor them. I would've given Mrs. Little's left arm to get inside that temple. It was calling to me ... and on more than one level.

"Let's head to the kitchen," I suggested. "I'm curious how a commune of this size handles food preparations."

"How do you know the size of our group?" Eric asked.

"It's something of a skill I've mastered over the years," I replied, refusing to let him intimidate me. "You'd be surprised at what I can accomplish when I set my mind to it."

"I probably would," Eric agreed. "The kitchen it is." He cut across the lawn, ignoring the walkways. He seemed determined to keep me off them.

As we neared the door to the kitchen building, I pulled up short and pointed at the ground. "What's this?" Someone — perhaps a child — had drawn in the dirt with a stick. "It looks like a Bigfoot drawing."

"If you know what it is, why ask?" Eric drawled.

"It looks like you have children here," Landon noted. "I don't hear any children."

"It's mid-morning," Eric noted. "Children are at school this time of day."

Landon's gaze was predatory. "What school do your children attend?"

"We have a school on the property," Eric replied. "I would appreciate it if you didn't interrupt their lessons. It's so hard to keep young minds focused."

The grounds were empty, telling me an alarm had sounded at our arrival and those most vulnerable had been secreted away. On top of that, the land felt ... sick. It was the only word I could describe for what I felt the moment we crossed onto the property. Something very bad had happened here. Whether it was a curse, wards that were meant to drive us away, or something else entirely, I couldn't say.

We were in the right place, though. I could feel it.

"Let's see the kitchen," I said. Now that I'd decided these people were responsible for what was happening, I felt emboldened. If the cult members moved on me, I would give them a lesson they wouldn't soon forget. "I love a good kitchen."

"Me too," Mom echoed, although she looked worried. She was out of her element, though she likely felt the sickness pounding back at us. "I'm at home in a kitchen."

"Here at Eden Mountain, we don't put emphasis on food," Eric explained. "We believe food is for nourishment, not enjoyment."

"Did you hear that?" I asked Landon. "It's for nourishment. No fun allowed when it comes to food."

He grinned at me. "I'm taking notes." He winked before turning to Eric. "How did you come up with the name? Eden Mountain is evocative ... but not entirely correct. There's no mountain near here."

"Not all mountains can be seen," Eric said on a sly smile when he opened the door to the kitchen. "This way."

I was relieved to find people at work. I noticed several things within seconds of surveying the room. The first was that all the workers were women. That wasn't surprising given the fact that we were dealing with a cult. They were often created as a way to subjugate women. Cooking was "women's work" after all. The second thing I noticed was that there was nothing processed in sight. No canned goods. No crackers. No bags of sugar or flour. Everything looked fresh.

"Where's your greenhouse?" I asked.

Fury fired in Eric's eyes. "What makes you think we have a greenhouse? I never mentioned a greenhouse."

"You didn't have to," I countered. "Everything in here is fresh. This time of year, you can get squash and corn easily enough. Those tomatoes and that lettuce are too fresh to be from a local market. You're growing it yourself."

Eric's left eye twitched, but he recovered quickly and graced me with a smile. There was nothing friendly about it. "You have a keen eye."

"I do," I agreed.

"There is more to our compound than what you see here," Eric noted. "We've ... expanded ... our efforts. We don't need to be on top of one another."

I nodded to Mom to watch Aunt Tillie before drifting closer to the stove. The woman stirring what looked to be soup on the burner appeared distinctly uncomfortable when I invaded her space. "Vegetable soup?" I asked in an effort to put her at ease.

It didn't work. She was completely focused on Eric, taking her cues from him.

"Don't worry, Lynn," Eric reassured her. "Our new friends simply want a tour. Tell them anything they want to know."

Lynn stared at her supreme leader a moment longer and then nodded. "Um ... it's soup. It's very healthy. No added ingredients. Just water and the natural juices from the vegetables."

Sounded downright bland, but it fit with the picture starting to take shape in my mind. "Do you work in the greenhouse too?"

"No." Lynn was leery, darting another look to Eric before continuing. "I'm assigned to the kitchen."

"Awesome." I smiled at her before moving along the counter. The setup was outdated. It looked typical for the period it had been built, but most of the appliances were old and worn. "Did you know Sid?"

"Who?" Lynn's expression was blank.

"Sid. This is his property."

"But ... ." Lynn looked helpless as she glanced back at Eric. If I didn't know better, I would think she was in pain. Maybe it was of the mental variety.

"It's fine, Lynn." Eric seemingly waved off the woman's worry as if it were nothing more than a pesky mosquito. "Miss Winchester is just curious."

"Ms. Winchester," Landon corrected.

"And maybe Mrs. Winchester-Michaels at some point," I added, my irritation momentarily getting the better of me.

Landon shot me a quelling look. "We talked about that." He wanted me to keep my maiden name because it struck fear in the hearts of our enemies. I was still trying to decide if that was the route I wanted to take.

"We'll talk about it again." I flashed a sincere smile in his direction before turning back to Eric. "How did Chester fit into all of this? Was he allowed to come and go, or was he a special guest star from time to time?"

"I have no idea what you're talking about," Eric replied, his expression remaining neutral. "I think you're confused."

Even though I wasn't technically in charge, Landon and Chief Terry had ceded the questioning to me. "Chester Hamilton's mother was a member of your group. She died a week before Chester. I believe they suffered from the same malady. If you could fill us in on how Astrid Hamilton grew sick, that would go a long way toward getting to the heart of matters."

Eric looked as if he was about to erupt. Before he could respond, however, Lynn did.

"That's not right," Lynn said. She looked puzzled. "Astrid transcended years ago. Chester wasn't a member. He was looking to become a member — as another son of Jasper — but he hadn't gone through the trials yet. His soul was unwashed when he fell to hell."

I stood rooted to my spot, a million thoughts raging through my mind. Finally, I slid my eyes to Eric. "Another son of Jasper? I didn't realize you and Chester were brothers."

"We weren't," Eric replied. "That was a rumor started among those in the flock because they were bored."

"But ... ." Lynn looked genuinely perturbed. She quickly silenced herself when Eric shot her a glare.

"There's some confusion as to what's happening here," he noted. "I think you're the one most confused, Miss Winchester." Why he insisted on focusing on me was baffling – and interesting. "Chester Hamilton was the son of one of our faithful, nothing more. If something happened to him, it has nothing to do with us. If you're seeking answers on an outsider, I really must stress that it's a mistake. We pay no heed to individuals who aren't members of our group."

"Right." I licked my lips and glanced at Landon again. He looked as intrigued as I felt. "I must be mistaken," I said. "Let's continue with the tour. I want to see everything."

"That's not allowed," Lynn argued, horrified. Now that she'd started talking, apparently she couldn't stop. "Our structures are private. Our beliefs are sanctioned by the Lord and related to us by the supreme leaders. Outsiders can venture no farther."

Well, that answered that question. I decided to push my luck. "Eric said only the temple and school are off limits." I looked to Landon for confirmation, barely managing to hold back a smile when he winked. "Isn't that what you said, Eric?" I made sure to use his first name because I knew he would find it irritating.

"Of course." Eric didn't miss a beat. "A full tour is in order. I'm nothing if not cooperative."

That remained to be seen. The only thing I knew right now with any degree of certainty was that he was furious. I couldn't wait to see how far I could push him. I wanted to crack that cool veneer of his like an egg.

24
TWENTY-FOUR

Eric showed us the cabins, most of which were arranged like barracks. They had bunk beds, and from what I could make out, the women and men slept separately. One of the cabins was reserved for children, and I quickly counted the beds. There were twenty, but only half of them looked as if anybody slept in them. That made me feel better, if only marginally.

Eric was more reluctant to show us his sleeping space, but he ultimately acquiesced with a bit of prodding. He'd claimed one of the cabins for himself — it was huge, so his space resembled a small apartment — and one whole wall was lined with bookshelves. I wanted to look at the books, but he kept cutting me off from them.

"You have interesting reading habits," I noted as Mom stood protectively next to Aunt Tillie. They positioned themselves in the middle of the room so nothing could fall on them. "This is quite the library."

I used my hip to box him out and grabbed one of the books. "*Jaws?*"

"Most of those books were donated to the previous owner," Eric said defensively. "I'm a proponent of reading as many books as possible, so I allow all of my congregants to borrow books as they wish."

"You mean Sid," I pressed.

"I believe that's what I said," Eric gritted out.

"You never refer to him by name. I'm curious how you got your hands on his property."

"Sid was a member of my flock," Eric replied easily. "He left the property to us."

It was a lie, not a very good one. "That should be easy enough to check, right?" I asked Chief Terry.

He nodded.

"He left it to me verbally," Eric insisted. "There might not be paperwork."

"Then this property might not be yours," Chief Terry replied. "It's going to suck if you have to give it up after all this work."

"We will not give up our home," Eric seethed, his temper making another appearance. "It's our right to live here."

"I guess we'll have to see." Chief Terry flashed a smile designed to keep Eric on edge.

"Why would you want to take this from us?" Eric demanded, taking a step closer to Chief Terry. That allowed me to get a better look at the books. "Nobody is using this land. It was just sitting here. We're repurposing it, making it better. How can that be bad for the community?"

"I didn't say it was bad," Chief Terry said. "If Sid died without a will, then the property will go to his parents."

"Then I guess we'll have to buy it from them," Eric growled.

"You can try," I said as I fingered several of the spines. "I know someone in town who will most likely outbid you to get her hands on this property."

"Oh, really?" Eric didn't look impressed. "Who is that?"

I debated if I wanted to answer truthfully and then realized it would be a good test. "Margaret Little. She's been buying up a lot of property."

Eric snorted.

"Do you know that name?" I asked.

"I'm aware of Margaret Little," Eric replied. "You act as if I'm some newbie to the community. We've been here for years."

"And yet nobody knew it," Chief Terry argued. "I just don't understand how that happened."

Eric held out his arms. "Perhaps you don't see as well as you think you do."

"We see just fine," I replied. "Mrs. Little does too. She'll snap up this property the second she realizes it might be on the auction block."

"Then I'll talk to Mrs. Little ... though I heard she was losing her mind."

And that's what I was waiting for. "Did you?" I felt as if my facial muscles were straining to hold my smile in place. "Where did you hear that?"

"The townspeople talk," Eric replied. "I was there to pick up some seeds for the greenhouse two days ago. A woman in the coffee shop said Margaret Little was losing her mind. She said she wouldn't be surprised if Margaret was locked up soon ... or perhaps fell victim to an accident at her own hand."

He had to be talking about Mrs. Gunderson. There was certainly no love lost between her and Mrs. Little — Mrs. Little had an affair with Floyd Gunderson years ago — but it wasn't the sort of information Mrs. Gunderson would offer to a stranger. "That's ... very strange. I wouldn't worry about Mrs. Little, though. She did seem to be struggling a few days ago but she got past it. Things are going well for her now."

Eric worked his jaw, absorbing the information. "Well, good for her. If she's feeling better, I'll certainly arrange a meeting regarding the property. I'm sure there's nothing out here for her."

"I'm sure." I pointed to the wall, where a framed piece of art hung over a king-sized bed. "What's the symbol in the art there?"

In truth, the art looked like an abstract. Someone had fashioned it with pastels before framing it, and there were a myriad of symbols embedded in it. Or, to be more precise, there was one symbol used over and over again.

"Symbol?" Eric feigned innocence. "I have no idea what you're talking about. One of my people made that as a gift for me. There's no symbol in it."

"Sure there is." I wasn't going to let him off the hook that easily. I strolled to the work. "Right here. And here. And here." I moved my finger around. "It's the same symbol. It almost looks as if someone tried to hide it in some of the patterns, but it's clearly there."

Eric was the picture of serene confusion. "I never noticed it."

I didn't bother looking at Landon and Chief Terry for the next part. They were letting me handle this, and rightly so. "I've had reason to research that symbol recently," I said.

"Really." Eric's smile widened into something more genuine now.

"It showed up at two separate crime scenes."

"What did you learn?"

"It was created in Greece thousands of years ago. It's a curse. People carved it into items, cursed their enemies, and then buried the item with the dead."

I watched Eric closely for a reaction and wasn't disappointed when his nose wrinkled, and his eyebrows hopped. He covered quickly. "Are you sure? That seems a bit far-fetched."

"Oh, I'm sure. It seems there was a cult that co-opted the symbol. Apparently, it's supposed to kill people with bad luck. It seems a strange choice to be woven into your artwork."

"Well, I'll have to ask the artist about it."

"I would love to talk to the artist. It's an interesting piece. Does he or she do commissions?"

"I don't believe so."

I pursed my lips as I studied some squiggled lines at the bottom of the drawing. "Astrid Hamilton. That would be Chester's mother, right?"

"I ... ." Eric's eyes flashed with annoyance. "Are you done here?"

"Almost," I replied. "How are you going to talk to the artist if she's dead. She is dead, right?"

"She moved on to another rung," Eric insisted.

"You still haven't told us where her body is," Chief Terry said.

"I have no idea where her body was buried," Eric replied. "We don't put importance on an empty shell. I'll have to ask my people and get back to you."

Chief Terry opened his mouth to argue further but I stopped him with a hand on his arm and a shake of my head. "There's no way we can just let this go without seeing the body," I said.

"Even though you're not a police officer," Eric growled.

"No, I'm not a police officer," I agreed. "I'm something else."

"What are you?"

"You'll find out." I moved closer to Mom and Aunt Tillie. "I think I understand everything that's happening here. We can arrange to come back tomorrow?" I addressed the question to Chief Terry. He nodded. "We'll come back then."

"I have to insist that you don't," Eric countered. "This is, after all, our property. If you want to come back, you'll need a warrant." He looked smug.

"No problem." Chief Terry returned the smile. "I'll get the warrant tomorrow morning. Does tomorrow afternoon work for a return trip?"

Fury dripped from Eric's dark countenance. "This is our land. We won't let you take it from us."

"I'll take that as a yes," I said to Chief Terry. "Thank you so much for your time, Eric. I look forward to seeing you again tomorrow."

With that, Chief Terry officially dismissed him and headed for the door. I moved with him and waited there until Mom and Aunt Tillie were with me, and we descended the stairs carefully. When I reached the bottom and looked over my shoulder, I saw Eric standing in the opening glaring at me.

"Have a nice day." I waved at him and then started toward the pathway to the parking lot.

"This isn't over," Eric called to my back.

I didn't bother looking over my shoulder. "Not even close," I agreed. "See you soon."

"THAT WAS A MASTER CLASS ON interrogation, baby," Landon said when we were on the path to the parking lot.

I slid him a sidelong look trying to decide if he was making fun of me and found him watching me with something akin to wonder. "Are you serious?" I asked.

"Absolutely."

"You're not making fun of me?"

"Bay, the only time I make fun of you is when I'm feeling frisky and I want to entice you, because you like to fight about small things and I like to make up." He smiled. "That right there, what you just did, was straight out of the academy. Where did you learn to do that?"

"I watched you."

He smirked. "Oh really?"

"I watched a lot of television with Aunt Tillie before you came into my life. She likes police procedurals."

"And soap operas," Aunt Tillie offered. "I'm a connoisseur of all things television."

"Of course, you are." Landon winked at her. "As for you, my favorite wife, I'm very impressed." He slid his arm around my waist but somehow overreached and his fingers tangled in Aunt Tillie's shirt. There was a terrific ripping as he clawed off the front half of her shirt.

"What in the hell?" Aunt Tillie stared down at her exposed bra.

Thankfully it was so big it was like a bathing suit top. "What did you do?"

"I didn't mean to." Landon looked horrified. "I don't even know how that happened." He refused to look anywhere but at Aunt Tillie's face. "I don't ... I didn't mean ... I ... ."

Aunt Tillie squared her shoulders. "I think you like what you see."

I slapped my hand over my mouth. If I started laughing, I wouldn't stop. That wouldn't help our situation.

"I can't even." Landon focused on the cloudless sky.

I looked around, debating, and then focused on my husband. "How about you give me your shirt?" I asked.

"What?" Bewilderment washed over his features.

"Your shirt. Aunt Tillie needs something to wear."

"So do I." He looked appalled.

"It's more appropriate for you to go shirtless," I noted.

"Says who?" Aunt Tillie demanded. "I look good without a shirt. Heck, I don't think I need a bra either. I only threw one on because I sensed something like this might happen. I wanted to be prepared for all possibilities."

"And a bra does that?" I asked.

"It's not just any bra." She thumped her chest, causing a hollow metal sound that took me by surprise.

"What is that?" I stepped closer and looked at the bra — really looked at it — and frowned when I realized it was something else entirely. "Is that a bulletproof vest?"

"It's a bulletproof bra," she clarified. "I made it myself. Do you like it?"

Like wasn't the word I would've picked. Still, I found it intriguing. "You made that yourself? Why?"

"I figure one of these days Margaret is going to lose it and try to shoot me. I want to be prepared for all possibilities."

"Because you're going to live forever, right?" She seemed to be perkier than she had been when we set out on our adventure this morning.

"Oh, no." She shook her head. "Nobody lives forever, Bay. One day I'll gladly cross over. I have people waiting for me there. I'm not done here yet. When I am, I'll know ... and you'll know too."

Her matter-of-fact tone wasn't what I expected. "Aunt Tillie ... ."

"Don't." She raised her finger to quiet me. "I can't leave until you guys are ready to go it alone. You're getting better, but you're nowhere near ready to lose me. I don't want you getting melancholy and whining. I'm not saying anything that should come as a surprise. I'm not ready to go yet. You're not ready to say goodbye. One day, I will be ready."

"What about me?" I whispered. "Will I be ready?"

"Of course not. But it's not about you. It's about me."

When I turned, I saw Landon had taken off his shirt and was holding it out to Aunt Tillie. It was weird seeing him shirtless in the middle of the woods — especially considering the crisp weather — but he shrugged back into his coat quickly and his smile told me he was mostly okay with the turn of events.

"This smells." Aunt Tillie made a face as she lifted it. "Do you secrete bacon pheromones or something?"

Landon didn't look offended. "If only." He looked to me. "What's the plan here, Bay? I get that we're on the right track. I understand our answers are here, but I don't know how this is going to play out."

"I don't either." I opted for honesty. "I don't know if Eric is behind what's happened, but at the very least he's involved." I glanced back at the temple. "I really want to see inside that thing."

Chief Terry slowed his pace. "Do you want to go back?"

I considered the offer – could we end this here and now? – and then shook my head. "No. Not right now. It's not safe." I glanced at Aunt Tillie. "When the fight comes, Aunt Tillie can't be anywhere near us."

"Hey!" Aunt Tillie's eyes practically bugged out of her head. "This is my fight."

"Yes, but your bad luck will affect our magic, and you know it. We have a window here. These people are the answer to the question. They're the reason this is happening. We still don't have all the pieces to put the final puzzle together. We need to talk a few things out."

"Are we really coming back here tomorrow?" Landon asked.

"I don't know yet. I need to think. I feel like I'm missing something important."

"You'll figure it out." Landon slung an arm around my shoulders, this time missing Aunt Tillie, and kissed my temple. "You were masterful, my little witch."

"Oh, geez." Chief Terry sounded like he was in actual pain. "This mushy stuff has to stop. It's going to give me an ulcer. It's also the reason I saw Tillie's bra. Haven't I suffered enough?"

"I heard that." Aunt Tillie's gaze was dark. "For the first time, Terry, you're on my list."

"What? Me? You never put me on your list."

"Well, you're on it now. How do you feel?"

"Terrified ... and kind of excited." Chief Terry rubbed his hands together. "What are you going to make me smell like? I suggest chocolate cake. That's Winnie's favorite and I can think of a few ways to make that fun."

My stomach rolled. "Oh, now you're the one who is being gross. How did I go from being the hero to being punished? That's not fair."

Landon laughed. "It sucks to be on the receiving end, doesn't it?"

"So very much." I paused when in front of the Bigfoot sign. "There's one thing that doesn't fit," I noted.

"The Bigfoot thing," Landon said. "Yeah, it's weird."

"I feel like I should know something," I admitted. "It's like ... right here." I tapped my forehead. "But I can't pull it out of my head."

"It will come to you." Landon tugged me toward the truck. "Come on. Let's get home. Something tells me we need to inform the rest of the family what's going on. You know ... just in case."

"Yeah. We need to get everybody together."

"I don't understand," Chief Terry said. "What do you think is going to happen?"

"I don't know. Maybe nothing. It's also possible Eric will move on us because he knows we're a threat. Either way, we have a baby, and there's strength in numbers. We need to be smart about this."

25

TWENTY-FIVE

We sent Aunt Tillie in with Mom when we got back to the inn. She was handling calls — Thistle and Clove wouldn't be happy about having to move back in, even if for a short time — and I set about wandering the property to ensure the wards were intact. Landon trailed behind, quiet as I pushed and pulled on the wards to be certain they'd hold.

When I finally finished, I turned to find him watching me. "What?" I demanded. "I'm just making sure that we'll be safe."

"I'm not giving you grief, Bay," he replied. "I'm just ... thinking."

"If you want pot roast for dinner you should head inside and make your request now. They'll start cooking soon."

He smirked. "I told her to make prime rib. She said they have a nice roast already."

"You like prime rib."

"I do, but it's your favorite roast. I want her to make it for you."

"Why?"

"You're doing all the work on this one. It turned out that way the last few times, but it feels even more dire this time. You work a lot, and I want you to be happy."

I tried to suck in a sigh ... and failed. "Landon, you don't have to worry about me. Given the things we've fought over the past few months, a killer cult seems minor."

He smiled. "How weird are our lives that you can say that and mean it?"

"Pretty weird."

He held out his hand and I automatically took it, letting him wrap his arms around me for a hug. "When I first met you, all I saw was a hot chick with attitude outside a corn maze," he said. "I felt a spark with you, but I thought it was all hormones. I didn't realize what it meant."

"What did it mean?"

"That you were my soulmate."

He'd used that word to describe our relationship so many times I'd lost count. He seemed open to the idea of destiny, often saying we were meant to be. Obviously, he was feeling philosophical today, so I decided to indulge him.

"When I saw you, I was irritated," I said, smirking when I felt his lips curve against my forehead. "I couldn't understand why you were with those guys. I knew you were different, and I was attracted to you — though I would've denied it with my dying breath back then — but I didn't know what was to come, either."

"It's a good thing we pushed forward even when we didn't know."

I bobbed my head and then drew back to study his face. "I might have to kill them, Landon." It was something that I never believed I would have to say when I was younger, but it seemed natural now. "If we manage to pin down who is involved, I might have to kill them to save Aunt Tillie."

"Do you expect me to talk you out of that?"

I hesitated and then shook my head. "I just ... it's hard for me. When I left Walkerville, I thought I was working toward the life I wanted in Detroit. I believed in my heart that I didn't want to be a witch and moving away from them was my solution to that."

"What do you believe now?"

"That I was always meant to be here, with you and them. I won't let Aunt Tillie die. One way or another, I'll figure a way out of this."

He gently brushed my hair from my face. "Bay, I never question that you'll do the right thing. I know I hurt you when I brushed off Chester Hamilton's suicide as a fluke, but I should've known better. I think part of me wanted it to be a plain suicide so we could remain happy in our bubble.

"I'm always happy with you," he continued. "Putting arbitrary limitations on our happiness is stupid. I knew better, but I couldn't stop myself."

"It's okay." I meant it. "I wanted it to be a straight suicide too, which seems horrible to say."

"You knew it wasn't. We could've gotten ahead of it then."

"Or we could've sat around spinning our wheels," I argued. "We didn't have anything to go on then. Now we do."

"And we're going to save Aunt Tillie. I promise you that. I won't let this family be harmed if I can stop it, but I think this is going to come down to you. I'm sorry that it always seems to happen that way lately, but I think that's destiny."

"Why is that?" I was honestly curious.

"Because you were always meant to be something spectacular. That's who you are. If this cult comes after us, I have no doubt you'll kick the crap out of them. You are always amazing, but what you're becoming ... it just blows me away."

He was so earnest it tugged my heartstrings. "We'll beat them. I still don't have it all worked out. I'll feel better when the whole family is under the same roof. Then I'll be able to think."

His snort was quick and loud. "Oh, Bay, it's cute that you still have a streak of naïveté."

My eyebrows moved toward one another. "Excuse me?"

"Tonight is going to be madness and mayhem, Winchester style. It's going to be a different sort of stress. It's also going to be a whole lot of love. I don't think you'll find the answers you're looking for tonight, but you will find the strength you need."

"I will?"

"Everyone you love most will be under this roof tonight. Unfortunately, the people you love most aren't always easy to love. They'll be all over the place, which is okay, because you inherently know how to fix things when a problem arises. It's when you overthink that things go astray."

It was an interesting observation. "You're saying I shouldn't strategize and just react. That backfires on us sometimes."

"And yet it always works out okay in the end. I have no doubt it will tonight." He pulled me in for another hug, his lips brushing my forehead. "You'll figure it out because you always do. I'm starting to think you don't know how to fail."

His faith bolstered me. At the same time, it made me uneasy. "I can't get complacent. We're missing something."

"You'll figure it out. You always do."

"I don't have a choice. I'm a badass."

"You're my badass." Landon tipped back my chin and gave me a kiss. It started soft and then grew more intense. It likely would've carried on, but the sound of someone clearing his throat behind us shattered the moment.

I found Chief Terry glaring at us. "What?" I asked defensively.

"You two make me sick." He shook his head and planted his hands on his hips. "Your mother wanted me to tell you to come inside. She thinks it's too cold for you to be fretting about wards. Obviously, you're keeping warm another way."

Landon chuckled as he slung an arm around my shoulders. "That's how we roll. Your interruption was timely, though. I need to run to the guesthouse and grab a few things because we're spending the night here. It's probably best to get it out of the way now."

I glanced at the sky. It was fall, so it was getting dark earlier. "I'll stay here. Just grab the basics. If we need more, we can go tomorrow.

We're here for the duration now. Until Aunt Tillie is saved, until the cult is out of business, we need to stick together."

"As long as there's food, I don't care where we stay." Landon winked at me. "I have you. I don't need anything else."

"You need pajamas for when you want a midnight snack," I argued. "You don't want to risk Aunt Tillie seeing you in nothing but your boxers. She already thinks you're hot for her after the bra incident."

Landon looked horrified. "Did you have to mention that?"

I had an idea. "While you're getting our stuff, I want to get a better look at Aunt Tillie's bulletproof bra. I might be able to work with it."

"To do what?" Chief Terry demanded.

"Landon gave me an idea a few days ago. He wanted me to come up with a spell to stave off heart attacks so he can keep eating whatever he wants. I can't do that, but I might be able to do something else."

"Well, now I'm intrigued." Landon gave me a quick kiss, this one more chaste. "I can get to our place and back in thirty minutes."

"And I won't eat all the cookies while I'm waiting for you."

"Good. I'm going to need a lot of sugar to get through this night."

I had no doubt he was right.

THISTLE WAS IN A MOOD WHEN SHE arrived with Marcus. I wasn't surprised — Thistle was always in a mood, after all — but her grouchiness was a sight to behold when she and Aunt Tillie faced off in the dining room.

"I can't believe you made a bulletproof bra and didn't tell me," Thistle hissed. "That's right up my alley. I would totally like a bulletproof bra. Why did you cut me out of the action?"

"Who is going to shoot you?" Aunt Tillie demanded. "You're too much of hermit to get shot. Until you decide to embrace your destiny as my mischief maker heir, you're stuck being you." She sat in her usual chair and eyed her silverware. "I need someone to cut my prime rib."

That was quite the shift in topics, and it forced me to look up from the bra. "What?"

"Are you kidding me?" Aunt Tillie was exasperated. "If the pieces aren't tiny, I'll choke. If I cut my own meat, I'll hurt myself with the knife. It's like you're not even trying to keep me alive."

I was caught off guard. "What are you even ... ?" I trailed off. "You're pretty vigilant these days," I said, changing course. "This curse actually worries you, despite your bold talk that you're not ready to go."

"I'm more worried that you're not ready to live without me," Aunt Tillie countered. "As for this curse, I'm not afraid at all."

"Then what was with all the talk about wanting to control your memorial?"

"I want to hear people tell me how great I am."

"You've stopped talking about that. Does that mean you're convinced we'll win?"

"Bay, I always know we'll win. Don't be an idiot. I'm still holding the memorial. I might time it for when the coven visits, but I'm holding it. I've decided I want to hear how people truly feel about me before I die."

Thistle raised her hand. "I'll tell you how I feel about you."

"I already know you love me and want to be just like me when you grow up," Aunt Tillie shot back, faux sweetness on full display.

"Oh, whatever." Thistle rolled her eyes until they landed on me. "Can you believe her? Even when she's cursed, she's a total pill."

"I'm not surprised," I replied as I fingered the material. "I also have an idea." I glanced up when Mom entered with a charcuterie board. She wouldn't admit it because the circumstances were less than ideal, but she loved having all of us under one roof. She was always happiest when she could dote on people. "I need to run to Aunt Tillie's greenhouse for some supplies."

Mom glanced at the window. It was almost dark. "If you're going, go now."

"I'll go with you," Landon offered. He'd returned with our overnight bags and had spent the past thirty minutes stuffing cookies into his mouth. He was a stress eater, and tonight promised to be stressful.

"I'll take Thistle." My tone was firm. "We need to talk about a few things." I flicked my eyes to the opposite door as Clove appeared with baby Calvin in her arms. "I'll take Clove, too."

"Where are you taking me?" Clove asked, instantly suspicious. "I just got here. I don't want to go anywhere. Besides, I'm not leaving my baby to go on a monster hunt."

"I want you to go to the greenhouse with me," I replied. "I need some ingredients. I have an idea. I don't think anybody should go anywhere alone. If the cult attacks tonight — and I think that's a distinct possibility — they'll likely come under the cover of darkness."

"If they're even ready to move on us," Thistle argued. "You clearly surprised them when you showed up out of the blue like you did. They might not be prepared to take us on."

"Probably not," I agreed. "I still want to be ready."

"That's always smart." Thistle didn't seem bothered about heading out to the greenhouse with me.

"Okay." Clove wasn't happy in the least, but she didn't argue. "But if we get attacked, I'm totally going to cry and whine. It's been a bit and I might be out of practice, but you've been warned."

"Oh, you're never out of practice when it comes to whining," Thistle drawled.

Clove smacked her arm. "You're on my list, and there's a whole greenhouse full of dirt out there. Do you really want to test me?"

Aunt Tillie gave Clove an appraising look. "Maybe I've been focusing on the wrong witch taking up my mantle as head mischief maker. Maybe it should be you."

Clove beamed at her — she was always happy to earn approval

from the older generation — and then she grasped what Aunt Tillie was saying. "Um ... wait."

I smirked as I stood. "I'll be right back," I promised Landon.

"If you're not, I'll come looking for you," he said.

"I'll keep him busy until you get back," Aunt Tillie promised. "He'll be cutting up my food and feeding me."

Landon scowled. "Why me?"

Aunt Tillie shrugged. "Why not?"

I WAS READY FOR A FIGHT WHEN WE stepped outside, but the night was quiet. I didn't sense anyone watching us as I led the way to the greenhouse, casting an illuminated magical net over our heads to light the way. We were quiet until we reached our destination, and then Thistle and Clove started bickering.

"You should let me keep the baby one night a week," Thistle insisted. "That way you can rest, and he and I can bond."

"You just want him to like you more than Bay," Clove argued. "That's your entire motivation for wanting to spend time with him."

"Oh, you're full of it," Thistle shot back. "I'm trying to help you."

They were both full of it as far as I was concerned. "Thistle likes the baby. She likes that he calms her frayed nerves. You should let her take him, Clove."

"What about you?" Clove's gaze was pointed. "Don't you want to take him?"

It was so Clove to worry about something like that. "Of course, I do, but right now I have to focus on Aunt Tillie."

"I get that. It's just ... what happens if you can't save Aunt Tillie?"

"That's not an option."

"It might become a reality," Thistle pointed out. "We only have a few days left."

I was determined. "We're ending this tomorrow. If we don't, then we'll just have to save Aunt Tillie the same way she did Mrs. Little. That will give us the time we need to figure things out."

"Who will absorb the curse?" Thistle demanded.

"My mom volunteered." I shifted my eyes to the pots. "I have a list of things we need. Let's gather them and get back to the house."

"Hold up." Thistle grabbed my wrist. "You're not thinking of taking your mom's place and absorbing the curse yourself?"

I didn't answer.

"Bay." Thistle sounded exasperated. "You can't do that. We need you firing on all cylinders. If it comes to that, I'll take on the curse. We can't afford for your luck to turn. It won't end well for us."

"She's right," Clove added.

Thistle scowled at her. "Thanks for agreeing I should sacrifice myself."

"You're welcome." Clove's smile was serene. "You said it yourself, we can't afford to let Bay take it on. Our mothers spend too much time in the kitchen. They could hurt themselves badly if they do it. It has to be you."

"We're not there yet," I reminded them. "I have every intention of ending this tomorrow. If I don't, then we still have a bit of time. Either way, we're not losing Aunt Tillie."

Thistle nodded. "I hate to admit it — and I'll deny it if you tell her I said it — but I'm not ready to say goodbye to the old bat. I know one day we will be forced to put her to rest, but not now."

"Definitely not," I agreed. "We're going to save her ... one way or the other."

26
TWENTY-SIX

The inn was rowdy all night, which was to be expected. Mom and the aunts filled us full of sugary goodness. We danced around and messed with one another, as was our way. The men watched indulgently from the table, but I didn't miss the fact that Landon restlessly walked the inn, checking windows and doors when he thought nobody was looking.

Nothing happened. Nobody moved on us. By eleven, we were ready for bed. The inn fell into comfortable silence, and I fell asleep quickly.

My dreams were hardly comforting.

I woke outside, in a place I vaguely remembered but couldn't identify. The trees were tall, the sun refusing to filter through the branches even though the leaves were starting to die and fall. There were no landmarks I recognized but the scene still felt familiar.

"Hello?" I called out. I expected a dream monster to find me and offer some cryptic threat. Initially I didn't find anything, and then the rustling of leaves had me jerking my head to the right.

It wasn't Eric Cadogen watching me. It wasn't even a shadowy faceless form. What I found standing under the canopy of red and yellow leaves was something completely unexpected.

Bigfoot.

"What in Hecate?" I shook my head as I regarded the creature. It didn't look as if it was about to pounce. It also didn't look as if it wanted to be friends. "Why are you in the center of this?"

Bigfoot cocked his head like a dog listening to his master. He didn't retreat into the trees or move closer. He just watched.

"What are you?" I had trouble wrapping my head around what was happening. "You're not the real Bigfoot. You're just a representation of ... something."

The creature didn't respond. A hissing somewhere behind me had my attention snapping in that direction. There, a dark wraith – all flowing black tendrils and ethereal menace – hovered and watched.

"You I expected," I said on a sigh as I studied the creature. "You're exactly the sort of dream monster that finds me regularly."

The wraith floated closer with another hiss.

"If you have a message, now would be the time to deliver it," I noted.

"You shouldn't be here," the wraith hissed. "You shouldn't be sticking your nose in business that doesn't concern you."

"It's not surprising you'd think that," I noted, running my tongue over my teeth and considering. "Did Eric send you?"

"Nobody sent me. You called to me."

That was a new tactic. "I didn't realize I called you. How did I do that?"

"You're a witch. Your voice echoes on the winds whether you control it or not."

"Interesting." I ran my thumb over my bottom lip and decided how I wanted to proceed. "There's magic at the campground, but I'm willing to bet it didn't originate there. That place was meant to offer serenity for those suffering the torment of a different sort of demon. I think Eric took it over because he had no other choice."

"I'm not here to talk about real estate." The wraith disappeared behind a tree. Rather than follow, I glanced over my shoulder. The Bigfoot remained where I had seen it last, motionless and watching. It reminded me of a sentry. "I'm here to warn you that you should back away from this. You'll die otherwise."

Even though I knew this was a dream, I recognized that the wraith was trying to warn me. Bigfoot, though, seemed to be on his own mission. I wanted to figure out what it was, but he refused to communicate with me.

"I think someone in Eric's group has access to magic," I said as I focused on the wraith again. "I think he started out as a low-level grifter. His family lost that farm — whether the story he told is true I can't say, but bits and pieces of it are — and it made them bitter. It also forced them to scramble."

The wraith didn't look invested in the conversation. She also seemed leery about letting things carry on too long. "I'm not here for this. I came to issue a warning. Now I shall go." She started to dissolve, but I didn't allow her to finish her escape.

"I don't think so." I'd never exerted my necromancer powers in a dream, at least not on purpose. I did now, stopping the wraith in her tracks. "We're not done talking."

The wraith's eyes widened, but no matter how hard she fought against my magic she couldn't overcome the power I exerted over her. "Let me go."

"Nope." I knew I sounded like a dictator readying to snap but I couldn't be bothered to care. "I'm not done with you. I want to have a discussion."

"There is nothing to say." The wraith moved her shoulders back and forth, fury evident. "Let me go."

"I said no." My voice was commanding, no-nonsense. Landon joked regularly about how he liked when I took charge. I was starting to grow into the power I'd always possessed, but it was the human part of me that was in control now. "I find it interesting that you have a female form. That either means Eric isn't supplying the magic, or that he's a total misogynist and believes women are evil and that somehow makes you scarier. Which is it?"

The wraith's red eyes went wide.

"I'm going with the likelihood that he's not magical." Now I was speaking to myself. "That makes sense. He was at Haggerty Road summer camp first, before his group relocated, and I don't know of any magical power spots out there. That means he likely absorbed a member into his group who had access to magic, and when he found out, he decided to bend her will to his."

"The supreme leader is a great man," the wraith insisted. "You don't know who you're messing with."

"Oh, I have some idea." I refused to get worked up about Eric. "I've dealt with men like Eric Cadogen before. I'm curious about a few things, though. For starters, was Chester Hamilton really his brother?"

The wraith's only response was to hiss.

"I bet he was," I continued. "He was the original target of the spell. Or, his mother was. I'm guessing she was part of Jasper Cadogen's cult long before her neighbor realized. Like all cults, Jasper preyed on the women for sex and the men for subservience and labor.

"Astrid got pregnant but told her husband he was the father," I continued. "He raised Chester, but the mother continued to spiral. She waited until Chester was an adult to leave her husband, but why? And why not take Chester with her if he was heir to the Cadogen cult? It's not much, but absolute power is always enticing."

"Let me go!" The wraith was shrill now, fighting my restraints with everything she had. I locked her down tighter.

"I'm guessing that even though she was a true believer, Astrid Hamilton recognized the danger associated with being Jasper Cadogen's son," I said. "Eric was the obvious heir, but if there was a brother, the cult members might split. Is Eric a benevolent ruler? I'm guessing not. That would've propelled the other members to push Chester forward as a substitute."

I didn't need the wraith at this point. I was figuring it out myself. I kept her trapped out of spite. "Maybe good old Jasper had more than one offspring. Maybe that's how you fit in. Eric would be the type to use a sister to get what he wanted." I nodded, agreeing with myself. "Yeah. It all comes back to Eric. He's not supplying the power, but he has control over whoever is."

"You don't know what you're talking about," the wraith spat. "You're involving yourself in something that you have no business being involved in. Witches are evil. They don't belong with the faithful. Hell, they're even below the faithless." Now she looked disdainful, almost humanly so.

"You're a reflection of the woman wielding the magic," I surmised. "She's real, as is her power. Eric exerts control over her. She's the one who started the curse, maybe because Chester stopped to visit his mother and Eric recognized how precarious his position was should somebody find out that there were two sons of Jasper."

"Let me go!" The wraith's voice was ragged now.

"I'm going to let you go." I made up my mind on the spot and started toward her, not stopping until I was directly in front of her. I made sure I wasn't so close that I inadvertently touched her or that she could touch me. "I want you to take a message back to Eric."

"I'm not here to run errands for you," the wraith spat.

"No, but you're going to run this one because he'll command it of you." I let loose a feral smile. "Tell him I'm coming for him, and by the time I'm done he'll have nothing left, not even his life."

I took a step back. This time the smile I graced the ethereal creature with was soft. "You tell him that for me."

The wraith's rage was palpable. She fought against my magic again but ultimately nodded. "I will share your feelings with the supreme leader."

"Awesome." I released her from my hold but kept a barrier up so she couldn't attack. "I look forward to his answering volley." With that, I turned away from her and focused on Bigfoot. Deep down, I knew it was stupid to refer to him that way. He wasn't Bigfoot. He was something else, a representation of something that I couldn't put a name to. Unfortunately, he was no longer in the spot he'd been standing when I'd started the conversation with the wraith.

Frustrated, I left the wraith to stew as it tried to get through the shield I'd erected to protect myself and walked to the tree line. I thought it would be a fruitless effort, that the creature would be long gone, but I found it standing several feet down an embankment ... and it wasn't alone.

"Do you like berries?" a female voice asked. "I can take you to some berries. I bet you like them. It's too bad you can't make your own berry crumble or shortcake, but berries are still good."

I recognized the voice. "Viola?"

The ghost, surprised, jerked her head up to look at me. "What are you doing here, Bay?"

"I was just about to ask you the same question." I started down the embankment, but the sasquatch — really, what else was I supposed to call him? — growled. I pulled up short. "What is he?"

"He's Bigfoot," Viola replied, her tone indicating she thought I'd asked a ridiculous question. "I told you he was in a bad mood."

"You told me ... ." I trailed off. Now that I had a chance to think about it, she had mentioned Bigfoot. That day I stopped in at the office to research Chester Hamilton, she'd led with her Bigfoot story ... and I'd dismissed her.

"Son of a witch." I viciously swore under my breath. Had the answers to my questions been right under my nose this entire time? "You need to be at the office in the morning," I warned. "I'll be there to talk to you."

If Viola was bothered about being bossed around, she didn't show it. "Aren't I always around when you need me?"

"I'll be there soon."

"You will," Viola agreed. "It's already morning. You just don't know it yet."

. . .

I ROCKETED TO A SITTING POSITION in bed just as the light began to eke around the curtains, a gasp escaping from my throat.

"Bay." Next to me, Landon stirred. When we'd fallen asleep, we'd been spooned together. He liked to be close so he could feel me in slumber. Now he seemed confused, and part of it likely stemmed from the fact that we weren't in our normal bed. "Sweetie, what is it?"

"It's nothing," I reassured him as I worked to calm my breathing. "I'm fine. Go back to sleep."

"Like that's going to happen." Landon's voice was a low rumble as he sat up and slid his arm around my back. I'd slept in flannel sleep pants and a T-shirt — which was more than I was used to sleeping in, but I wanted to be prepared — and Landon slipped his hand beneath my shirt to rub my back. "Tell me what you dreamed."

I swallowed hard, the images from the dream darting back and forth as I tried to make sense of them. "Eric Cadogen sent a dream wraith after me."

"I don't know what that means," Landon said.

"It means someone in his flock is magical. I'm not sure who — I'm guessing he didn't let us see whoever it was out of fear — but it's someone close to them. He's using her power to attack us."

"Didn't we already know that, or at least suspect it?"

I nodded. "Yeah, but there's more. Bigfoot was in my dream too."

Now Landon cocked his head. "Bigfoot?"

"I told you those signs meant something," I insisted.

"Yeah, but ... if you're about to tell me that a wacky cult leader managed to capture and train Bigfoot to use as a foot soldier, I'm afraid that's too much, Bay. I can believe in witches ... and ghosts ... and vampires ... and even freaking pixies. I can't accept a trained Bigfoot."

"It's not really Bigfoot," I reassured him. "It's something else. It's ... a symbol." Was that it? It felt right. "Whoever Eric has wielding magic for him, she's seen the signs. One of the creatures she's created as a sentry of sorts looks like Bigfoot. It has a purpose."

"What purpose?"

I held out my hands. "I'm not really sure. It's important that we figure it out, though. All of this — Eric's murderous ways and Aunt Tillie's curse — will be solved today."

"How can you know that?" Landon brushed my hair over my shoulder and kissed my neck. He was cuddly in the morning, especially when he was feeling vulnerable. News that I planned to go to war in a few hours made him feel vulnerable.

"I issued a warning through the dream wraith last night."

"But ... how can you be sure the dream wraith was real?" Landon asked. "I'm not doubting you. I know you're a masterful witch and I'll be with you regardless, but I'm curious about how you know."

"I used my magic on the wraith. I had to make her stay. That means it was more than a dream."

"But what about Bigfoot? I don't understand how he figures into this."

That made two of us. "I'm not sure, but I know who to ask."

When I didn't respond, Landon made a "come on" motion with his hand. "Don't keep me in suspense."

"Viola. She's known about at least part of this since the start. The day I went back to the office to research Chester Hamilton, she was there and was talking about Bigfoot having a bad day. She's been aware from the start."

Landon shook his head. "I thought you said Viola is a loon."

"She is, but she was in my dream. She knows something."

Landon sighed. "Well, that means we need to go into town." He looked at the window. "Let's get cleaned up, get some breakfast, and head out. I think it's best everybody else stays here."

I agreed with him wholeheartedly. "We're close, Landon. I just need the final piece of the puzzle."

"Then we'll get it for you." He was matter-of-fact. "I'll be with you, Bay, until the end. Don't even try to get rid of me."

"I would never do that." I beamed at him. I was suddenly feeling light and free. "How does a big platter of bacon sound?"

"It sounds like a trick."

"Did I mention that I might've figured out a way to protect your heart from your glutinous ways when I was working on Aunt Tillie's bulletproof bra last night?"

Landon's eyes narrowed.

"It's true. I have an idea to keep you with me forever."

"Don't tease me," he warned.

"You still have to watch yourself," I said. "You can't do whatever you want whenever you want. There will always be consequences. But first we need to take care of the cult. Then we'll talk about your bacon fetish."

"Sounds like the perfect after-battle activity." He swooped in for a kiss.

"Then let's finish this. I think I know what to do. I just need confirmation."

"Then let's get it. I'm dying to see how this all plays out."

He wasn't the only one.

27
TWENTY-SEVEN

Landon and I went to the newspaper office after breakfast. Nobody questioned where we were going, or what we were doing. Aunt Tillie's bad luck had ratcheted up enough that she'd broken three dishes at breakfast and somehow stabbed herself in the hand with a fork. My aunts and mother were making her their focus today under the guise of planning her non-memorial memorial service. That left Landon and me free to focus on what needed to be done.

"I'm going to pull up records on Eric Cadogen and his father," Landon said as he settled on my office couch. "There might be something we can use."

I nodded as I booted my computer, frowning as the silence of the building hit me. It was possible Viola wasn't here. Unlike my previous office ghost Edith, Viola was known to wander. "I'm going to find Viola."

Landon lifted his chin. "You're not going to leave the building to find her?" He looked alarmed at the prospect.

I shook my head. "I'll call her here if I have to. She might be in the kitchen watching television. I'll check."

Landon looked as if he wanted to say more but he nodded. "I'll be here when you need me."

Not if, but when. It made me smile. "Just dig," I instructed as I dropped a kiss on top of his head. "I'm ending this today."

"I'm sure Cadogen wants the same thing. You shook him yesterday. He doesn't strike me as the sort of guy who will take that lightly."

"Ego is everything with him. He needs me out of his life just as much as I need him out of mine."

I left Landon to his research and headed to the kitchen. The sound of the television hit me when I walked through the door, and I was happy to find Viola watching some sort of talk show.

"Oh, you don't even know what you're talking about," she grumbled at the television. "Term limits are a scourge on society. If somebody is doing a good job, they should be rewarded for it."

I stared at her ethereal back a moment. Viola showed no signs of wanting to pass on. She still had one foot firmly in the world of the living. Would she always be that way? "Hey."

She didn't look up at my greeting. "Can you believe these guys? It's like they don't even understand how the world works."

"I don't have much interest in politics right now," I admitted. "I need to talk to you."

Viola slowly tracked her eyes to me. "Let me guess, your family is in turmoil and you need me to fix it."

"Why would you say that?"

"That's the way it always is with you."

"I don't think I ask you to fix my family."

Viola cocked a dubious eyebrow. "How many times have you summoned me to swoop in and save them?"

"That's a bit of an exaggeration." I was suddenly uncomfortable. She wasn't entirely wrong. "Today I need information."

"Awesome. I'm a fount of information."

"You're ... something." I moved to the Keurig and turned it on to warm up. Coffee couldn't possibly hurt. "About two weeks ago you mentioned Bigfoot and how he was living in the woods."

"Yes."

"Tell me more about that."

"About Bigfoot? Well, you're in luck. I know tons about Bigfoot. I watch a lot of informative shows and he's a star in fifty percent of them."

"But most people don't believe he's real," I said.

"Most people are morons."

I didn't disagree. "Viola, Aunt Tillie is in trouble. Somehow, Bigfoot plays into it. I need to know what you know."

"Well, it started decades ago," she said. "Many people here think we have the Dogman, not Bigfoot, but they're the same."

I had to tug on my fraying patience. "I don't need a tutorial on Bigfoot. I need to know about the Bigfoot you saw."

"Oh." Viola looked momentarily perplexed. "He's been hanging around in the woods. He doesn't look like I expected — I always knew I would see Bigfoot one day — but he's hanging around."

"Where did you see him?"

Viola shrugged. "In the woods. He wanders around. Sometimes I follow."

"In the woods where?" She was on my last nerve, but yelling would be a mistake. She shut down when I yelled.

"Out by your place. Out by the Dandridge. Over by the stable."

I frowned. "By my family."

"I guess I hadn't thought about it like that, but yes."

"When did you first see him?"

"Oh, I think it was about three weeks ago when I first crossed paths with him on the bluff by The Overlook. I was spying on Tillie — she is a pip — and he walked through that clearing up on the hill."

"Where we perform our rituals?" My mind was churning.

"I guess. I don't know much about your rituals. He was up there watching her. She was doing some sort of spell. I'm guessing it was the spell to make all those unicorns fart. There was a lot of magic swirling about and then I saw him. He was in the shadows."

"And he looked like Bigfoot?"

"What else would Bigfoot look like?"

"I'm having trouble wrapping my head around this. Was he furry?"

"No. He was more ... smoky. Do you remember that show that was on a few years ago? *Lost.* It had a smoke monster. That's what Bigfoot is. He's a smoke monster."

"So, he's not really Bigfoot."

"No, he's Bigfoot." Annoyance lined her features. "Why would I say he's Bigfoot if he's not really Bigfoot? Come on."

"Bigfoot isn't a smoke monster." Irritation bubbled up. "Bigfoot is an animal."

"And so is this."

"But ... ."

"It's a smoky animal," she snapped.

I reminded myself that she'd always been a bit of a wild card, even in life. She couldn't be other than she was, and if I expected her to be easy to deal with, I was wrong. "Let's start from the beginning. Tell me exactly what you saw."

"He was smoky. His eyes were red. He watched Tillie and then took off. After that, I saw him popping up more and more. He was watching the Dandridge a lot, seemed interested in that baby. His favorite place to visit is the bluff. I swear he's looking for something."

"What?"

Viola held out her hands. "Probably magic. He's a magical being. He probably wants the magic so he can pass for human and get out of the woods. It's boring to be in the woods constantly. There's no *General Hospital* out there. That's why I keep coming back here."

"Did you ever see him wield magic?"

"No. He was down at Hollow Creek one day with his friend. They poked around for a long time. I think they were looking for the magic, but they didn't find any. At least not that I saw."

His friend? What in the ... ? "Bigfoot has a friend?" I asked.

"Yes."

"Another creature?"

"It was a man ... and a woman. So I guess it's fair to say he has friends. I don't want to sell him short."

Now we were getting somewhere. "Show me."

"Show you what?" Bafflement had Viola's eyes narrowing.

"What you saw."

"How am I supposed to do that?"

"Just ... let me see the memory." It was the only way I could figure this out. "Let me inside your head. I'll be gone quickly, and you can go back to your show."

Viola was conflicted. "Um ... how do I know you won't turn me into a Stepford Wife while you're in there? My brain is a gift to the world. If you scramble it, everybody loses."

"I promise not to scramble it."

Viola pursed her lips. "You could just do it if you wanted to, force your way in."

"I would rather not." I didn't add that I would if she gave me no other choice.

She let loose a sigh. "Fine. Go in and take a look. Knock yourself out."

"Thank you." I moved closer to her, narrowing my eyes as I began to wade through the swamp that was her mind. "This won't hurt."

"You've said that before."

"Have I ever lied?"

"No, but there's always a first time for everything."

"Not this time. I swear. We have a battle coming, Viola. I need to see."

"I already said you could. Just get it over with. I want to go back to my shows."

It was the only invitation I needed. "Just hold still. It will be over before you know it."

· · ·

LANDON WAS STILL ON HIS TABLET WHEN I returned to my office.

"Did you find her?" he asked, not looking up.

I nodded. "She's not seeing Bigfoot."

His lips quirked. "I never thought she was."

"It's a wraith of some sort, a spirit yoked by a witch. Viola showed me the witch. I think ... I think it's Chester's mother."

Landon glanced up, perplexed. "I thought she was dead."

"Death would be better in this case. She looks ... ragged. She's been infiltrated by some sort of dark magic. She no longer looks human."

"Why would Cadogen lie to us about her being dead? That opens him up to scrutiny."

"Is it worse to try to pawn her off as dead or try to explain why he has an inhuman woman serving as his right hand?" I thought about the temple. "He keeps her inside that thing he built. He controls her somehow. Maybe the symbol is part of it. She made that piece of art for him."

"But what about Bigfoot?" Landon asked. "How does he play into this?"

"It's a wraith that looks like a monster. It doesn't really resemble an animal, but it's not human. I think he uses it as a sentry of some sort, a protector. He put up the signs at the campground to explain away the creature's presence if somebody else should see it. That's why they embraced the Bigfoot mystique."

Landon rubbed his chin. "Well, I managed to find some information too. There is no death certificate for Jasper Cadogen. He'd be in his seventies if he was still alive, but I don't think he is."

"No." I shook my head. "Eric killed him."

"Probably because Eric wanted to be in charge," Landon agreed. "He wanted the power of the cult to wield. I have no idea how he killed Jasper, or where the body is, but I believe he's dead. Unless he's the creature that's running around."

"That's a thought." I sank onto the couch next to Landon,

considering the possibility. Ultimately, I shook my head. "There's no way Eric left his father alive. Even in that state, there would always be a chance that he could break from the spell and go after his son. Eric wouldn't risk that."

"So we're dealing with Eric as the mastermind," Landon said. "He and Astrid were working together. They got their hands on magic. They used that to their advantage, created the sentry, and ... what? What's their end goal?"

"It has to be money," I said. "Money and power fuel all these guys. Can you get a look at Eric's banking information?"

"Not without a warrant, which we don't have and I'm reluctant to get. If we're going to go out there and put an end to this charade, we have to be careful. We don't want the state police breathing down our necks and asking questions we can't answer."

"No," I agreed. "I wish we had more information on the people working with Cadogen."

"There's the woman in the kitchen," he noted. "We might be able to find her."

I'd almost forgotten about Lynn. "Can you look her up?"

"As long as you cuddle with me on the couch when I do."

I gave him a dubious look but settled in at his side, resting my head against his shoulder as a million scenarios flew through my head. Eventually, Landon came up with something.

"Here we go. Lynn Huntington. There are some legal documents here, and they mention the cult by name. That's how I found them. I searched for both."

"What do you have?"

"She's been with the cult five years. She joined under Jasper ... and her husband Chuck Huntington had to file an injunction to stop her from taking money from their accounts to give to the cult."

"I bet that happens with a lot of people."

Landon was solemn. "There are divorce documents here. The divorce wasn't contested but Lynn never showed up in court. The husband won control of their money and custody of their children. She got almost nothing because she didn't fight his lawyers."

"And once her access to money was gone, she somehow ended up in the kitchen," I mused. "I'm guessing that the more money you funnel into the cult — or Eric — the higher you climb on the hierarchy ladder. He keeps talking about rungs. There has to be a reason."

"That makes sense."

"Only Astrid is different. She had access to magic somehow. Maybe she was a born witch and didn't realize it. Maybe Eric somehow figured it out. I just don't know how that works."

"Maybe it doesn't matter how it works," Landon argued. "Maybe all that matters is that we know the basics, including the fact that Chester Hamilton was likely Jasper Cadogen's son. I'm guessing Chester tracked down his mother, likely looking for answers, and given the way she'd been changed, Eric was worried about any interaction. He arranged for Chester's death. He needed it to look like an accident or suicide, something that couldn't be tracked back to him. He didn't bank on you being present for Chester's demise."

"Maybe that was by design. Maybe Astrid worked the spell in a specific way. That's why it spreads the way it does."

"Or maybe you just want to believe she's doing all of this against her will," Landon countered. "You don't want to think she actively conspired against her son because that offends you."

"Offends me?" I scoffed. "Why would I be offended?"

"Family is everything to you and the thought of turning on them makes you angry."

He was right. "I just don't know what to think about Astrid. She's our wild card. The wraith thing is going to attack us when we go to the camp. He's a mindless being and we'll have to stop him. Astrid, though, I just don't know what to think about her."

"*When* we go out there?" Landon arched an eyebrow. "I don't remember talking about a return visit."

"She's in that temple," I said. "We can't fight her on our turf unless Eric releases her to fight us. I think he will do that, but we don't have time to waste. We have to go to her."

"I don't know, Bay." Landon looked pained. "How are we going to work this? We can't take Aunt Tillie out there again. You saw her this morning. It's too dangerous."

"She has to stay at the inn with my mom and aunts. I can't tell them what's happening because they'll want to tag along. If they do, Aunt Tillie will find out what we're doing and it will be over before it even starts."

"Who will help you?"

"Maybe I don't need help. Maybe I can do it on my own."

"I don't like the idea of you being the only magical being out there. What if something goes wrong?"

I understood his trepidation, but I needed to keep my family safe. "It's best to keep the team small. Besides, I'm never alone. I can always call on ghosts to help."

Landon grimaced. "Do you plan to tell your family what you're doing?"

"No. You and I should head out there alone. We can let them do their own thing. They'll be happier not knowing. They can keep Aunt Tillie safe, and we can do the rest."

"Ugh. I don't know."

"It's the best course of action," I insisted. "I want my family safe. We have a better chance of sneaking on the property. I can handle this."

"I'm not saying you can't, sweetie, but you're missing one tiny detail. Your family is the most important thing to you. It's the same for me, but you're my family. I can't help feeling that if we go out there alone, we'll be vulnerable. Isn't there some way we can take at least one person with us to serve as backup?"

"The only one who we can risk taking is Thistle, but it's better she be at the inn. She'll help keep everybody there in check."

"I wasn't thinking about Thistle. I was thinking about Scout. She's uber powerful."

I hadn't considered tapping our half-pixie friend. She was indeed powerful. "This isn't her fight," I replied. "This is my fight."

"She likes to fight." Landon was firm. "She's good at it."

I pressed my lips together, debating, and then sighed. "Fine. I'll call her. I'm handling this myself if I can. She'll just be backup."

"I'm fine with that. I just want all our bases covered. Let's make sure we can end this now. I don't want to have to retreat and regroup. Let's finish this."

"I'll get her on the phone and then we'll head out. I want to end this. He won't expect us this early in the morning."

"Let's hope not, because if he has a trap ready for us, all bets are off. I want to win as badly as you, but I don't want to be reckless."

"I learned how to fight from Aunt Tillie. I'm not reckless. I'm always prepared." I patted his knee. "You'll be feeling great in two hours when this is behind us. Trust me."

"There's nobody I trust more. That's why I'm going along with this half-baked plan. If you believe you can handle it, I have faith in you. Let's get it done."

28
TWENTY-EIGHT

Scout Randall met us on a side road with her boyfriend Gunner Stratton in tow. They didn't look bothered about being called for a fight, calmly eating chicken as they leaned against a motorcycle.

"Isn't it a little early for chicken?" Landon asked, his nostrils flaring.

"It's gas station chicken and it's awesome," Scout replied as she licked her fingers. "Give us a rundown of what's happening here."

I laid it all out for her in succinct fashion. She merely nodded.

"Doesn't sound so bad."

Landon made a disgruntled sound. "I love how you never think it sounds bad."

"I'm an optimist." She slapped his shoulder hard enough he glared. Her grin was impish. "I've been dealing with much bigger problems in Hawthorne Hollow. We've got a vampire problem not going away any time soon. We're happy for the distraction."

"We are," Gunner agreed. Like Landon, his hair was long and it gave him a dangerous look. "What do you want us to do?"

"I want to handle this myself," I insisted. "Landon wants me to have backup. Aunt Tillie is in trouble, which is fueling all of this. I just ... need this to end today."

"We're all for protecting Tillie," Scout offered. "She's too cool to lose."

"Definitely," Gunner agreed. "I'm guessing you want us to sneak through the woods to get to the property and then we'll have a showdown with the head guy where he mwuahahas his way to death. Then we have a shadow wraith to deal with and some sort of enslaved witch. We've faced far worse."

His breakdown of the situation made me chuckle. "That's it in a nutshell."

"It's fine," Scout reassured me. "You're the lead here. This is your show. I'll help where I can."

"There are going to be a lot of innocents there," I warned. "I don't know where their heads are, but I would rather not hurt them unless I have no choice. They've been taken advantage of. They might not realize it, but they're victims in all of this too."

"We've got it." Scout bobbed her head. "Believe it or not, I've dealt with a few crazy cults in my day. There was one in Detroit that worshipped rats. They funneled magic into a controlled infestation, but as a side effect they created a six-foot rat that started eating people. That was far worse than this could possibly be."

I shuddered. "Why did you have to tell me that? Now I'll have nightmares."

"You and me both." Landon was horrified. "What is wrong with you?"

"Oh, so many things." Scout's smile never diminished. "Let's do this."

"I just ... thank you for coming." I meant it. "I owe you."

"No, you don't." Scout was firm when she shook her head. "You've helped us. We help you. That's what friends do."

"Definitely," Gunner added. "If you want to pay us back, ask your mother to cook pot roast for dinner tonight. That's all the thanks we need."

"I'm pretty sure that can be arranged," I said. "My mother loves you."

"Just not as much as me," Landon said. "I'm her favorite. Don't go getting any ideas."

Gunner's smile was lazy. "I'll try to refrain."

SCOUT THREW A MAGICAL BUBBLE around us. She was adept at providing camouflage. As a shifter, Gunner had his nose in the air the entire walk. He seemed intrigued ... and a bit agitated.

"There's a current of something underneath this place," he noted as we rounded the final corner and approached the temple — I still had trouble calling it that — looming above our heads. "They're definitely up to something funky here."

"Definitely," Scout agreed, her eyes narrowed. "What's with the teepee?"

"That's the temple," I explained. "At least their version. I know it's weird."

"Cults are always weird." Scout didn't look bothered in the least. "Once, when I was on Belle Isle for training, I ran into this cult. It was only three people, but they were trying to manifest sharks in the Detroit River to eat their enemies. Now those guys were weird."

I could do nothing but shake my head. Scout had a story for everything. "We need to get inside. Once we do, you can drop the bubble and we'll see how things play out."

"Got it." Scout flashed me a thumbs-up. She was far more intrigued by the cult. "How many people are here?"

"We don't know," Landon replied as he squeezed my hand. His anxiety had ratcheted up several notches during our walk to the campground. He was practically bouncing now that we'd reached our destination. "Cadogen made sure to hide his numbers from us when we were here last time."

"Sounds typical." Scout made a face. "Lead the way, Bay. I'm dying to see what's inside."

She wasn't the only one.

Even though I knew Scout built her bubbles to be soundproof, I stepped lightly as we drew nearer. The campground was eerily quiet, though I could make out several figures moving between buildings. None looked in our direction. Cadogen likely didn't explain why we'd visited the previous day and because he'd promised them protection under the guise of supreme leadership, they had nothing to fear.

There was a sentry at the opening of the temple. I was still debating how to handle him when Scout's hand shot out, breaching the camouflage barrier, and slapped into the side of his face.

"*Dormio*," she intoned.

The man, dressed in workmen's overalls, began sagging to the ground. Gunner caught him before he hit, drew him inside the bubble, and hoisted him over his shoulder.

That left the entry clear for us, and I didn't hesitate to step inside. What I found was straight out of a nightmare.

"What in the ... ?" I was breathless to the point I barely noticed when Gunner dropped the unconscious man on the ground.

Scout lowered the camouflage and immediately moved to the cage in the center of the space. There, the dark female wraith from my dream floated. If hate and anxiety could take form, they would be the thing that had once been a woman.

"This is quite the cage," Scout noted as she eyed the lock. "Don't touch that," she warned Landon when he reached out for the lock. "You'll be cursed to within an inch of your life."

Landon slowly drew back his hand and turned to me. "Is this what you expected?"

Not even close. I was too busy taking in the symbols that had been painted on the walls to immediately answer him.

"Bay." Landon was alarmed. "Look at me."

I slid my gaze to him and forced myself to focus. "I figured it would be some sort of trap. I just didn't realize it was going to be this sort of trap."

"What sort of trap is it?"

"Something dark," Scout replied. "There's so much dark magic in here I don't know where to start."

"Start by letting me out," the shadow witch demanded in her snake-like voice. "Free me."

"I don't think that's a good idea," Gunner replied. "You've got bad intentions written all over you."

"Nobody was talking to you, mongrel." The wraith witch dripped with hate. "Your kind should be wiped from the face of the planet. You never should've been born."

"Have you been talking to my mother?" Gunner deadpanned.

I shot him a surprised look, but Scout caught my eye before I could say anything and slowly shook her head. There was something going on with him, bubbling under the surface, but now wasn't the time. Her message was clear.

"You're Astrid Hamilton." I opted to take control of the conversation. I moved closer to the cage, but not so close that the being inside could reach through the bars and snag me. "You're at the bottom of all of this."

"I'm no one now," the shadow seethed. "I'm nothing."

"But you were Astrid Hamilton at one time."

The creature nodded. When she looked at me again, it was to grace me with an appraising look. "And you're the witch on the hill."

"One of them," I agreed. It was obvious she knew who I was, so there was no sense dragging things out. "You've been watching us."

"I don't care about you." Astrid went back to pacing. Or, well, the closest she could manage without physical feet. "I don't care about any of this." She wrapped her ghostly fingers around the bars and shook them. "Let me out!"

"Don't let her out," Scout warned. "This thing ... she's murder wrapped in the sort of package that can straddle worlds. I don't even know how something like this happens." She looked amazed. "Are you telling us you were a human once?"

"Not for a long time," Astrid replied. "I shouldn't be here. This isn't my world any longer."

"Was it ever?" I asked.

Astrid didn't respond.

"Listen, we're willing to help you," I started.

"We are?" Gunner didn't look thrilled at the prospect. "I don't think that's our responsibility."

I ignored him. "We'll help you cross over. We'll help you find where you're supposed to be. You have to help us first."

"How do I do that?" Astrid's serpentine voice made my skin crawl.

"Tell us what the deal is with Eric. We know he's behind this."

"Of course, he's behind this. He's evil."

I kept my voice measured. "Tell me how this happened."

"How does anything happen?" Bitterness dripped from Astrid's black lips. "I was fooled by a man. That's how all of these stories start."

"Jasper Cadogen," I surmised. "You were involved with him. Did it start before you married Fred Hamilton?"

"Years before. Jasper was married to Eric's mother. He said divorce was a sin, but love was forever."

"And you fell for that?" Gunner made a tsking sound. "Never fall for the cult leader when he says things like that."

Astrid threw herself at the bars, but she was bound tight.

"Gunner, normally I enjoy having you along for these things," I said. "I'm not sure you're helpful this time."

"In other words, shut up," Scout said. Her gaze never moved from Astrid. "So, you married a dude and Jasper stayed married to his wife. You kept banging him, got pregnant, but told your husband the child was his. Then what?"

"I wanted my happily ever after." Astrid's shoulders sank. There was no hint of the woman in the wraith's features, but the sadness was real. "I tried to live the life Jasper wanted but failed. He let me join the commune but said I couldn't bring Chester."

"Because Eric was the prince apparent," I surmised. "He was being groomed for leadership."

"Yes." Astrid was morose. "Jasper couldn't see him for what he was. But I could. His mother was evil before him. She taught him how to be worse than she managed to make herself."

"Did Eric's mother know about you?" I asked.

"Jasper said she didn't, but I knew better. I thought she was the barrier to my happiness. I was wrong. It was always Jasper. He wasn't who I thought he was, but that didn't stop me from loving him."

In the end, she'd turned out to be a flawed woman who couldn't see the truth. Part of me felt sorry for her. The other part knew we would have to end her. We couldn't let her roam free. She was too dangerous. "Tell me the rest."

"Jasper kept saying that the only way for us to be together was for Elizabeth to die," Astrid replied. "I knew he was leading me down a dark path. I didn't care. As the supreme leader's mate, she had elevated standing, servants. I was in charge of feeding her. I started poisoning her food."

"You were her servant?" I asked.

"Jasper personally assigned me to her."

"Sounds like a great dude," Scout muttered, shaking her head. "How long did it take for the poison to work?"

"Months. I didn't realize that Elizabeth was aware that I was with Jasper. I thought we were okay. She was working against me the entire time I was working against her."

"She cursed you," I deduced. "She turned you into this."

"Truthfully, I turned myself into this. She warned me there would be dire consequences, but I didn't care. I pushed forward, and the day she died the magic she was born with passed to me ... only with a twist. I didn't know she was a witch. I only knew that I was different from the moment she died."

"Sounds like karma," Scout mused, shaking her head. "What happened then?"

"Jasper used me to get what he wanted. He immediately started up with one of the younger women in the group. I realized after the fact that he'd been with her for months, all the while stringing me along. I wanted to kill her too, so I did. By then, my soul had blackened. There was very little of what had been human left inside me. That's when Eric found me."

My stomach constricted. "And he convinced you to kill his father."

"It didn't take much convincing. By that point I hated Jasper as much as I loved him. I cornered him in the woods, took my revenge, and when he died, he took the last part of my soul with him."

It all made sense. Eric's mother had been a dark priestess. Jasper likely married her because he recognized that she could use her magic to elevate him. Then things had spiraled because nothing would ever be enough for him. When Eric came of age, he stepped in and took control.

"Why did you curse your own son?" I asked, pushing the conversation forward. Dwelling on the past was going to get us nowhere.

"Eric ordered me to," Astrid replied. "I was bound to him through his mother's blood. She secreted her blood into my food in the months before she died. That created a bond that could never be broken."

"Blood magic," Scout noted as her eyes drifted to me. "It always goes bad."

I nodded. "Who came up with the idea of the curse?"

"Eric. I'd long since pushed Chester out of my mind. I wanted him with me at first. He was Jasper's son, but by the end I knew he was better off without me. When he showed up here looking for me, I tried to protect him. But Eric controls me. He wears the talisman around his neck. I cannot fight his orders because of it."

I thought back to how Eric had been dressed the day we met him. He'd been wearing a turtleneck. If he'd had a talisman on him, it was hidden beneath his clothes. "Why did you create the curse so it transferred from person to person? Why not just kill Chester and be done with it?"

"That was my attempt to escape." Astrid turned rueful. "I

thought if someone magical figured out what I was doing they would come. And you did ... but you fell victim to his plan just like everybody else. He knows you're here."

My blood ran cold. "Excuse me?"

"He knows you're here," she repeated, weariness evident. "He has his new minion with him, and you will fall."

"You mean the Bigfoot thing."

Astrid made a face. "It's not Bigfoot." The denial, said with equal parts annoyance and frustration, was the first time Astrid had sounded human since we'd entered the temple. It made me smile.

"I know. It's something else. He made it look like Bigfoot."

"He wanted people to be afraid. He told me I had to help him create it. He swore he would let me go if I did. As always, he was lying. He'll never let me out of here."

"We will," I promised. "We won't let you run free, but we'll help you move on."

"I just don't want to be here. I want all of it ... gone."

"We can fix that, but you have to help us with Eric. His reign of terror ends today ... as does your curse." I was firm. "Someone I love very much is suffering from that curse. I need you to end it."

Astrid regarded me for a long time. Ultimately, she nodded. "If you break the binds tethering me to this cage, I will end the curse."

I smiled at her. "Just give me a second."

"Where are you going?" Landon demanded when I headed for the door.

"You heard her." I slowed my pace. "Eric is outside. He thinks he's won. I'm going to disabuse him of that assumption."

"Bay." Landon scrambled to catch up with me. "You know, as much as I love that you have faith in your abilities, sometimes I think you're starting to channel Aunt Tillie. It terrifies me."

"I'll be fine." I slid my eyes to Scout, who was grinning. "Right?"

She nodded. "The bigger they think they are, the easier they fall. I'll go out through the back."

"And do what?" Landon shouted.

"I'll handle Bigfoot." She rubbed her hands together. "Wow. There's something I never thought I would say. I can't freaking wait." With that, she disappeared toward the back of the temple, Gunner on her heels.

"It's okay," I reassured Landon. "I know exactly what to do now."

29
TWENTY-NINE

There were only a handful of people outside when Landon and I emerged. Eric stood at the front, two men flanking him. Lynn from the kitchen was two paces behind. She looked worried.

"I take it you followed in your father's footsteps for some things," I noted as I inclined my chin to Lynn. "Does she think she's going to climb the rungs like Astrid?"

Eric narrowed his eyes. "Someone has been talking out of turn."

"No. She's just sick of her circumstances and doing your bidding."

"She'll get over it." Eric was blasé. "Just out of curiosity, how did you get on our grounds without anybody noticing? I have sentries posted throughout the woods."

"That's interesting." I matched his tone. "We didn't see any of them when we came through."

"Well, so much the better." His smile was feral. "You should not have come back. This ground is consecrated. You don't belong here, and when you die here, my guess is nobody will come looking."

He was full of himself, and it made me smile. "How do you think this is going to play out?" I scanned the area looking for the shadow creature, but it was nowhere to be found. That likely meant it would approach from the rear. Behind the temple, however, it would run into a bit of a surprise. I had no doubt that Scout could easily handle it.

"I think you're going to tell us exactly who knows what and then we're going to quietly end this," Eric replied. "If you give me a list, we'll make sure it's painless."

"Did you forget who you're dealing with?" Landon demanded. "You can't expect to off an FBI agent and get away with it."

"You'd be surprised what I can accomplish when I set my mind to it. I'm the supreme leader. I have dominion over this land."

"And yet you earned none of it yourself," I said. "What exactly would you have if your mother hadn't cursed Astrid? I'll tell you what. Nothing. You wouldn't have had a single thing."

"Who is Astrid?" Lynn asked blankly.

"Shut up," Eric snapped, causing the woman to shrink back. "You're here to be a witness. Nothing more."

"Yeah, don't get on his bad side, Lynn," I called out. "He won't hesitate to order his shadow witch to kill you."

"Shadow witch?" Lynn's nose wrinkled in concentration. "I don't understand."

"That's how Eric wants it," I explained. "He doesn't want you to know the source of his power. He doesn't want you to understand that he's not doing any of it. That creature he has caged in the huge teepee is doing it all."

"What is it you think you know?" Eric demanded, fear flitting through his eyes. We'd obviously made it further than he anticipated on our fact-finding mission, and that was cause for concern.

"I know that your father liked to romance young women," I replied. "I know that he had an affair with Astrid Hamilton, fathered her son, and then convinced her to kill your mother. Your mother was aware of at least some of it, and she tied Astrid's fate to her own with blood magic. When she died, Astrid lost her soul ... and you became her master."

"I'm master of all here," Eric said smugly.

"You're master of nothing but deceit," I shot back. "You've been using Astrid's magic, magic supplied by your mother, to kill people and hoard money for years. You used her to kill your own father."

One of the men serving as a guard balked. "You cannot tell lies on our grounds!"

"I guess it's good that I'm not lying, then," I said. "Eric is power-hungry. He uses magic and curses to get what he wants. He forced Astrid to kill her own son because he feared Chester would try to claim what he believed was his."

"It is mine!" Eric snapped. "You don't know what you're talking about."

"Unfortunately for you, I do." I was over this conversation. "Astrid cast the curse that killed Chester, concocting it so that it would spread. She likely sensed magic was close and hoped someone would discover what was going on. That happened when the curse spread to my great-aunt."

"Then perhaps you should be worrying about her," Eric sneered.

"That's why I'm here. I'm going to end this right now."

A sly smile spread across Eric's face. He had one of those faces that wasn't handsome. It wasn't ugly either. It was forgettable, and if I had to guess, his greatest fear was being forgotten. "I know something you don't," he whispered in taunting fashion.

"I don't think so." I kept my serene smile in place. "If you think your shadow creature, the one you had Astrid fashion after Bigfoot so you could hide it more easily, is going to sneak up behind me and end this for you, you have another thing coming."

Eric's eyebrows hopped. "How ... ?" He trailed off and collected himself. "I don't know what you're talking about."

"Then let me explain it for your followers. Eric had Astrid create another minion. It's a creature without a soul, all black magic and teeth. He uses it as a sentry and spy, and to control all of you. He's a bad man, but his reign of terror is about to end."

I strode forward, causing the men on either side of Eric to flex, one of them emitting a low growl. They weren't my problem, so I used my magic to scatter them to the side, tossing them into the bushes as if they were nothing. They would be sore the next day, but they would be alive.

Eric took a step back when I stopped in front of him. "What are you?"

The way his voice shook caused me to grin. "Didn't Astrid tell you?" His fear was palpable though. "I think you should know that she set this up. She arranged things so that she had a chance to pay you back ... and she did it well."

"Lars!" Eric barked. "Where are you?"

I didn't look over my shoulder at the sound of footsteps. I didn't have to.

"You mean your little shadow sentry?" Scout called out, her magic hitting my back like a warm blanket as she loaned her calm to me. "Yeah, we met him behind the building. He went bye-bye."

I smirked as genuine fear coursed through Eric. He liked to wield power, but when it came time to stand on his own two feet, he was incapable of fighting his own battles. "You're on your own now, Eric," I offered. "How does it feel?"

"No!" He vehemently shook his head. "I'm not done." He feinted right to get inside the temple to order Astrid to kill us. There was no way I would allow that to happen.

My hand shot out and I grabbed the chain peeking out from around his neck. I tugged hard, breaking it, and brought up the metal talisman that had been hidden under his shirt. I was grim as I regarded the glinting metal. "Well, this is familiar." It was the same symbol that had appeared on the victims' hands.

"That's mine!" Eric fruitlessly reached out to reclaim the talisman, but Landon grabbed him around the throat.

"I don't think so." There was warning in Landon's tone. "If you even think of touching my wife, I'll make you pay."

I studied the talisman and then turned to Scout. I threw the necklace to her, and she easily plucked it out of the air. "Can you do something with that?"

She flipped the talisman over and nodded. "It should be easy enough. I can free the wraith, end her torment, and that should be enough to free Aunt Tillie and remove any other curses that have been cast."

"Then do it, please." I smiled at her before turning back to Eric. "We have a few more things to discuss. I'd like to be able to head home within the hour, though. I want to check on my family."

"And get pot roast." Gunner demanded.

"I believe pot roast will be on the menu."

"Awesome." He pumped his fist and then fell into step with Scout as they returned to the temple. "These are the sort of assignments I like — fast and not particularly dirty."

"They are fun," Scout agreed as they disappeared.

When I turned back to Eric, I saw Lynn inching away. She recognized that her supreme leader had lost and the only thing she wanted now was to escape. "Hold up," I called out to her, grimacing when she froze in place. She feared me, which felt out of place given everything that happened. There was nothing I could do about it, so I pushed past the disappointment that I was the bad guy in her story. "Spread the word. The Brotherhood is over. Everyone, all the people here, need to disperse and go home."

"And they need to do it by noon tomorrow," Landon added. "Because I'll be showing up with an entire truckload of agents and police officers. This isn't your land. You all need to go back to your lives ... or figure out something else to do. I don't really care what it is."

Lynn swallowed hard. "I don't understand this."

"You're not meant to. This was never an authentic place or community. You need to understand, everything Jasper and Eric built was lies. None of it was real."

"But ... it felt real." Her tone told me she was lost.

"It wasn't. You need to come to grips with that. Do it somewhere else because this is no longer your home." I didn't look at her again, instead focusing on Eric. Landon had a firm grip on him. The supreme leader had been relegated to tears and sniffling. "As for you, I can't let you go, and we can't risk putting you behind bars."

"What do you suggest?" Landon asked. He looked worried. "I know he's got it coming, Bay, but I don't want you to kill him. You'll suffer for it."

"I have no intention of killing him." I glanced around and grinned when something caught my attention. I stepped forward and grabbed the Bigfoot lawn gnome partially hidden in the bushes. I'd seen it the first day when we were walking the path. "I thought maybe I would do what I did with Brian," I said, referring to another man who had tried to kill me. "You know, death isn't always necessary."

Landon smirked. "You're going to trap his soul in that?"

"I am."

"And then what?"

"I thought I'd give it to Aunt Tillie as a gift. I think she'll like it."

Landon let loose a hearty chuckle. "Sounds like a perfect gift."

IT TOOK US TWO HOURS TO CLEAN UP the mess at the campground. Scout and I had to combine our magic to destroy the talisman. Astrid paced her cell as we worked. When it was ultimately destroyed, her form began to solidify. By the time she dropped to the floor of the cage, lifeless, she was nothing but a hollowed-out husk.

"We'll have to take that with us," Landon said. He had the garden gnome clutched to his side. "There's no explaining that when I bring the troops out here tomorrow."

I nodded. "Yes, well, I can't wait to carry it through the woods." The thought made me sick to my stomach.

"Don't worry about that." Scout reached through the bars of the cage and touched what remained of Astrid Hamilton. The husk disintegrated into a pile of dust in an instant. "There was nothing left of her at the end. Hate fueled her and magic tethered her to Eric. She was gone a long time ago."

I nodded, swallowing the lump in my throat. "Let's check outside."

The campground buzzed with activity. The men who had stood guard next to Eric had regained consciousness and were no longer in the bushes. The remaining cult members were packing up and heading out. None of them looked in our direction.

"It might be stupid to let them leave," Landon noted. "They could come back and try to avenge Eric."

"They won't." I shook my head. "I think they all knew what he really was. They were just too afraid to admit it."

"I hope you're right."

I briefly leaned into him before snagging the lawn gnome. "I'm done here. I want to go home."

Landon kissed my forehead. "Then let's go."

Gunner and Scout followed us on their motorcycles. I was just leaning into victory when we arrived at The Overlook, but the feeling of peace didn't last as the voices of annoyed people assailed our ears when we pushed through the front door.

"Ah, sounds like business as usual," Gunner said with a grin. "I smell cake."

Landon perked up. "What kind of cake?"

"The kind you eat."

"I wouldn't be opposed to cake." Despite the rumble his stomach let loose, he waited for me. We made the long walk down the hallway together. "You're okay?" he asked in a low voice as we approached the source of the noise.

"I'll tell you in a moment," I said as I pushed past him into the dining room.

There, everybody I loved most in the world sat around the table. Thistle and Mom were adding bourbon to their coffee. Twila was trying to shove cookies into multiple mouths. Sam and Marcus had their heads bent together as they looked at a catalog. Clove and Marnie gushed over Calvin. At the head of the table, Aunt Tillie stood on her chair, barking out orders, and behind her Chief Terry shook his head.

"Get down from there," he ordered as he fixed Aunt Tillie with a stern look. "Just because you claim the curse is gone doesn't mean it is."

Relief washed over me. I'd expected Aunt Tillie to recognize the moment the curse had been removed. I was gratified to realize I was right. "It's gone?"

Slowly, multiple sets of eyes tracked toward my group.

"Where have you been?" Mom demanded. There was annoyance in her eyes, and something else. It might've been pride.

"We had a few things to take care of." I smiled at her before focusing on Aunt Tillie. "You're okay?"

"I'm perfect," Aunt Tillie replied. She jabbed a finger in Chief Terry's direction without looking at him. "You want to keep your hands to yourself, Sparky. I don't need you telling me I can't stand on my own chair. This is my kingdom, and I'm the queen."

I couldn't hide my smirk. "Scout and Gunner helped us run our errands. We're all done at the campground."

Mom worked her jaw. "Part of me wants to yell because you went alone. The other part is grateful you're okay."

"Go with the part that wants to cook pot roast for dinner," Gunner said. "That's what I would do if I were in your shoes."

Mom shot him a fond smile. "Well, nobody is missing any limbs, and everything appears to be back to normal." Her eyes darted to Aunt Tillie and her smile slipped. "Mostly. Pot roast sounds like a fine idea."

"Awesome." Gunner swiveled his hips like young Elvis. "I love this house."

"What's that?" Aunt Tillie asked, pointing to the garden gnome in my arms.

I handed it to her. "I got you a present."

Wrinkles creased Aunt Tillie's forehead as she accepted it, confusion evident. Then she broke out in a big smile. "It's a nice gift," she said. She didn't come right out and say what it was. She wouldn't want my mother to know in case she ordered it destroyed. "It's not even Christmas."

"Not for a bit," I agreed. "I thought you deserved an early gift. I mean ... you did save Mrs. Little's life at great risk to yourself."

"Turns out the risk wasn't that great." Aunt Tillie eyed me speculatively. "I can't believe you fought without me. I didn't think you were ready."

"I've fought without you before."

"Not by choice." She hesitated a beat and then grinned. "You're growing into quite a witch. I guess that means the second phase of your training can commence. We can use whatever you're planning with my bulletproof bra when we start your lessons."

My heart skipped. "Wait ... what?"

"Yes, there's still more." Aunt Tillie beamed at me. "As soon as we hold my memorial, we'll start your training. It's going to mean big things for this family."

"But ... why am I being punished? I saved the day. That deserves red velvet cake and ice cream. Not ... whatever it is you're suggesting. I don't want to be tortured by spending time with you."

Aunt Tillie's smile was gone in an instant. "You're on my list."

Landon laughed as he slung an arm around my shoulder. All the tension he'd been feeling since before we headed out to take on the Brotherhood had seemingly disappeared. "And all is right with the world."

"That's easy for you to say," I groused. "You don't have to take lessons with Aunt Tillie. Seriously, how did this even happen?"

"You're definitely on my list," Aunt Tillie intoned darkly. "You'll rue the day."

Oh, I was already there.

Printed in Great Britain
by Amazon